Unraveled

Heidi McCahan

Snug Corner Cove Press

Book Layout © 2014 BookDesignTemplates.com
Cover Design by Lynnette Bonner of Indie Cover Design
Cover Photos iStock Photo and People Images

Unraveled/ Heidi McCahan. – 2nd ed.
ISBN 978-0-692431948-

For My Parents, Dave and Nancy

"For I know the plans that I have for you, declares the Lord, plans for welfare and not for calamity to give you a future and a hope."

—JEREMIAH 29:11, NAS BIBLE

C'mon, girl. Don't give up on me now," Lauren Carter pleaded, both hands on the wheel as she maneuvered her beloved Honda Prelude toward the curb. With one last pathetic sputter, the engine died and the car rolled to a stop three driveways short of her own.

Lauren sagged against the faded gray upholstery, the weight of her predicament tying her stomach in knots. With an ominous hiss, a plume of steam billowed from under the hood. Great. Now she'd have to look for a job close to the light rail station. Or else act like a real Oregonian and start riding her bike. She grimaced, dismissing the notion as quickly as it came.

Blowing an errant curl from her forehead, Lauren eased the car door open and slipped out of the driver's seat. Heat radiated off the pavement as she circled around the front of the car and opened the passenger door. Today marked Portland's twelfth straight day of record- high temperatures. No one could remember late

June being this hot. She may very well sleep downstairs tonight. Her bedroom AC unit flaked out yesterday.

Lauren scooped her smartphone off of the passenger seat. A text from Mom illuminated the screen.

Found Granny wandering around town this morning. Can't leave her alone for 1 minute. Sending your brother to meet your flight. See you soon. XOXO

She swallowed hard against the lump rising in her throat. Granny's dementia seemed to worsen each day. Mom texted twice this week already. First she found Granny fiddling with a broken cell phone, insisting it was a remote control. Then there was the tea party she hosted in the middle of the toy aisle at the General Store. It'd almost be funny if it weren't dear Granny.

Lauren gritted her teeth. Maybe this wasn't the best time to bring Holden home to meet her family. Visions of her fiancé, with his monogrammed cuff links and Italian leather loafers, pursuing her disoriented grandmother along a muddy gravel road sent a shiver down her spine. She'd avoided this trip for far too long, using every excuse she could think of. Staying far away meant she could forget the mistakes of her past. Almost.

But the requests for help came more frequently in recent weeks. And Holden's refusal to set a wedding date without meeting her parents ... well, who could argue with that? Add exquisite manners to this list of things she loved about him. With a heavy sigh, she shouldered the straps of her worn, faux-leather purse and glanced at her phone again. Only an hour to finish packing the half-empty suitcases she'd left sprawled open on her bedroom floor. *Get with it, girl.*

Lifting a plastic shoe box off the floorboards, a hollow ache filled her chest. Dr. Putnam gave them plenty of notice before he closed his practice, but it didn't seem real until they cleaned out the office and locked the door today. Seven years as his medical assistant and all she had to show for it was a few pictures and a stethoscope. A flyer promoting Portland State's College of the Arts was tucked in the side of the box. She smiled at Dr. Putnam's subtle hint. He never stopped encouraging her to pursue her passion. Unlike Holden, who patted her hand and told her she didn't need to worry about her education, or lack thereof, anymore. He would take care of everything.

Everything. Lauren nudged the door shut with her hip. Becoming Mrs. Holden Kelly offered opportunities she'd only dreamed of. Like getting out of the aging townhouse she shared with Monique. She frowned at her roommate's electric blue Jetta hogging the narrow driveway. What happened to the Friday night chick flicks and the occasional splurge on a pedicure? Now they were barely speaking after Monique neglected to pay the water bill. Again.

A rivulet of sweat trickled down her spine as she fumbled for her house key.

"I'm sorry," she lamented to her once-pink begonias. Despite her best efforts at gardening, they sat shriveled in their clay pots on the top step. *Should've gone with the pansies.*

Sliding her key in the lock, Lauren turned sideways, and heaved her shoulder against the old wooden door while giving the doorknob a forceful twist.

The landlord refused to change out the temperamental lock. Or fix much of anything, for that matter. The heat wave would break long before he ever stopped by to look at the air-conditioner.

One more nudge and the door flew open. Lauren stumbled into the entryway, her tennis shoes colliding with a pile of shopping bags.

"Seriously?"

She slid Monique's purse out of the way with her toe. Hot, stuffy air enveloped her as she trudged up the stairs to the second floor. She couldn't wait to trade her scrubs for a sundress. "Monique?"

The unmistakable sound of muffled crying greeted her. This couldn't be good. When she got to the top of the stairs, she found Monique in the living room, back pressed against the red overstuffed sofa and her long legs stretched out on the yellow and red striped area rug.

"What's wrong?"

Monique sniffed and dabbed the corners of her almond-shaped eyes with a tissue, even though her long, thick eyelashes retained every coat of mascara. Strands of ebony hair slipped from the bun at the nape of her neck and framed her heart-shaped face. The girl managed to look exotic even when she was emotionally distraught. So not fair. A cropped pink T-shirt and black running shorts emphasized her lithe dancer's body.

"I reinjured my stupid knee. Now I can't dance tomorrow night."

Depositing her purse and the shoe box on the end table, Lauren sank to her knees next to Monique. "What's so special about tomorrow night?"

Monique leveled her gaze at Lauren. "Cirque de Soleil. They've hired me for the remainder of the tour."

"Can't they find somebody else until you recover? An understudy?"

Monique rolled her eyes. "Please. This isn't some summer drama production. If I don't dance, I don't get paid."

"Could I have a look?" Lauren extended her hand toward Monique's knee. "Maybe I—"

"No." Monique's French-manicured fingertips batted Lauren's hand away. "I'll just wait for Holden. He said he'd be here in a few minutes."

Her breath caught in her throat. She eased back on her heels, gnawing on her thumbnail. "When did you talk to Holden?"

Monique reached for her phone. "I texted him, told him I really need him to call something in for me."

"Call what in?" Holden was a surgeon. Yes, he'd reconstructed her ACL, but he wouldn't prescribe Vicodin now. Would he?

"Percocet. Vicodin. I don't care. Anything for the pain."

That's ridiculous. She bit back a snide reply and got to her feet. "I guess I better finish packing then."

She hurried to her room, still reeling from Monique's flippant request. As if all she had to do was ask and he'd oblige. Whatever. She shook her head and flipped the switch for the ceiling fan. Peeling off her sweaty scrubs, she slipped her favorite yellow sundress over her head. There. Much better.

She tossed her discarded scrubs at the white plastic laundry basket, missed, and leaned down to pick them up. A pair of black stilettos sat forgotten next to the basket. Monique was kind enough to loan her the shoes, she could at least express a little gratitude and return them. She groaned inwardly. Dropping the clothes in the hamper, she hooked her fingers through the ankle straps and ventured back toward the living room. Judging by the cadence of her voice, Monique was engrossed in a conversation on her phone. Lauren retreated, pausing outside of Monique's bedroom.

Clothing adorned almost every flat surface in the room. Monique's preferred fragrance lingered in the air. Parking the shoes next to a tower of boxes on the floor of the closet, Lauren turned back toward the door. Sunlight streaming through the window glowed amber through an empty prescription bottle lying on the beige carpet.

Before she could ponder how this one action might change everything, she leaned over and snatched the bottle from the detritus of lipsticks and concealer that spilled out of Monique's cosmetics bag.

Her breath hitched in her throat as she read the label. An empty bottle of Percocet, prescribed a week ago, by none other than Dr. Holden Kelly. Monique's surgery was almost nine months ago. But dancers had to work through the pain, right? Monique was always complaining about something. Maybe she'd injured her hip or her back. There had to be a good explanation. Holden would never—

"Hello? Anybody home?"

Holden. Her heart hammered against her ribs. He was early. The bottle slipped from her trembling fingers and Lauren raced from the room, meeting her fiancé at the top of the stairs.

Holden's brilliant white teeth contrasted sharply with his olive complexion as he offered a half smile and leaned in for a kiss. Her scalp prickled. She teetered on the precipice of indecision. Confront them both? Wait until they were alone?

"Hey." She brushed her lips against his and forced a smile.

He produced an oversized coral gift bag with stiff peaks of white tissue paper protruding between the handles. "For you."

Warmth spread through her chest. "What's this?"

"A little something for our trip. Go ahead. Open it."

The bag was heavier than she expected and the distinctive scent of leather teased her as she separated the tissue paper and looked inside.

"Oh, Holden." She whispered, lifting an apple green Kate Spade purse out of the gift bag. "How did you know?"

"I watched you window-shop while we were waiting for our table at Papa Haydn's the other night."

She ran her hand over the understated silver clasp, slid the zipper open and admired the interior. The joy of receiving such a luxurious gift overshadowed her previous concerns. She pressed her hand to his cheek. "You shouldn't have. Thank you."

He pressed his hand over hers, the lines at the corners of his chocolate brown eyes crinkling as he smiled. "You're worth it, babe. I—"

"I hate to break up the love fest, but I could use a little help here," Monique said.

Lauren dropped her hand, the tender moment lost. She stepped away from Holden.

Holden's smile faded. "Duty calls."

"Thank God you're here, Holden. I don't know what I would do without you." Monique threaded a crumpled tissue through her slender fingers.

Please. Lauren gnawed on her lower lip and took a seat on the end of the couch while Holden knelt beside Monique. "What seems to be the problem?"

He traced the perimeter of Monique's knee cap with his fingers, nodding as she gave a dramatic play-by-play of the afternoon's events. He frowned, manipulating the knee into a flexed position.

Monique sucked in a breath and stiffened, clutching the sleeve of his pinstriped button-down.

Holden studied her face. "Sorry. Did that hurt?"

She nodded, another tear sliding down her cheek. "Can't you just give me something?"

"Let me check one more thing. You may have subluxed your patella."

"If I don't dance tomorrow, I'm not sure how I'll make rent on my studio." Another tear coursed down her cheek. Lauren thought about the shopping bags lying in the hallway downstairs. This story didn't make sense.

"I can call in some Vicodin." Holden pulled out his iPhone. "Then I need to see you in my office when I get back from Alaska."

Lauren's pulse kicked up a notch. More pills? "Holden, are you sure that's a good idea?"

He glanced up from his phone, one eyebrow arched. "Why?"

He didn't get it. She tilted her head. "You've given her a lot of pain meds. What happened to the Percocet you prescribed after surgery?"

Holden pressed his lips into a thin line. "You heard her. She's got to earn a living."

Lauren's chest tightened. Her eyes darted to Monique. Was that a smirk? It vanished as quickly as it appeared. She thought about the empty bottle lying on the floor in the other room and leaned toward her roommate. "I'm worried about you, Mon. Nine months is a long time to still be on this stuff."

Monique shrugged. "It's not a big deal. I'll rest after—"

Holden held up one finger to silence them both while he spoke to the pharmacist. Lauren seized the opportunity to glare daggers at Monique, who conveniently avoided eye contact by picking at a loose thread on her shorts. *Unbelievable.*

"Same pharmacy, right? The one on 23rd?" Holden rose to his feet, reaching down to help Monique up.

She struggled to stand, clinging to Holden's outstretched hand as if her life depended on it. "That's the one."

"Your prescription will be ready in an hour."

"Thanks, Holden. You're the best." Monique's hand lingered on his arm just a little too long. Anger coursed through her veins as Lauren stood up to challenge her. "Just a min—"

His phone rang and he pressed it to his ear, barking out a terse greeting.

"Have a great trip," Monique called over her shoulder, hobbling toward the stairs.

Lauren couldn't even muster a response. That girl was up to no good.

Turning toward Holden, she watched the color drain from his face. He released a string of obscenities, pacing like a caged animal while he raked a hand through his dark hair.

"On my way," he grunted, then pocketed his phone.

"That was the hospital." He jangled the keys to his new BMW. "I replaced this guy's knee this morning. He just had a heart attack. Flat-lined. I gotta go."

No. "Wait. We—"

"I might have to catch a later flight. We'll talk later." Then he was gone.

The front door slammed closed behind him. Lauren flinched. There was one flight from Portland to Anchorage tonight and he was supposed to be on it. With her. She'd grown accustomed to his work interrupting their plans but this was surreal. He was her lifeline now.

She drew a ragged breath, taming the wave of anxiety that threatened to engulf her. She could do this. It was time to put on her game face. Reaching for her new handbag, she cradled it against her chest. Regardless of what her friends and family thought about her leaving home or what they said about her after she'd left, this was her chance to prove she'd made a great choice. If Holden couldn't make it to Alaska, that meant more quality time with her parents and her brothers. Not to mention her beloved Granny.

Twenty minutes later, both suitcases were crammed full. She squeezed her hairdryer and toiletries in before tugging the zippers closed. One more thing, her most prized possession. She sank to her knees and slid a small white box from its hiding place under her nightstand. She only allowed herself to view the contents once a year. It was self-protection, really. Her heart ached as she ran her hand across the smooth, unadorned lid. *Lord, I know I have no right to ask, but please protect him. Show him that he's loved.*

Only the whir of the ceiling fan answered back. Typical. He hadn't responded to the dozens of other requests she'd flung toward heaven. Why would today be any different?

A lone tear slipped from her cheek and plopped on the box that housed the only evidence of her past. She wiped it away with the hem of her skirt. Tugging a pale blue T-shirt from her dresser drawer, she wrapped it carefully around the box and slid it down inside her tote bag. Rising to her feet, she drew a ragged breath and glanced around her room one more time. Then she towed her luggage out into the living room, found her phone, and searched for a taxi service.

By the time the cab pulled up, she was waiting on the curb, sweaty and disheveled. As the driver loaded her suitcases in the trunk, she glanced up the street toward her deserted car. They'd come a long way from an old log house on Alaska's rugged coast to busy, eclectic northwest Portland. Not just in miles, either. It felt like a lifetime since she crossed the mighty Columbia—just a girl, her faithful car, and a life-changing secret—and fell in love with the skyline silhouetted against the breathtaking backdrop of Mount Hood. Now she was headed back to the one place she'd tried so hard to avoid ... home.

CHAPTER TWO

Lauren touched Granny's locket to her lips, but the metallic coolness offered little comfort. She eyed the white paper sack in the seat pocket in front of her and willed the twin-engine Cessna toward solid ground. *Please land, please land, please land.* While soupy fog and limited visibility were probably nothing for the pilots in the cockpit, she'd never been a fan of the bumpy decent into her hometown.

Gray asphalt appeared below the rain-streaked window next to her and the plane landed with a bounce before barreling toward the mountains that hemmed the runway. Lauren clenched the seat in front of her until the plane rolled to a stop next to the flat-roofed cement building that served as the airport.

"Sorry about that landing, folks," the pilot said through the loudspeaker. "Welcome to Emerald Cove, Alaska. Local time is 10:15 a.m. We sure appreciate you flying with us today. Bags can be claimed inside momentarily."

She sagged against the window, the plastic cool against her skin. Finally.

The cabin filled with chatter and activity as all twenty passengers tried to stand at once. Cell phones chimed and fragments of conversation mingled with the whine of the plane's propellers. Lauren retrieved her iPhone from her new Kate Spade purse. Sucking in a breath, she glanced at the screen. Who stands their fiancée up and doesn't even bother to call?

Cut him some slack. The voice of reason whispered in her head.

Jaw clenched, she stood and freed her tote bag from the small overhead compartment. He better have one heck of an apology whipped up. A little groveling wouldn't hurt, either. Clutching a bag in each hand, Lauren joined the line of passengers crowded in the narrow aisle. They inched toward the exit, slowed by an elderly couple fumbling with their winter coats and carry-ons.

Lauren stepped out of the plane and onto the steep stairs. Sheets of rain pelted her face. She gasped and put up a hand to shield herself from the deluge.

"Of course it's pouring. Perfect." Sweeping her wet, unruly mane of curls out of her eyes, she descended to the tarmac. A man clad in yellow rain gear stood outside the automatic doors and beckoned impatiently, waving his greasy-gloved hands over his head. The other passengers stumbled toward him like a small herd of stunned animals. Lauren trailed after them, cringing as water sloshed into her peep-toe wedges.

Inside the airport, she swiped the water from her face and followed the pack to the black conveyor belt that snaked through baggage claim. Men in plaid button down shirts, worn jeans, and steel-toed boots mingled with senior citizens, eager to begin their Alaskan adventures. A noxious odor of gasoline and stale coffee permeated the waiting area. Yep, still smelled exactly the same.

Rivulets of water dripped down her sundress as she spotted one of her black suitcases wedged between coolers and toolboxes.

"Excuse me, please." She pressed into the crowd, chasing after her luggage as it cruised away. She lunged for her suitcase and tugged on the handle. It didn't budge and she lost her balance. A large, warm hand grasped her elbow, saving her from an embarrassing fall.

"Easy, there," a deep voice said, "why don't you let me help you?"

Her pulse quickened and her breath caught in her throat as she regained her balance and stared up into cornflower blue eyes.

A mixture of surprise and recognition flashed across the man's face.

"Blake?" Was it really her childhood sweetheart?

He seemed taller, shoulders broader than she remembered. Sandy blond hair crowned his forehead in disheveled spikes. A faint pink tinged his high cheekbones. She let her eyes rest on the stubble that clung to his angular jaw. A hint of his cologne lingered in the air, catapulting her back in time to a warm, spring night that changed everything. *No. Not now.*

"Hello, Lauren." His lips pressed together into a tight smile. "It's been a long time."

"Yes, it has." She shivered at the sensation his strong, capable hands were sending down her arm. No, that was crazy. It couldn't be his touch. She glanced down at her wet, rumpled skirt. She was just cold. Dry clothes and hot coffee would warm her right up.

"Can I give you a hand with those bags?"

Lauren stepped away, tipping her chin. "No, thanks. I got it—"

Blake scratched his head. "Is somebody picking you up?"

She scanned the faces of the people nearby. "I thought my brother Matt would be here."

Blake yanked a large suitcase off the belt and parked it at her feet.

She raised her eyebrows. "How do you know that's mine?"

"Purple ribbons on the handle. You always loved purple."

Heat rushed to her cheeks at his recollection and she dipped her head, wondering what else he remembered about her. "I sent him my flight info. Maybe he didn't—"

The familiar chime of an incoming text message interrupted her and they both reached for their phones.

Sis, found Granny wandering downtown again. Taking her home now-late to pick you up.

"Oh, no." Lauren's stomach plummeted to her toes.

"Everything okay?"

"It's my grandmother. I—I'm not sure what's going on. Matt's taking her home."

"I could give you a ride," Blake said. "I got what I came for." He held up a large Fed Ex envelope with his left hand.

Lauren glanced at his ring finger.

No wedding ring.

She hesitated. His kindness was the last thing she deserved. After all this time, the guilt still managed to seep in, no matter how many times she shoved it aside. "I can wait for Matt. Really. Thanks for the offer, though."

Blake quirked one brow, eyes locked on hers. "It's just a ride, Lauren."

She glanced away, keenly aware of her pulse pounding under the weight of his stare. What harm could come of a short ride through town with an old friend?

"All right." She smiled for the first time since her flight left Portland. "I'll let Matt know."

"Is this yours, too?" He nodded toward the suitcase gliding toward them on the belt, a frayed purple ribbon twisted around the handle.

"Yes." She shivered again at the memory of his hand on her elbow.

Blake effortlessly stacked both of her suitcases on a luggage cart while Lauren fired off a quick text to Matt. Tucking the envelope inside his navy blue raincoat, Blake leaned on the luggage cart's handle, propelling it toward the parking lot and into the downpour. He stopped next to a new charcoal gray Toyota truck with an extended cab and a canopy on the back.

"Where's the old Chevy?"

"Sold it." He heaved her bags into the back of the truck.

"You loved that thing."

He slammed the lid shut. "Too many memories." His gaze held hers as he moved closer, jaw tightened, and opened the passenger door.

Her cheeks warmed again and she scrambled into the truck, a slide show of their times together in that old truck playing in her mind. So awkward. Suddenly she wished she'd waited for Matt.

Blake closed the door and jogged around the front of the truck. As he slid into the driver's seat, Lauren's eyes fell on a glossy brochure lying on the dashboard.

"Emerald Cove Rafting and Kayaking. What's this?" She stared at a photo of a bright red raft careening through river rapids. Water sprayed up over the nose of the raft, dousing the wide-eyed passengers in their shiny yellow rain gear.

"My brother and I started a new business together." Blake pulled the envelope from inside his jacket and placed it behind her seat. She wiped her hand on her skirt and picked up the brochure. The guide paddling the raft leaned into the rapids. She recognized the ruddy cheeks, the cavernous dimples. "Is this *you*?"

He frowned. "Don't sound so surprised."

"I thought—well, I heard¬¬ you taught in a little village school somewhere. You were always so good with kids, coaching basketball and everything. I'm sure they adored you."

"I'm still a teacher. I would love to coach basketball again, if Mr. Hoffman ever retires. But six years in Tyonek was long enough." His eyes flicked between her and the windshield. "It was time to come home. Perhaps you can relate."

She dragged her fingers through her tangled curls. "I'm not staying."

"Just here to plan the wedding?" Blake nodded toward the ring on her left hand. "Nice rock, by the way."

Pain knifed at her heart as she studied the two-carat diamond solitaire Holden chose for her. Flawless and nestled in a platinum setting, just as she hoped it would be.

"My fiancé thought it was time he met my family." She forced a bright smile but her heart quaked. Never in a million years did she expect to spend her first few minutes back in Emerald Cove with Blake, talking about her absent fiancé.

Blake studied her. "Let me guess. He couldn't make it?"

She nodded and stared out the window. "He had an emergency."

Lady Antebellum's song "Dancing Away With My Heart" came on the radio and Blake jabbed at the power button.

"Not a country fan anymore?"

"That song's overplayed," he muttered.

Not that she would admit it to him, but that song elicited the same response from her every time it came on the radio. Even if they were her favorite band, those particular lyrics worked a number on her heart.

"I saw your dad the other day at the hardware store. He said you're a nurse now?"

She shook her head. "Not quite. Just a medical assistant."

"That's not the same thing?"

She smiled. "No."

"Why do I feel like there's more to this story?"

She shrugged. "There might be. But let's talk about you. Tell me more about this rafting and kayaking thing."

"I see you, avoiding the question. That's cool."

"Some might call it avoiding. I prefer re-directing."

He shook his head, a smile playing at the corners of his mouth. "Whatever. We can talk about me. We opened Memorial Day weekend. I can't believe how quickly things have taken off."

As Blake regaled her with an instant replay of his first few weeks as a small business owner, Lauren stole a glance out the window, eager to get a glimpse of her hometown.

Oversized recreational vehicles crowded the two-lane highway, lumbering toward town. The windshield wipers kept a steady rhythm through the incessant drizzle. A pungent aroma of salmon and saltwater filled Lauren's nostrils. As they approached Emerald Cove's one and only traffic light, she studied the four corners of the intersection. The same bank, gas station, hardware store and motel still occupied prime real estate, and welcomed weary travelers to one of Alaska's premier destinations.

Blake brought the truck to a stop as the light changed from yellow to red.

"When did they put in a real traffic light? Remember when it just flashed yellow all the time?"

He nodded. "Apparently it caused a huge uproar. People got into fights after city council meetings, neighbors stopped speaking to each other ... Crazy, right?"

Lauren shook her head. "Small town politics. What's everybody so wound up about?"

"I think it's more about the motivation behind the change. Once the cruise ship passengers started coming on shore, the intersection was so backed up the shuttle vans couldn't get through. Passengers complained they didn't have enough time to shop. Hence, the new light."

Lauren craned her neck to see around the motor home in front of them. "Shopping? What shopping?"

Blake laughed. "You'll see."

The light changed to green and they cruised down Main Street. *Whoa.* Storefronts once deserted now had a fresh coat of paint, modern signs, and flowers in the planters. Despite the gloomy weather, several couples mingled on the sidewalks.

"Is that a new clothing boutique? Who opened a Thai restaurant?"

"Voila." Blake made a sweeping gesture with his right arm. "The new and improved Emerald Cove."

"Change is good, isn't it?"

"I don't know." He shot her a meaningful glance. "You tell me."

Lauren's heart lurched in her chest. "What do you mean?"

He flipped on his blinker and turned off Main Street onto Hillside Drive. "Change is hard, especially if people can't deal with the fallout."

She reached for the locket again, tugging it back and forth across the chain. "You aren't just talking about tourists and cruise ships, are you?"

Blake cut his eyes toward hers and his gaze lingered on the locket. "Maybe I'm not. I want—"

"Don't. Please." Her pulse pounded in her ears. "I can't do this today." She clenched her clammy hands into fists and turned away. This was a huge mistake.

An uncomfortable silence blanketed the cab. "I'm sorry," Blake said.

She nodded, not trusting herself to speak. There he was, always the selfless one, apologizing to her. Bile rose in her throat. If he only knew the truth. The hurt and shame she tried to outrun threatened to engulf her like a tidal wave. Panic welled up inside, her legs trembling as she fought the urge to open the door and jump out. They couldn't know. She simply couldn't let anyone find out.

Gravel crunched under the tires as they left the asphalt behind and meandered through a dense forest. The narrow road carved out by her grandparents more than fifty years ago hugged the hillside. Catching a glimpse of the amber-stained logs and rust red metal roof of her childhood home, the memories came rushing back—all the times he'd driven her up this hill, one hand on the wheel, the other slung across her shoulders. *Don't.*

Brushing aside the images of her life entwined with his, she focused instead on the blue green waters of the cove stretched across the bay, where the mountains on the other side seemed to rise into the heavens. Snow-capped, razor sharp peaks protruded from a shifting cloudbank and a lone ray of sunshine reflected off a fishing boat in the distance.

The Inn at the Cove sat in the middle of a narrow peninsula, nestled against a backdrop of stately Sitka spruce. The front yard jutted out into the quiet waters that lapped against the rocky shoreline. Adirondack chairs still circled a fire pit and the porch swing swayed in the breeze. Mitchell, Lauren's golden retriever, bounded off the top step and charged toward the truck, barking.

Her mother rounded the corner of the house in a faded red gingham shirt and worn khaki pants, carrying a bag of mulch. She dropped the bag to the ground and squealed with delight as Lauren slid out of the truck. Mitchell planted both paws on her hip and slathered her fingers with wet, sloppy kisses. She laughed and scratched him vigorously behind both ears. "It's good to see you, too, Mitchell."

Lauren gently pushed Mitchell away, raising her eyes and hesitantly gauging Mom's expression. While she expected to find hurt and disappointment lingering in her mother's brown eyes, she found them brimming with tears of joy. As if she couldn't wait another moment, Mom enveloped her in a tender hug.

"Hello, Mom." Her voice caught in her throat. Mitchell's tail berated her legs. She squeezed her eyes shut. *Home.* She tried so hard to pretend she didn't need it or wouldn't miss it. But the warmth of her mother's embrace melted away the façade of self-reliance she had carefully crafted.

Pulling back, Mom examined her from head to toe. "I can't believe it. Has it really been three years? You look wonderful, love. A little soggy, but wonderful." She smiled through her tears. "So glad you're here."

Lauren could only nod in agreement, swiping the back of her hand across her damp cheeks. In eight years, she'd come home once. For Pop's funeral three years ago.

The truck canopy slammed shut and both Mom and Lauren glanced toward Blake unloading luggage onto the front steps. Mom's mouth curved into a knowing smile as she turned her gaze back to Lauren.

"Your fiancé couldn't make it?"

"Don't ask," Lauren shook her head. "I'll tell you later."

Mom furrowed her brow. "I see." She moved toward Blake. "Blake Tully. It's been too long. So nice to see you again."

"Hi, Mrs. Carter. Where would you like these?"

"Oh, dear. Lauren's room isn't, well, Lauren's anymore. I'm afraid you'll have to put those up in the loft. Do you mind?"

"Not at all." He disappeared into the house.

Lauren followed Blake and Mom through the front door. The aroma of fresh-baked chocolate chip cookies made her mouth water. Remnants of a fire glowed in the fireplace, and two well-loved brown leather couches flanked the stone hearth. The head from the first moose her brothers ever shot still hung above the mantle, as though he kept watch over the comings and goings in the great room.

Lauren's eyes traveled up to the balcony that spanned the width of the room. Blake stood near the top of the stairs, looking over the hand-carved railing, holding her suitcases. When their eyes met, she remembered the many evenings Blake had spent in this very room, watching movies or playing their families' own ridiculous version of highly competitive Uno. Did he remember, too?

She glanced away, pretending to study the guest book flipped open on the hall table. Only a few entries were listed for the whole month of June. *That's a problem. We should be booked solid.*

"Smells wonderful, Mom. Are you expecting anyone?"

"Yes, one young couple coming in on the evening ferry. Would you like something to eat? You must be starving."

Slow, deliberate footsteps on the hardwood caught Lauren's attention. She looked up. Granny shuffled toward the kitchen. The old woman paused and clasped her hands together.

"Mallory, I've been looking all over for you." Granny moved closer and waved a frantic hand. "You must come quickly. Mother says the baby will be here in a matter of minutes. Come."

CHAPTER THREE

A plate shattered on the kitchen floor and Lauren jumped, her pulse racing. Her eyes darted between Mom and Granny. Mom stood at the kitchen counter, shards of her favorite blue ceramic platter littering the hardwood around her. All the color drained from her face.

"Mom? Are you okay?"

Mom just stared at Granny, a spatula dangling from one hand. She clamped her mouth and swallowed hard, but didn't speak.

"Granny? It's me, Lauren. Remember?" She stepped toward Granny and took one wrinkled, trembling hand between both of hers.

"No, no you're Mallory. The baby will be here any minute and Mother doesn't want you to miss it," Granny insisted, her eyes cloudy with confusion.

Lauren's stomach clenched. *Why is she calling me Mallory?*

"Let's sit down." She guided Granny into a chair and glanced at Mom. *A little help here.*

Mom cleared her throat and pulled a cup out of the cabinet. "How about some hot tea, Mother?"

Granny twisted in her chair and eyed Lauren, arranged her cardigan sweater just so and fished a tissue from her pocket. "Yes, I suppose tea would be nice."

"It is so nice to see you again, Granny. I love blue on you. It matches your eyes." Lauren hoped to draw her grandmother back to lucidity.

Granny smiled and patted Lauren's hand. "Thank you, dear. That's a lovely handbag you have there." She tipped her head toward Lauren's purse.

"Thank you. It was a gift from my fiancé," Lauren said.

"How thoughtful." Granny smoothed the fabric of her skirt over her knees and bracelets jangled at her wrist. Her beautiful silver hair was carefully combed and tucked into a small bun at the nape of her neck. Granny hadn't given up her fastidious concern for her appearance. Lauren smiled. Pop used to tease her about her fondness for cashmere sweaters.

Two little girls with tousled blond curls chased each other into the kitchen, one squealing with delight while the other snatched at her sister's blanket.

"Emmy and Ava, freeze." Mom stepped in front of them, planting her feet firmly in their path. "There's a broken plate on the floor and I don't want you to hurt your feet. Can you say hello to Aunt Lauren?"

Both girls were speechless, blue eyes wide with wonder as they peeked around Mom's legs. These curious toddlers looked nothing like the baby pictures that adorned her fridge back in Portland. If it weren't for Facebook and Matt's blog, she wouldn't even recognize them. Her heart ached. She missed so much.

Lauren offered a tentative smile. Ava inched closer and tugged on a strand of Lauren's hair.

"Cookie?" Emmy asked, her chubby arms outstretched toward Mom and the kitchen counter. Mom handed her a chocolate chip cookie from the cooling rack. Ava wandered over to investigate, mirroring her sister's actions.

"Here, let me sweep up." Lauren went to the pantry and got the broom and dust pan. "I didn't know the girls were here. Where's Matthew? I thought he'd hang around to say hello."

"He planned to wait for you. Then Angela called. Sounds like Joshua fell and might need stitches. There's never a dull moment in that house." Mom loaded a plate with cookies and brought it to the table.

Before Lauren could dump the contents of the dust pan into the garbage, Emmy had removed all of the plastic cups and plates from the bottom kitchen drawer. Lauren blew out a breath. Mischievous little things. As if on cue, Ava upended Lauren's bag and scooped up the mascara and powder compact with great interest.

"Oh!" Emmy gasped, her little mouth ringed with chocolate as she examined Lauren's iPhone.

"Um, I'll take that." Lauren dropped the dustpan and snatched the phone from Emmy's grasp. "Thank you."

Emmy's lower lip turned down, and she released an ear-splitting wail.

Oh no. Lauren glanced at Mom. Now what?

"Girls, let's give Aunt Lauren back her things, please. I'll help you." Mom kneeled down next to the girls.

Still whimpering, Emmy and Ava obeyed.

"I'm sorry, honey. Why don't you go get settled." Mom looked up at Lauren and handed her a tube of lip gloss that had rolled across the floor.

Lauren nodded in agreement. A hot shower was calling her name. She collected her re-organized bag from her nieces and headed for the loft.

Blake stood at the bottom of the stairs, brow furrowed as he studied his phone. He glanced up as she came closer. "Mission accomplished. Two bags delivered."

"Thank you. And thank you for the ride."

Blake shrugged. "No problem." He smiled. "It is nice to see you again, Lauren. I hope you enjoy the time with your family."

Lauren watched him saunter through the kitchen, admiring the view from behind as he snagged a cookie on his way out the front door. Her heart stuttered.

All that paddling suits you.

Good grief. *Still engaged, remember?* Putting those broad shoulders out of her mind, she climbed the stairs to the loft. A queen-sized sleigh bed covered with a handmade quilt in patterns of turquoise and chocolate took center stage. A once-empty niche under the window was now a built-in window seat, warm and inviting with a tufted cushion and several overstuffed pillows. Lauren smiled with delight as she sank onto the cushion, tension melting from her neck and shoulders. She was at the end of the house, tucked under the peak of the roof with an unobstructed view of the water. Out in the distance, the rich green curve of the shoreline gave way to the barrier islands that protected the small community from the harsh waters in the Gulf of Alaska.

"Do you like the new upgrade?"

Lauren twisted away from the window. Mom leaned against the door frame, an expectant smile brightening her features.

"It's amazing." Lauren rubbed the silky tassel on one of the pillows between her fingers. "I think I could sit here for hours."

"I know the feeling. I hope it makes up for not being able to sleep in your old room. I'm sorry about that. After your grandfather died, it was easier to move Granny here than have to worry about her living alone. Your room was most convenient. With her memory issues it doesn't seem wise to move her again."

"I don't expect you to move Granny just for me. What's going on with her memory? Why is she talking about Aunt Mallory?"

Mom's smile disappeared. Her green eyes filled with sadness. "Dr. Wheeler says it's a classic case of dementia. Her short-term memory is poor, but her long-term memory is still quite sharp. Today's hectic. I'm sure that adds to her confusion. And Mallory, well, that's a story all in itself."

"Do tell."

Mom sank down on the bed. "I know we've never talked much about my sisters before." She shook her head. "Our whole world changed in an instant."

"Mallory died in an accident, right?"

"Snuck out with her boyfriend. They were racing snow machines, going way too fast. There was a terrible collision. Neither survived." Mom shivered and looked away.

Lauren cringed. "That must have been awful."

"Mallory was always a bit of a problem child."

"What do you mean?" *And why haven't we talked about this before?*

"Mallory was a young mother, pregnant by the time she was sixteen." Mom whispered.

The hair on the back of her neck stood up. Goosebumps pebbled the flesh on her arms. Lauren leaned forward, eyes wide with disbelief. "Where was the baby?"

"My parents took care of her. This house wasn't always a bed and breakfast, you know. Women delivered at home all the time. I think that's what Granny was alluding to when she tried to rush you out of the kitchen. Mallory delivered here."

Lauren swallowed hard. "What happened to her? The baby?"

Mom's eyes filled with tears. "She was adopted."

Her heart lurched in her chest. Yearbook photos of teammates and childhood friends flitted through her mind. Did she grow up with her cousin and not even know it?

"Who adopted her?"

"A young couple who thought they couldn't have children." Mom's voice broke on the last word. "I'm sorry I'm so emotional. My parents were heartbroken. My Dad never talked about Mallory again. Today was the first time I've heard Granny say her name in years."

"Wait. What about your other sister? Jane? Does she still live in San Diego?"

Mom nodded. "Her boyfriend was transferred there and she left with him. She was so angry that our parents wouldn't let her keep the baby."

"They just left? Nobody tried to stop her? I can't believe Pop didn't track them down."

Mom wiped the tears from her cheeks. "My parents and Jane argued for days. When they weren't yelling, Mother was crying in her bedroom. I think when Jane left they simply felt relief. I know that sounds harsh now but they desperately needed to grieve."

"So that's it? Aunt Jane runs off to San Diego and never comes back?" Lauren twisted a ringlet of hair around her finger.

Mom sighed. "She pops up from time to time."

"Pops up? Like visits?"

"She sends letters or e-mails, bragging about her latest trip to Venice. Then last week it was all about how she'd be here soon to start helping out."

"What makes her think you need her help?" Lauren felt a muscle in her jaw twitch. *The nerve of this woman.*

"Arrogance, I suppose. Or maybe guilt because she never had a chance to say goodbye to Pop. I can't figure her out. But I would welcome her help with Granny, especially now."

"Are you sure? She doesn't sound like she'd be much help." Lauren shook her head in disgust. Her parents had poured themselves into the bed and breakfast for more than twenty years. An estranged relative couldn't just waltz in and take over.

Mom smiled wanly. "I meant financial help, sweetie. Long term care for dementia patients is expensive."

"Mom, you can't be serious." A high-pitched screech interrupted their conversation. Mom stood quickly and ran toward the noise.

"Sounds like the twins are having a disagreement. I better go check. Thank you for coming home. We really need you." She blew Lauren a kiss as she descended the stairs.

Lauren fell back against the cushions on the window seat and closed her eyes, rubbing her palm across her forehead. This was more drama than she could handle, especially on the heels of an already exhausting twenty-four hours. What was that verse? *The sins of the fathers will visit the sons.* Or something like that. Apparently she wasn't the only one in this family trying to make amends for her past.

CHAPTER FOUR

Blake propped his arms on the counter and scanned the spreadsheet, probing for gaps in their budget. Inquiries for rafting and kayaking excursions flooded their inbox. The new website received dozens of daily hits, and the first three weeks of the season were booked solid. His heart swelled with gratitude. Thank you, Lord. They'd anticipated some success, given the surge in cruise ship traffic. But this— he shook his head, double-checking the numbers again— went way beyond even their most optimistic projections.

His brother Jeremy spun around in the desk chair and crumpled a piece of paper. "We could just chuck the whole thing and buy a time share in Maui."

"Uh-huh." Okay, insurance was on track but payroll—a wad of crumpled paper popped him in the temple, and he flinched. "Hey."

"Seriously, dude. What's with you today? You haven't heard a word I've said."

Blake sighed and tried once again to discard the memory of those long auburn curls and a yellow sundress. "Sure, I heard you. You booked six reservations this morning."

"I said that, like, ten minutes ago. Dang, what happened at the airport?"

"Nothing." *The incredibly hot Lauren Carter wearing some dude's ring, that's what.*

He'd blinked twice at baggage claim to realize she wasn't a dream. He grabbed her elbow and she stared up at him with those bottomless green eyes. It was her, all right. Suddenly he was twenty years old again, heartbroken as he watched her Honda Prelude disappear around the bend.

The hurt awakened, like a bear from hibernation. He'd spent almost a decade trying to get over her. He was beginning to wonder if he might need a decade more.

A bell chimed and Tisha McDowell, their first official employee, wedged the front door open with her hiking boot then scooted in carrying a loaded cardboard coffee carrier.

"Compliments of your baby sister next door." She smiled, sliding the trio of grande mochas onto the counter. Megan had scored a summer job as a barista in the new coffee shop. Although she begged her brothers for a chance to paddle a kayak, their parents feared for her safety and insisted she was too young.

Jeremy took a long sip then set his cup on the desk. "Man, she makes a good mocha."

Blake wrapped his fingers around the warm paper cup and tipped it to his lips. Extra strong java with a jolt of chocolate, just the way he liked it. "Not bad for a girl who'd rather be paddling," he agreed.

"Speaking of paddling, when's my next run, boss?" Tisha leaned over Blake's shoulder and the ends of her long ponytail tickled his forearm.

Blake stiffened and clenched his jaw as she tapped her fingernails on the desk, *rat a tat rat a tat*. Her breath was hot on his cheek. He tried not to squirm. *Ever heard of personal space?*

"Looks like one short run at 4:30, family of five wants to kayak around the bay for an hour," Blake kept his eyes on the screen, staring at the reservation and praying Tisha made a quick exit.

"Great! I'm all over it. Catch you later." She grabbed her coffee and sailed back out the door.

Jeremy chuckled. "That isn't the only thing she's all over."

Blake narrowed his eyes at his younger brother. "What are you talking about?"

"Dude. She would be all over you in a second if you didn't sit there like an iceberg. What's your problem, man?"

Blake grinned. "No problem here." Jeremy loved to aggravate him. And he was good at it. But not this time. He shook his head. *You're way off on that whole Tisha thing, little brother.* He grabbed a thick stack of brochures off the counter and reached for his keys. "I've got to deliver these to the ferry terminal, I guess their rack is empty already. I'll be back in a few."

Jeremy dismissed him with a wave. "I'll hold down the fort."

Five minutes later, Blake pulled his truck into the ferry terminal and cut the engine. He had just enough time to drop off these brochures and head over to the warehouse to make sure Tisha had everything she needed for that four-thirty run.

A new Lexus SUV pulled into the space next to his. Blake's heartbeat stuttered when he recognized the school superintendent, Alan Maxwell, in the driver's seat. Although Blake checked the school district's website faithfully since he moved back, no one had posted an opening for a head basketball coach at the high school. *Well, there's no time like the present. Couldn't hurt to ask, right?*

He scooped the brochures off the passenger seat and jumped out of the truck. Slamming the door, he mustered his most professional smile and waved to his new boss.

"Hi, Mr. Maxwell. How's it going?"

In his plaid flannel button down and spotless Levi's, Mr. Maxwell looked like he'd just stepped off the pages of LL Bean. "Afternoon, Blake. How's business?"

"Can't complain. We've got more business than we can handle most days."

Mr. Maxwell hitched his thumbs in his belt loops and rocked back on his heels. "Good, good. Keeps you out of trouble, I guess."

Blake's stomach clenched. "Trouble, sir?"

"C'mon, son." He clapped Blake on the shoulder. "No need to pretend with me. I'm well aware of your history. Just glad to hear you're keeping your nose clean."

Blake chewed on his lower lip, his blood pounding in his ears like a freight train. "I can assure you, sir, those days are behind me."

"Of course they are. Now if you'll excuse me, I need to buy—"

"Wait." Blake put up a hand to stop him. "I'd really like to be considered for Mr. Hoffman's position, when and if he decides to retire. I know—"

"Whoa. Slow down, there. Don't get me wrong, I'm thrilled you're teaching history this fall. But coaching?" A thin smile stretched across his weathered features and he shook his head slowly, as if that would make the words more palatable. "You're gonna have to earn my trust, son." With one final pat on the shoulder, he turned away.

Blake watched him go, seething inside. What was that all about?

Lord, why did you call me back here? You know I want nothing more than to coach again. If you've forgotten the mistakes I've made, why can't he?

***

LAUREN SAT UP, startled awake by the opening notes of Katy Perry's "Firework". Groggy and disoriented, she glanced around the loft. That's right. *Home.* Sliding off the window seat, she reached for her bag and dug past her wallet, baggage claim stubs, and an Altoids tin.

"C'mon, where is it?" The blue glow of her cell phone appeared and she studied the screen. Holden. Her heart stuttered in anticipation. She needed to hear his voice. Surely he'd offer to catch the next plane out.

She sighed, swiping her finger across the screen. "Hello?"

"Hey, you." His voice was husky, confident. She waited for the rush of warmth that usually accompanied that timbre. Huh. Nothing.

"Hi." She sat down on the edge of the bed.

"I'm sorry I didn't call sooner. Things are kind of crazy here."

She hesitated. "What kind of crazy?"

"They're opening an investigation. One of the surgery techs says I left a sponge in this guy's leg."

Lauren gasped. "You're kidding."

"I wish I was. Listen, there's—"

Here it comes, she thought, rubbing the back of her neck. *He's bailing.*

"Look. About the other night, it wasn't what you thought. I don't know what Monique has told you, but I've only done what any other doctor in my situation would do. Does that make sense?"

There it was. The subtle defensiveness. It had been cropping up more and more lately. Lauren swallowed hard and gathered her courage.

"And the golf pro at the country club? What's the story there?" She'd seen medications change hands on more than one occasion during their golf outings. This was new territory for her, challenging him. The steely silence that greeted her was a strong indication that he was as surprised as she was.

"Whose side are you on, anyway?"

Bile rose in the back of her throat. "This was your idea, Holden. You said we couldn't set a date until you met my family. You're supposed to be here. With me. Now." She hated how her voice had risen dangerously close to a whine.

Muffled voices in the background distracted him. A pregnant pause ensued. Was he with someone? Her scalp tingled. "Holden? Who are you talking to?"

"Sorry. Something's come up. I gotta go."

"If you're really sorry you'll catch the next flight."

"Seriously?" He muttered an obscenity under his breath. "You have no idea what I'm up against here, Lauren. I'll call you later."

Then the line went dead.

Lauren pulled the phone away from her ear. That's it? Tossing her phone into her bag, she flopped back onto the bed and stared at the ceiling. How did they get here? Where was the charming, suave Holden she'd fallen in love with?

"S-s-sister? You up there?" a male voice hollered.

Lauren flinched, her heart pounding in her chest. Seth.

"Lo-lo!"

Lauren smiled as Seth barked the nickname she hadn't heard in years. She rolled off the bed and opened the door. At the bottom of the steep stairs, she found her youngest brother. His beard was grizzly and untamed, blond hair cascaded to his shoulders in matted curls.

Squealing with delight, she flew down the stairs and jumped in his waiting arms. He swung her around, laughing as her feet left the ground. He was six years younger but he outweighed her by a hundred pounds.

She smelled the musky, sour odor of a man who missed quite a few showers.

"W-w-what are you doing here?"

She pouted. "Can't a girl come home and check up on her baby brother?"

"S-s-sure you can." He smiled. As the oldest, she tried to mother her brothers from the minute they came home from the hospital. Matthew resisted but Seth basked in the glow of her attention. She taught him to sing when his words froze on his tongue and knocked the boys on the playground flat on their backs when they taunted him. Nobody messed with her baby brother.

"Come sit down and tell me all about your latest adventures." She tucked her arm in the crook of his elbow and they settled on the couch closest to the fireplace.

"C-c-can't tell you. Top secret." Seth smirked and leaned out of reach as she swung a fist in the direction of his bulging bicep.

"You smell like you've hiked for days." She fanned her fingers in front of her nose. "Where have you been?"

"Me and Toby staked a k-k-iller claim. This c-c-could be the m-m-mother lode." He always stuttered more when he was excited.

"That's incredible. How long will it take to excavate?"

He stroked his beard and stared at the ceiling. "About—"

A thump followed by a muffled cry interrupted their conversation. Seth's eyes, wide with fear, met hers. *Granny.*

Lauren and Seth tripped over each other racing down the hallway to Lauren's old bedroom. Mom knelt on the floor, stroking her mother's forehead. Granny lay crumpled beside the bed, legs askance and her slip peeking out the hem of her skirt.

"Mom?" Lauren touched her shoulder. "What happened?"

Granny moaned a low, guttural sound that turned Lauren's stomach.

"I don't know." Mom's eyes darted to Seth and back to Lauren. "I was making the bed in the next room and I heard this awful noise. She must have bumped her head as she fell."

"Sh-sh-should I call 9-1-1?" Seth asked.

"Did you check her pulse?" Lauren dropped to her knees and reached for Granny's wrist. *Airway, breathing, circulation.* A very faint pulse fluttered under her fingertips. "I've got a pulse. Granny, can you hear me?"

Granny moaned again but her eyes didn't open and her complexion remained ashen.

"Please, dear Lord." Mom whispered. "Let her be okay."

Lauren swallowed hard and surveyed the rest of Granny's body. Her ankle was twisted at an abnormal angle. She cringed and straightened Granny's skirt with trembling fingers. "I'm worried about her leg. I think we should call an ambulance rather than move her ourselves."

"Got it." Seth reached for his cell phone and keyed the numbers in.

"Does she have a history of falling? Ever had a seizure?"

Mom dabbed at a cut on Granny's forehead with a tissue. "She's fallen before, but I've never seen a seizure. Why?"

"The EMT's are going to ask. It might help to have a list of her meds, too."

"It's all in her chart at the hospital," Mom said. "I'm going to ride with her in the ambulance, anyway."

Lauren frowned. "Wait. What about the guests?"

Mom offered a weak smile. "That's where you come in."

Seth ended the call and stuffed his phone in his pocket. "A-A-ambulance c-c-coming."

"Mom, I haven't helped out since I was in high school."

"Not much has changed, honey. You can probably run this place with your eyes closed."

A wave of panic welled up inside. Lauren sagged back on her heels. "I don't know—"

"It will all come back to you, I promise. You—"

"Mom?" A man's voice called out from the living room. "Anybody home?"

Seth turned and poked his head into the hallway. "W-w-we're in here."

Heavy footfalls echoed on the hardwood and Matt came into the bedroom, stopping next to Seth. Worry clouded his features as he stared at Granny on the floor. He raised his blue eyes to meet Lauren's gaze. "Hey, sis. What's going on in here?"

"Granny fell a few minutes ago. We're waiting on the ambulance." Lauren stood and stepped gingerly away from Granny, slipping her arms around Matt's waist. "Good to see you again."

He pulled her close and planted an affectionate kiss on the top of her head. "I'm glad you made it. Sorry I couldn't meet your flight. It's been a crazy day."

"That's okay. How's Joshua?"

"He's fine. Nothing a few staples couldn't fix. I'm a little worried about Granny, though. Think we should splint that ankle?" He knelt down and gently placed a hand on Granny's leg.

"Lauren says we shouldn't move her, but whatever you think—" Mom stood and reached for another tissue from the box on the dresser.

"Mom, the ambulance will be here in a minute. Let the professionals do their job." Lauren put a hand on Matt's shoulder.

"I think it's pretty obvious that leg's broken. What if she tries to move it?"

Lauren's chest tightened. *Always trying to micromanage.* "She's breathing and has a pulse, Matt. That's what matters right now. We could do more harm than good trying to—"

The blare of sirens blanketed any further discussion as the ambulance pulled up outside. Lauren ran and opened the front door for the paramedics. Her breath hitched in her throat. Jess Ferguson, Blake's best friend, stood on the porch. He looked confident and professional in his crisp white shirt and navy blue pants. The EMT waiting next to him resembled a girl who was a year behind her in school. Tiffany. Tiffany Lambert.

"Lauren?" Jess's brown eyes widened. "Holy smokes. It's been a long time. We're responding to a call about—"

"Hi, Jess. Tiffany. It's my grandmother. She's back here." She directed them to the bedroom, breathing a sigh of relief as Matt stepped out of the way and let the paramedics take charge of Granny's care. Her heart ached as Granny was strapped to the stretcher and loaded into the back of the ambulance. Mom climbed in behind her and blew Lauren and her brothers a kiss. Lauren managed a weak wave before the ambulance doors slammed shut.

Matt glanced at his watch. "I can still pick up the guests from the ferry but there's no way I can stay here tonight. Ang will kill me."

"I think I'm on for tonight. Unless you want to step up to the plate and take a swing at serving breakfast?" Lauren gave Seth a playful nudge.

"N-n-no way." Seth held up both hands and backed away, a look of panic in his eyes. "It's all y-y-you."

"Right. All me." How hard could it be? Greet the guests, fix a little breakfast, then send them on their way. A cool breeze blew in off the water and Lauren shivered, trying to ignore the way her stomach twisted in an anxious knot.

CHAPTER FIVE

L auren knocked a stack of metal lids over and muttered under her breath as they clattered onto the kitchen floor. She was up with the sun to fix breakfast for the guests, a caffeine headache encircling her skull in its vise-like grip. Wrestling her mother's ancient electric griddle from the cabinet, she rubbed her bleary eyes and studied the recipe on the Bisquick box. In her world, breakfast meant a carton of yogurt topped with granola. Her father reminded her late last night that guests expected, and paid for, something more substantial. Surely she could produce pancakes for two.

He had come home around midnight and wrapped his only daughter in a warm hug, then followed it with grim news from the hospital. Granny's fall resulted in not only a mild concussion but also a broken arm and ankle. Mom had left a few instructions scribbled on the back of an envelope. She must have already gone back to the hospital. Hopes of rest and rejuvenation dashed, Lauren accepted her assignment as temporary innkeeper. *Come on, you've got this.*

The first egg she touched refused to come out of the carton. She tried again and half of the shell came off in her hand, dripping sticky egg white down her arm. *Or not.* Reaching for a paper towel, she tipped the open carton of half and half on its side. A white river flowed across the granite countertop. *Fabulous.*

"Sure smells good in here."

Lauren's head shot up, hands full of kitchen towels as she raced to soak up the sticky mess oozing down the side of the cabinet. The young couple from Chicago hovered in the doorway, eyes wide with surprise. She pasted on a smile and gestured toward the empty chairs at the table.

"Please sit down, have some coffee." Her father had set the table and programmed the coffee maker before he went to bed, buying her valuable time.

"Are you the owner's daughter or..." The man trailed off, pressing his wire rimmed glasses back up on the bridge of his nose.

Lauren tossed the soggy towels in the sink and reached for the carafe of coffee. "I'm Lauren. My parents couldn't be here this morning. My grandmother fell—it's a long story. Do you take cream and sugar?"

"Yes, please."

"Chilly this morning." The woman shivered, drawing her navy blue cardigan tighter.

"Sure is." Lauren set two steaming mugs of coffee in front of them and then scrambled to open a new carton of half and half. She really needed to get those pancakes started.

"Did you grow up here then?"

"Uh-huh." She kicked the refrigerator door shut, balancing butter, orange juice, and a bowl of fruit salad in her arms.

"How do you sleep with all of this light?" the woman asked, wrapping both hands around her coffee mug and sipping it slowly.

"Get used to it, I guess." Dang. Forgot the bacon. The package sat on the counter next to the stove, still unopened. Might have to skip that this morning.

"Knock, knock." Blake stood in the doorway of the kitchen, rapping his knuckles on the doorframe.

Lauren's heart skipped a beat. She dropped the measuring cup in the pancake batter. "Good morning, you must be Mr. and Mrs. Baird." He leaned across the table, giving the man a hearty handshake. "Blake Tully. It's a pleasure to meet you."

"Todd Baird and this is my beautiful bride, Melissa." He slipped his arm around his wife and gave her a tender kiss.

"Congratulations. We hope your honeymoon in Alaska is unforgettable." Blake smiled and raised his insulated coffee mug toward Lauren. "Good morning. Mind if I get a refill?" He paused next to the coffee maker.

"What are you doing here?"

He smirked as he tipped the carafe into his mug. "Believe it or not, I'm helping you out."

She furrowed her brow. "Really? How so?"

"It seems your folks include complimentary transfers with all their reservations. I thought you might need an extra driver this morning."

She poured the pancake batter onto the griddle and tried to avoid Blake's gaze. His eyes matched the blue polo shirt that hugged his broad shoulders and she couldn't afford to be distracted. She wanted to be annoyed.

"I am quite capable of driving my guests wherever they need to go," she said, heat rising on her neck as she noticed the Bairds had stopped talking. They sipped their coffee, watching the conversation over the rims of their coffee cups.

Blake leaned back against the counter and crossed one long, lean leg over the other. "My mom works nights in the ER. She told me your grandmother was admitted. This seems like a lot for you to take on your second day back."

She resented his implication that she couldn't handle a challenge. On the other hand, she'd made a real mess of breakfast. Two guests generated at least one load of laundry, not to mention the cleaning and vacuuming. If Blake handled the driving she might finish the chores before lunch and have the afternoon to visit Granny.

"Looks like Blake will handle your transportation this morning." She glanced at the Bairds, then back at the pancakes bubbling on the griddle. "Remind me of your plans?"

"Helicopter ride this morning and sea kayaking after lunch," Melissa said.

"Perfect. No rush. Whenever you're ready, we'll be on our way." Blake remained propped against the counter, casually sipping his coffee. The weight of his expectant stare propelled her around the kitchen; serving the pancakes, loading the dishwasher, and wiping down counters. She needed to thank him. She owed him at least that much for helping her and her family out in a crisis.

But a trace of annoyance niggled its way up into her gut, sifting in with the shame and guilt she already carried. He waltzed in like he owned the place, calling the guests by name and playing tour guide. Did he not remember her cruel words and thoughtless actions? Why was he showering her with kindness?

"So, Lauren. What does your father do for a living?" Melissa forked another bite of pancake and waited for an answer.

"He's a State Trooper."

"Hey, isn't there a show about those guys on TV?" Todd nudged his wife and smiled.

"How long has your family run the B & B?"

Good grief. *What's up with the inquisition?* "Um, they started the year after I was born. So this is their twenty-sixth season." Lauren opened the cabinet, reaching for a clean mug. If she didn't get some coffee in the next fifteen seconds, her head just might explode.

"And did your dad build this place himself?"

Blake cleared his throat and slid a napkin next to her elbow. Lauren glanced at the message he'd scrawled in all capitals: TRAVEL WRITER. PLAY NICE!

Oh no. She raised her eyes to meet his. Blake arched one eyebrow. So that explained the questions. Lifting the carafe in the air, she flashed her most hospitable smile. "My grandfather built it, actually. Can I get you some more coffee?"

"That must have been quite an adventure," Todd said, covering his cup with his hand. "I'm okay, thank you."

"I'll take another half cup, please." Melissa smiled and raised her mug toward Lauren. "What do you think sets your place apart from that of the competition?"

Lauren poured the coffee and wracked her foggy brain for a witty comeback. Did Melissa know the Inn was struggling this season? Or was she merely making conversation? "I think it's tough to compete with cruise ships and their all-inclusive packages. But for those guests who desire a truly unique and authentic experience, I believe we offer exactly that." She reached for the empty pancake platter. "Can I get you anything else?"

"I think we're all set," Melissa said.

Lauren returned to cleaning up the kitchen, hoping her response wouldn't come back to haunt her later in print. Maybe she shouldn't be speculating about the state of the family business when she hadn't even been home twenty-four hours yet. While she second-guessed her response to Melissa's question, Blake kept the conversation flowing with a story about one of his many recent adventures on the river.

Before long, chairs scraped back and silverware clattered as the Bairds shrugged into their fleece-lined outerwear. Lauren wished them well and walked with them to the front door.

Blake followed them out but turned back, studying her for a moment.

"What?"

"You've got a little something on your face. Right here." He pointed a finger at his cheek. "Looks like pancake batter."

She rubbed her hand quickly across her cheek then studied her fingers. How embarrassing.

"Lauren?"

She sighed and looked up at him.

"You're welcome." He winked and reached for the door knob.

She balled up her fists, stomped her foot, and growled as the front door clicked shut.

***

BLAKE SMILED AS he drove the newlyweds away from the Inn. The pancake batter on her cheek, mass of fiery red curls piled on top of her head, half and half dripping off the counter; it took every ounce of self-control he could muster not to laugh out loud. She still tried to handle everything on her own. Some things never change.

Blake glanced in his rear view mirror as the Bairds huddled in the van's middle seat. If he was supposed to dazzle Melissa Baird the travel writer, he had better get busy. Although snuggled up against her new husband, she didn't appear too interested in the scenery. He could squeeze in a quick drive-by of some popular attractions before dropping them off for their helicopter ride.

Melissa met his eyes in the mirror. "Do you know much about the Inn?"

"A little. What else would you like to know?"

"I'd like to hear more about the family's history, the building, how it became a bed and breakfast. I didn't get to ask a lot of questions. Lauren seemed too distracted."

Blake spotted a black bear and two cubs frolicking on the rocky beach and pulled the van over for a closer look. While the Bairds scrambled for their camera, he turned the question over in his mind. The Carter family's bed and breakfast, once the reigning favorite in Southcentral Alaska, had faltered in recent years, something Lauren had definitely alluded to. His parents told him the increase in cruise ships making port calls put a significant dent in the Inn's reservations. Granny's health issues probably weren't helping the situation. He couldn't air the Carters' dirty laundry to a stranger, particularly a travel writer and also his customers for an afternoon of sea kayaking.

"The Carter family has a rich history here. The bed and breakfast evolved out of a desire to share their unique location with others. I've heard it said that people laughed when the family claimed that land. Look at it now. You couldn't ask for a more amazing view." Blake tried to give just enough information to satisfy her curiosity.

"What about you and the redhead? What's the story there?" Melissa prodded, pulling a notebook and pen from her satchel.

Blake turned in his seat to look at her. "Excuse me?"

"C'mon." Melissa's eyes twinkled. "The chemistry between you two was palpable. Think you'll ever get together?"

Clearly the novelty of black bears was lost on her. He turned back around, put the van in gear and headed for town. "No, I don't see that happening." He didn't tell her that he spent many a night alone, dreaming of nothing else. But that dream was fading. She belonged to someone else now.

CHAPTER SIX

L auren tucked a stray curl behind her ear and stuffed wet sheets into the dryer. The dirty bathroom beckoned her but she ignored it in favor of a second cup of coffee. How did her mother do this every day? She felt exhausted already and the day wasn't even half over.

She poured half and half into her mug as a blur of red sweat pants and spiky blond hair flew into the kitchen.

"Hiiiii-yaa!" Her nephew Joshua high-kicked and karate chopped his way past her chair.

"Whoa." Lauren glanced at her nephew. "Let me see those staples."

"Got five, right here." Joshua leaned over and pointed at his scalp. Lauren winced. Gross. Emmy and Ava scampered in, waving identical stuffed monkeys. Their mother, Angela, brought up the rear. Dark circles underlined her brown eyes as she cradled baby Gavin in her arms.

Lauren stood and extended one arm toward her sister-in-law, giving her an awkward half-hug. The baby's head brushed her arm and she retracted her arm, as though she'd been burned. "Hi, Ang." She pasted on a smile, while her heart thundered in her chest. She'd avoided babies at all costs, always making up creative excuses not to assist with the post-partum appointments when she worked with Dr. Putnam.

"It's so good to see you, Lo. I couldn't believe it when Matt told me you were back in town." Angela slid onto a kitchen chair and dropped her overstuffed diaper bag like a boat anchor on the floor. "How long you staying?"

Lauren shrugged. *At least until this mess with Holden blows over.* "I was supposed to be here for a week. Now that Granny's in the hospital, I guess as long as they need me. Want some coffee?"

"No, thank you," Angela looked down at her sleeping baby. "Not when I'm nursing. Caffeine upsets his stomach."

Lauren made no effort to hide her surprise. "Seriously? How do you function?"

Angela offered a weak laugh. "Somehow we make it through."

"What's Matthew up to this morning?" Surely he wasn't still asleep, foisting these children on his young wife.

"He's working on his sermon. Pastor Tom is on vacation so Matt gets to preach tomorrow. I'm really excited for him." Angela's eyes brightened, her enthusiasm pushing aside the fatigue for a moment. She dipped her chin and planted a kiss on Gavin's tiny forehead.

Lauren smiled at the mental image of her brother Matthew in the pulpit. Hard to believe the same boy once scrawled Angela's name on the water tower in red spray paint.

"You should come tomorrow."

"I don't think so." Lauren shuddered. She hadn't darkened the door of Emerald Cove Community Church since the weekend of Pop's funeral.

"Why not? Everyone would love to see you."

"God and I aren't exactly on speaking terms."

"I'm sorry to hear that—Joshua! Put that down, please," Angela said. Joshua came into the kitchen with his arms wrapped around a pan full of rocks and pebbles.

"But I found gold! Like Uncle Seth!"

"It doesn't belong in the kitchen." Angela stood and thrust baby Gavin into Lauren's arms. "Here, hold him for me."

Before she could protest, her new nephew lay in the crook of her elbow. A tingling sensation started in her chest, while black spots pocked her field of vision. The faint sweet scent of Pampers, the soft cotton blanket against her forearm and the perfect little fingers tucked into a tiny fist brought the horrid memories rushing back. Her heart ached and she tamped the images back down into the deepest recesses of her mind. Gavin yawned and his eyes fluttered open. He studied her with his gray blue eyes. Lauren froze. *Where is Angela?* She could not keep holding this baby.

Angela reappeared with Joshua in tow. "Good grief. He is fascinated with Seth and his gold mining stuff."

"I want to go hunting for gold, Mom. Can I? Can I? Pleeeaase?" Joshua whined, yanking on Angela's hand.

"Did s-s-s-omebody say gold?" Seth bellowed and grabbed Joshua from behind. Joshua squealed as his uncle tossed him high in the air.

Gavin wailed and Lauren held him at arm's length, her heart pounding. "Take him."

Angela giggled and scooped him up. "What's the matter, Auntie Lauren?"

"I don't do babies."

"Oh. Well, I was sort of hoping—"

Seth's growls erupted from the floor as he prowled on all fours and pretended to grab each of the twins. They giggled and side stepped his beefy arms, squealing with delight as they toddled in circles around him. Joshua yelled at the top of his lungs and jumped on his uncle's back.

Angela's lips were moving but her voice was drowned out by Gavin's cries.

Lauren massaged her temples and closed her eyes. "I can't hear you, Ang. What?"

"I was hoping you could watch the twins for me," Angela called over the ruckus.

Oh, no. No way. Lauren shook her head emphatically. "I don't think so."

Angela's eyes brimmed with tears and she turned away.

Lauren followed her into the hallway. "What's wrong?"

Angela swayed back and forth, pressing a pacifier into the little pink bow of Gavin's lips.

"It's nothing, really. Forget it."

"Then why did you ask?"

Angela sighed. "I'm supposed to take Joshua to a birthday party. The girls need naps. Mike and Debbie watch the kids whenever. I thought you'd be okay."

"I'm not my parents, Ang. I'm terrible with kids. Who is going to make the bed and clean the bathroom? I haven't seen Dad this morning and Mom is still at the hospital."

"The girls sleep really well here. You can do your chores while they nap."

Lauren bristled. *Your chores.* She chose her words carefully. "I've kind of got my hands full, Ang. What if they wake up and need something? "

"Then turn on a show and give them a snack. They'll be fine."

Lauren hesitated. She wanted to help, but this request was testing her patience. "Maybe Matt could work on his sermon while the girls nap?"

"He won't. I already asked."

Surely Angela understood. The business came first. "I'm sorry. I can't help you today."

"Don't worry about it. I'll figure something out." Angela stared at Gavin and avoided eye contact with Lauren.

Lauren nodded and grabbed the bucket of cleaning supplies from the hall closet. Brushing past her young sister-in-law, she tackled the bathroom with vigor. She clenched her teeth as she scrubbed the bathtub, anger bubbling up inside like hot lava. How could her brother be so selfish? It did not take all day to write a sermon. His family needed him. The ringing telephone interrupted her thoughts. The Inn couldn't afford to miss any potential customers, either. She dashed for the kitchen and snatched the cordless on the fourth ring.

"Thank you for calling the Inn at the Cove. How may I help you?" Huh. Funny how that greeting her mother drummed into her head as a preteen rolled right off her tongue.

"Yes, I want to make a reservation." The woman's voice was cool and crisp.

"Um, okay, one moment please." *Where was the reservation book?* Shuffling through a stack of papers on the counter, she uncovered a giant desk calendar with names scrawled inside the oversize squares. *It's time to embrace the 21st century, Mom.* She envisioned a spreadsheet, rectangles marching across the page in formation, carrying the details of each reservation. She could design it this afternoon. "Which dates are you interested in?"

"I want the loft next weekend."

Lauren paused. "I'm sorry the loft is occupied."

"But I've been there before. That's the room I want. When is it available?"

"I'm sorry. It is occupied indefinitely. We have a lovely King bed with a private bath available." Lauren scribbled *check website* on a Post-it note.

"By the way, this doesn't sound like Debbie. Who am I speaking with?"

Lauren hesitated. "This is Lauren. May I have your name, please?" A sharp intake of breath followed by a beat of silence was the only response. "Hello? Are you still there?"

"Yes, I'm here. Just in shock. Lauren, this is Jane Watson Merrill Montgomery. Your aunt."

Lauren's stomach plummeted. Mom would flip if Aunt Jane stayed at the Inn. "Oh. H—hello, Aunt Jane. What a ... surprise."

"Yes. Likewise. Please tell Debbie she can expect me on Friday. I suppose that King bed will have to do." Jane reluctantly parted with her cell phone number, then hung up without saying goodbye.

Lauren puffed her cheeks and blew out a breath, flustered by this turn of events. She cringed at the thought of adding any more stress to Mom's already overflowing plate. *Maybe we can convince Jane to get a hotel room.* While she was writing the reservation on the calendar, the phone rang again. Glancing at the caller ID, she recognized her mother's cell phone number. Oh boy. This would not be fun news to share.

She punched the talk button. "Inn at the Cove."

"Hello, sweetheart. How's it going today?"

"Just fine until a few minutes ago."

"Oh no. What happened?"

Lauren drew a deep breath. Here goes nothing. "Aunt Jane called. She's coming on Friday and wants to stay here."

"You're kidding. What did you tell her?"

"I didn't know what to say. We had a room available so ... I'm sorry, Mom."

"Don't worry about it. We'll figure something out. Friday's still a few days away, right?"

Lauren carved a rectangle around Aunt Jane's name and number, taking her frustration out on the pen and paper. First the breakfast fiasco, then she'd hurt Angela's feelings, and now this. Couldn't one thing go her way today? "Maybe I could call her back, tell her I made a mistake."

"No. We have to face this music sooner or later."

"How's Granny?"

"Surprisingly well, all things considered. I'd like for her to get some rest. And I need a shower. Would you mind coming to pick me up?"

"Sure. Are you ready now?" Tucking the calendar back under the stack of papers, she sifted through the basket of keys and snagged the spare to her mother's minivan.

"Give me about ten minutes to speak with Dr. Wheeler."

"Okay, see you soon." She clicked the off button and dropped the phone on the counter. After checking the laundry and re-starting the dryer, she climbed the stairs to the loft and grabbed her bag. Rummaging for her lip gloss, she dabbed on a fresh coat as she went back down the stairs. The television was on in the front room and the little girls were mesmerized by Sesame Street. Angela had fallen asleep on the couch with Gavin in her arms. A pang of regret knifed her heart as she stared at the sleeping baby.

Seth smiled up at her from a tower of Legos he was constructing with Joshua. "Going somewhere?"

"Mom wants me to pick her up at the hospital." She gestured toward the children. "Are you okay watching them?"

He shrugged. "Sure. We're the men and we rule this house. Right, Josh?"

Joshua grinned and kicked the tower of Legos over. "Right."

Lauren shook her head and slipped out the door before Seth could change his mind. Hopefully Angela and the kids would be gone when they got back and she could talk to Mom about a new reservation system and maybe even upgrading the website. If they had any hope of booking more reservations, she needed to make changes   as   soon   as   possible.

CHAPTER SEVEN

Granny sat propped up in her hospital bed, staring out the window. Her legs were concealed by a beautiful afghan. One arm was casted and the other arm leaned against the table, pulled close to her body. Her hand splayed across her open Bible.

"Granny?" Lauren whispered as she stepped closer.

Granny turned her head, blue eyes clear and bright. She smiled. "Hello, my dear."

"I was so worried about you. How is your head?" Lauren planted a gentle kiss on her grandmother's forehead and sat on the edge of the chair beside the bed.

"Oh, this old noggin will be just fine." Granny rapped her knuckles against her temple.

"What's this I hear about your arm? Dad says your ankle is broken, too?"

"My, news travels fast around here. Don't you worry. I will be back on my feet in no time at all."

The door opened and a nurse wearing pale blue scrubs and a broad smile stepped in. Lauren's stomach plummeted. Shannon. They used to finish each other's sentences, words spilling out all over the place. She lost many a phone privilege when her mother caught her huddled under the covers, gabbing into the wee hours.

She pulled out her stethoscope and glanced at Lauren. Her broad smile faltered and she stopped. "Oh my word. Lauren Carter? Is that you?"

Lauren swallowed hard. "Hi, Shannon. How are you?"

"I'm good. What brings you back to town?" Shannon lifted her stethoscope from around her neck and started checking Granny's vital signs.

"I came to see my family, help out a little bit with ... things." It was partly true, anyway. She squirmed in her chair. Eight years gone by and not a word exchanged. Her chest tightened and she bit down hard on her lower lip. How did you make up for walking away from your dearest friend?

"Well, I know they are glad to see you. Right, Mrs. Watson?"

"Of course, dear. My you are a pretty thing. Have you met my grandson?"

Shannon giggled. "Yes, I know Seth. He's a little young for me."

Silence filled the room as Shannon pressed her fingers to Granny's wrist and watched the clock. Lauren fidgeted with the straps on her handbag, wracking her brain for any nuggets of information Mom might have shared about Shannon. "Have you worked here long?"

"About two years, I guess." Shannon made a note in Granny's chart. "I worked in Anchorage for a little while, waiting on Jess to figure out what he wanted to do. But I hated it. Big city life wasn't for me."

Lauren nodded, thinking about all the little things that made Portland feel like home. "I guess it's not for everyone."

Shannon held her gaze for a moment, blue eyes questioning. "Well, we're creatures of habit around here. We still get together at Jess's sometimes. A bunch of us will be there tonight if you want to stop by."

"I can't." She tipped her head toward Granny. "There's no one to watch the Inn."

Shannon glanced down at Granny's chart, and then closed it gently. "If you change your mind, things usually get going about eight."

"Thanks." If her friends knew what she'd done, they wouldn't welcome her back quite so easily.

Shannon reached for the door, but turned back. She took a breath and Lauren leaned forward expectantly. Her pulse quickened as she braced herself. *Go on, say it. I deserve it.* Instead, Shannon clamped her mouth shut and her lips formed a weak smile. She slipped out the door, taking her unspoken message with her.

Lauren gnawed on her thumbnail and tried to dismiss the regrets barging back in. Her friends still got together at Jess's house. How many Saturday nights had she missed? Trucks circled up, tailgates down as the bonfire launched sparks into the pale blue sky. It didn't matter. She didn't belong here anymore. Bonfire days were over. She met Granny's eyes and offered her a smile.

"You need to get home and care for that little one."

Lauren's heart lurched in her chest.

"Granny, I —"

"Go on." Granny shooed her toward the door with a rapid flick of her fingers. Lauren's knees quaked as she pushed up from the chair.

"I'm fine here. You get on home. That baby needs you."

Lauren nodded and moved toward the door. Hot tears pricked her eyes. A lump filled her throat. The old familiar ache squeezed her heart. If only Granny knew the truth.

Maybe she does.

"That's impossible." Lauren cringed. She didn't mean to say that aloud. She glanced over her shoulder. Granny's eyes were already closed.

She stepped out into the hallway, pulling Granny's door shut behind her. The unmistakable baritone voice of Dr. Wheeler boomed down the hallway. He needed to know about Granny's sudden and unpredictable lapses into the past. Maybe he could adjust her medication. Lauren's heels tapped out a staccato rhythm on the linoleum as she approached the nurses' station. Before she could get his attention, Dr. Wheeler clutched his cell phone and dashed toward the ER. The meeting would have to wait. But the nurse could probably tell her where to find Mom.

"Sweetheart?" Mom was walking toward her, brow furrowed. The letters on her sweatshirt were cracked and fading, her short brown hair matted on one side. A smudge of mascara emphasized the fatigue in her eyes.

"Hi, Mom."

"Your face is flushed. What's going on?"

Lauren pressed her lips into a thin line, shaking her head slowly. "I don't get it. One minute she's totally with it, then the next thing out of her mouth makes zero sense."

"Oh, honey, I know." Mom pulled her close and planted a kiss on her forehead. "I'm sure she's glad you stopped by. C'mon, let's go home."

Lauren frowned and followed Mom down the hall toward the waiting room. Maybe it wasn't her place to worry about Granny's meds. She'd only done a short rotation on the Psychiatric floor during her two semesters at Portland Community college and probably knew just enough to be dangerous. But there had to be some explanation for Granny's cryptic comments.

"Did you hear me?" Mom glanced back over her shoulder, eyebrows raised.

Lauren shook her head. "I'm sorry, I didn't."

"I asked if you wanted to drive?"

"Sure." Lauren pulled the key to the minivan from her bag and followed Mom outside. Fog had rolled in again, hiding the mountains in shrouds of billowing gray and white clouds.

"I really appreciate your help. I'm sure it's not easy to drop everything and come back home." Mom climbed in the passenger side of the minivan.

Lauren circled around to the driver's side, buying time to formulate her answer. This wasn't the best time to let her parents know that the man who wanted to marry their daughter was quite possibly in a heap of trouble. But the reality was that without Holden, she couldn't survive in Portland on her own. Sliding into the driver's seat, she propped her bag on the console between them.

"Is something else bothering you? Besides Granny, I mean?"

Where to begin? Lauren wet her lips. She didn't have to tell Mom everything. Just enough to get a fresh perspective. "Things aren't going well with Holden. I-I don't know where we went wrong. One day I'm dating a handsome, successful surgeon and almost overnight, he morphed into this distracted, paranoid person that I hardly recognize."

"He's probably under a lot of stress. Long hours, little sleep. Maybe he needs a vacation."

"That's the thing. This trip was his idea. He—" She cut her words short and stole a glance at Mom.

Mom managed a weak smile but the hurt in her eyes was unmistakable. "It's okay, honey. You've made it pretty clear that you don't want to spend a lot of time here."

"It's just … complicated. I've been gone so long and things haven't turned out like I expected. And now I'm not even sure I can marry him. I feel like all of my plans are unraveling."

A shadow crossed Mom's face, but she quickly recovered and shaped her lips into a gentle smile. "Maybe the Lord has something better in mind."

"I doubt it. He's never seemed too concerned with me."

"Now you know that isn't true. Jeremiah twenty-nine eleven is engraved on that locket of yours for a reason. Do you remember what that verse says?"

Lauren's fingers fluttered to her throat where she found the locket and caressed the tiny letters engraved on the back. She nodded.

"It says 'For I know the plans for you; plans to prosper and not to harm. Plans to give you hope and a future.'" Mom reached over and squeezed her shoulder. "Don't give up on Him."

That verse seemed a long way from her reality now. She deserved to be forgotten, cast aside, after the mess she'd made of things. How could anyone love her if they knew what she'd done?

Her heart as icy as the glacial peaks on the horizon, she turned the key in the ignition. *Click, whirrr.* Then nothing. *Great.*

Mom groaned and pressed her hands to her face. "Not again."

Lauren got out and circled the car, as if the solution would materialize with a quick inspection.

"So this has happened before?" She rubbed her arms vigorously. She hoped somewhere in her overstuffed suitcases she managed to pack at least one sweater. In her rush to get to the airport, she must have left her jacket in the hall closet.

Mom got out of the van, holding her cell phone. "This van is so temperamental."

"Why don't you get Chip to look at it?" Chip Harvey repaired everybody's cars for as long as she could remember. She loved visiting his shop with her Dad when she was a little girl. Mr. Harvey walked with a limp but he always ambled over to the tiny waiting area that smelled like motor oil and Windex to offer her a lollipop. She would snatch the candy from his outstretched hand, trying to ignore the black grime that caked every fingernail. He always let her watch Scooby Doo on the miniscule black and white TV while they waited.

Mom chewed the corner of her lip. "Chip passed away. His kids didn't want the shop so it closed. We haven't made the time to find someone else. Seth can usually get it running again, anyway."

Lauren swallowed hard. The older Harvey girl was in her class. Beth. She married the Clawson boy right after graduation. She shook her head. It would be hard to lose a parent so young. When things settled down at the Inn she would drop by Beth's house, maybe bring flowers.

"Let's track down Dad. He can swing by and give us a ride."

"I'm freezing, I'll wait inside," Lauren said. They abandoned the minivan and scurried back to the hospital as a light rain began to fall.

A carafe of coffee beckoned from a side table in the waiting room. Lauren filled a Styrofoam cup and held it close, letting the steam warm her face. Dad wasn't answering his phone so Mom had moved on to other options.

The clock on the wall ticked closer to three p.m. Lauren started to pace. Guests could arrive at any time and the beds still weren't made. Seth could not be counted on to check anybody in, much less prep the rooms.

"Seth can come get us," Mom said, dropping her phone in her lap. "Matthew will stay and greet the guests until one of us gets home."

"I hope Angela gets the kids out of there."

Mom stared, eyes twinkling. "Do you think my grandchildren are bad for business?"

"Customers invest in an Alaskan vacation. They purchase an experience. I don't think toddlers eating goldfish crackers appeals to them. We need to manage our presentation. Blow them away with a unique first impression." Lauren felt her adrenaline pump as she envisioned the possibilities. "What about hors D'oeuvres and complimentary wine in the afternoon? Or a hot chocolate bar and s'mores by the fire pit for a more casual feel?"

"Wow." The corners of Mom's lips twitched. "I can see you've given this some thought."

"It's basic marketing, Mom."

"And I thought you were a medical assistant." Mom patted her hand. "I appreciate your input, love. We have always been a family business. Kids underfoot keep me young."

Mom was missing the point completely. "But I think—"

"Oh, look. There's Seth's truck. Let's get out of here." Mom was out of her chair before Lauren could finish her objection.

Lauren sat motionless for a minute, teeth pressed into her lower lip. She didn't expect Mom to shoot her ideas down so quickly. It didn't take an expert to figure out that the Inn was struggling. Still clutching her coffee cup, she followed Mom back out to the minivan.

Seth had already popped the hood and was leaning over the engine, bushy brows knitted together.

"Thanks for coming, sweetie." Mom patted him on the arm and leaned in next to him. "What do you think?"

Seth scratched his scruffy chin and shrugged. "Don't know yet. C-c-could be the starter. Just p-p-put in a n-n-new battery last month."

Lauren sighed. "Want to try jumping it?"

Seth grinned. "We could give it a shot. You a m-m-mechanic now?"

"No, smarty. I just drive an old car."

"C-c-cables are in my truck."

Lauren set her coffee on the hood of Seth's battered maroon Ford Ranger and opened the rusty toolbox mounted behind the cab. She carried the cables back to the minivan and offered them to her brother.

"You busy later?" Seth clipped the cables on the battery.

Lauren glanced at Mom, who shrugged. "Not really. Why?"

Wiping his hands on his caramel-colored Carhart pants, Seth pulled his keys from his pocket. "P-p-party at Jess's tonight. I want you to c-c-come with me."

Lauren's heart lurched. Two invitations within an hour. Were Shannon and Seth in on this together? "I don't know, Seth. I've been gone a long time."

"Don't matter."

The curious stares wouldn't be a problem. But what if people started asking questions about why she left?

That could get dicey. "Who goes to those parties anymore?"

The words were out of her mouth before she even gave them a second thought. Seth's wounded expression made her wince.

"Me." He brushed past her to lift the hood on his truck.

She groaned and shook her head. "That's not what I meant."

Mom slipped her arm around Lauren's shoulders. "He misses you, you know. Just wants to hang out with his big sister before you disappear again."

"I'm not going to disappear."

"He doesn't know that."

Lauren watched as Seth fiddled with the cables then turned back to give them instructions. She couldn't bear to hurt his feelings. Her stomach hardened, but she would take that over the disappointment etched on Seth's forehead.

"Seth." She squeezed his elbow. "Thanks for inviting me. I'll come with you."

A wide smile broke through the storm cloud hovering on his face. His eyes lit up as they bumped fists. "Sweet. Now let's get this c-c-car s-s-started."

She smiled. If only she could cast her cares aside as easily as Seth.

CHAPTER EIGHT

B lake grunted and hauled the last sea kayak onto the rack in the warehouse. He spent the entire afternoon with the newlyweds, paddling all over creation and answering a bazillion questions. Every single muscle ached. A hot shower and some take-out from the Thai place, maybe kick back and catch a few innings of the Mariners game on TV...the perfect end to a grueling day.

Jeremy pulled up in his truck, one arm dangled out the open window and a wide grin stretched across his face. "What up, bro?"

"I'm about to call it a night. What are you up to?" Blake tossed his hat on the hood of the truck and pulled on a well-loved University of Alaska sweatshirt.

"Jump in. Everybody's headed for a party at Jess's place."

"Not everybody. I'm going home. It's been a long day, man."

"What if I told you a certain redhead might make an appearance?"

"How do you know?"

Jeremy winked. "Seth sent me a text. Said he talked her into going."

Blake hesitated. He couldn't resist. "Meet me at home. I need a shower. And I'm driving."

Jeremy laughed and drove off, tires spewing gravel.

An hour later, Blake eased into his favorite spot in front of Jess's cabin. Close to the bon fire with an unobstructed view of the lake. The water reflected the purples and blues of Mt. Greer, a few dollops of snow still clinging to the mountain's craggy peaks. Two trumpeter swans glided gracefully near the shore, a fluffy brood of cygnets trailing in their wake. It turned out to be a beautiful evening after all.

Blake grabbed a Coke from the cooler and settled onto his tailgate. Seth Carter's unmistakable guffaw rang out from the crowd gathered around the fire. He was always the life of the party. Blake watched Jeremy fist-bump and high-five his way to the food.

Shannon came out of the cabin with a tray of cookies and Lauren followed with chips and salsa. Blake's heart thrummed in his chest as he took in the dark washed jeans and pale blue V-neck sweater hugging her curves. She'd tamed her curls and they cascaded over her shoulders in bouncy ringlets. His eyes fell on the delicate hollow near her collarbone where he used to plant kisses. She caught him staring and a slow heat crawled up his neck. He smiled and raised his Coke in her direction. *Real smooth, genius.* She returned his smile but remained planted next to Shannon.

"You saved me a seat, how thoughtful." Tisha plopped down on the tailgate next to him, red wine sloshing out of her glass. "Oops!" She giggled. "Party foul."

Blake groaned inwardly as she scooted closer. Heavy floral perfume mixed with alcohol descended like a storm cloud. He glanced at Lauren. She watched, eyebrows raised, until Shannon touched her elbow and motioned toward two empty lawn chairs.

"So tell me about growing up in the wilderness of Alaska." Tisha flung her arm dramatically toward the woods then let her hand linger on Blake's thigh.

Are you kidding me? The fire popped and crackled, laughter rang out. He watched Lauren nibble on a carrot stick, her plate balanced on her lap.

"You're a wonderful girl, Tish. But let's try to keep this professional, shall we?" He removed her hand from his leg and placed it gently in her lap.

"C'mon." Tisha pouted. "Don't be a party pooper. Tell me a story and I'll behave."

It took every ounce of self-control he could muster not to get up and run. But he couldn't embarrass her or himself in front of everybody. Besides, until they trained another employee, she was indispensable.

A few of the girls Blake had grown up with gathered around Shannon and Lauren. He could tell by the squeals of delight and Lauren's extended arm that they were admiring her ring. That chafed him pretty good. "Why don't I introduce you to some of the ladies here tonight? I'm sure they would love to meet you."

Tisha wrinkled her nose. "Doubt it. They're all about that redhead. Who is she, anyway?"

Blake's chest tightened. He glanced over at Lauren again. Now that was a story, all right. But not one he felt like telling.

"I'll tell you what. How about⌐⌐"

"Wait." Tisha pointed toward the road. "Who is that?"

Blake turned and looked. A tall, dark-haired guy in jeans and a bomber jacket climbed out of a taxi in Jess's driveway. He pushed his aviator sunglasses on top of his head, surveying the crowd that circled the fire. When his eyes landed on

Lauren, he slammed the door of the cab and started toward her. Somebody had turned off the radio. It was so quiet, Blake could hear the grass squeak under the guy's fancy brown shoes as he cut across the yard. The hair on the back of Blake's neck stood up. This looked an awful lot like trouble.

***

"LO-LO?" JESS TAPPED her shoulder. "Do you know that guy?"

Lauren's heart pounded in her chest. *Holden. It couldn't be.*

She dropped her paper plate and it landed face-down, smearing Ranch dressing on the toe of her boot.

Ignoring the mess, she stood and closed the distance between them in several quick strides. A look of fierce determination brewed in his eyes. "What are you doing here?"

"You told me if I was sorry, I'd catch the next plane out. I chartered a flight. We need to talk." He glanced over her shoulder. "If you aren't too busy. I wouldn't want to interrupt. Your mother said I could find you here."

She stared in disbelief. "When did you talk to my mother?"

"A few minutes ago. I tried to call you when I landed but you didn't answer. So I went to your house. Very rustic. Too bad I can't stay." Holden offered a sad smile.

Lauren swallowed hard. "What do you mean you can't stay?"

"Can we talk? Privately? Please, Lauren. This is important."

She glanced around at her old friends, staring, slack-jawed at her fiancé. "C'mon. Jess used to have a couple of chairs down on the dock. We can talk there."

Holden followed her down to the small wooden dock that jutted out into the lake. Two rocking chairs, sporting fresh coats of white paint, sat side by side. Lauren sank into one of the chairs, her fingers trembling as she tucked a loose curl behind her ear.

"What's going on?"

Holden still stood, staring out at the lake. "It's complicated."

"Is this about you dispensing medication?"

He turned, eyes narrowed. "What did you see?"

The blood drained to her toes. So there was something going on. She swallowed hard. "I'm not stupid, Holden. I watch you. The way you talk to the bartender at Papa Haydn's. When you take me there for dinner—it's like you have something that he wants. And he'll do anything to get it."

Holden swore and kicked a rock. It skittered off the edge into the pond. "What else?"

She chewed her lower lip, heart thundering in her chest. "What do you mean?"

"What else do you know?" Holden started to pace. "I need to know if you've talked to anybody else, seen anyone hanging around your apartment, following you home. Anything."

Lauren laughed, but it came out nervous and forced. "Have you lost your mind? Nobody's following me, Holden. That's crazy."

Holden stopped pacing and dropped into the chair opposite hers. His eyes darted back toward the crowd. Then he leaned close, his voice barely a whisper. "Here's the thing. I'm in a little trouble. I need to go off the grid for a while. I hate that

I've dragged you into this, but⊓ I think it's better if we don't see each other anymore."

His news sucked the breath right out of her. "Dragged me into what?"

Holden leaned forward, elbows on his knees. "I'm trying to be honest. Really. But I can't tell you everything because I need to protect you."

She snorted. "Please. Do you hear yourself right now?" A slide show of day trips to Cannon Beach and romantic dinners in the Pearl District played through her mind. He was so good to her. And a surgeon, for crying out loud. How could he possibly be in trouble?

Wait. Monique. Goosebumps pebbled her flesh. "Does Monique have anything to do with this?"

Holden dropped his chin to his chest. "Monique's been addicted to painkillers since I operated on her knee last fall. She promised me she'd quit."

Lauren gasped. "Holden. How could you?"

He slid from the chair and knelt at her feet. He reached for her hand, but she shrunk back. Her stomach turned. "Believe me, she's the least of my worries right now. This is exactly why I need to go away for a while. It's not that I don't love you, babe. But I'm no good for you. Not like this."

This couldn't be happening. Hot tears pricked her eyelids. But she wouldn't give him the satisfaction of seeing her cry. "Just go," she whispered.

He hesitated.

Oh. Of course. The ring. She twisted it off her finger, bypassed his outstretched palm and chucked the diamond into the lake. It landed somewhere behind him with a gentle ploop.

Tilting her head, she forced herself to meet his gaze. "If you want it back, you'll have to swim for it."

He squeezed his hand shut and stood slowly, his complexion pasty white. "I guess I deserved that. Goodbye, Lauren."

She remained seated, watching the ripples from her ring expand in concentric circles across the lake and disappear. Just like that. Game over. Once she heard the crunch of gravel under his feet, she shifted in her chair to watch him go. Without a backward glance, Holden marched toward the taxi still idling near the road. When the tail lights were out of sight, she sagged against the back of the rocking chair and wept.

***

BLAKE STUFFED THE last bag of trash into the can outside of Jess's garage and dug in his pocket for his keys. He waved to the last car load of his friends pulling out of the driveway. *Getting way too old to stay out past midnight.* Matthew Carter preached a heck of a sermon and he needed to get his butt in the pew to hear it, first thing in the morning.

"Hey." Jess jogged toward him, pointing down toward dock.

His heart shimmied when he recognized the unmistakable silhouette of Lauren still sitting in the rocking chair.

"Go talk to her, man. Nobody's said a word to her since that guy left."

Blake nodded. As he got closer to the dock, he could see her shoulders trembling and she swiped quickly at her cheeks. She was huddled against one armrest, knees pulled up under her chin.

"Go away," she said, shivering.

Blake lowered himself into the other chair and stretched his legs out in front of him. He tipped his head back and admired the pale pink streaks brushed against the baby blue sky.

"It's a beautiful night. Where's lover boy?"

"O-o-on his ch-ch-chartered plane," she stuttered, teeth chattering.

"Want to talk about it?" Blake shrugged out of his fleece jacket and handed it to her.

She shook her head, cocooning inside the jacket as fresh tears glistened on her cheeks. Blake resisted the urge to reach over and brush those tears away. It killed him to see her cry.

"C'mon, I'll drive you home. Seth left with Molly Simmons." He stood and jangled his keys.

She walked in front of him, wordless, across the yard to his truck. He liked the way she looked wrapped up in his jacket.

He held open her door, breathing in the sweet scent of her shampoo as she brushed past him. With a last wave to Jess, he jogged around the truck and slid behind the wheel.

"I know what you're thinking and I don't want to hear it," she muttered as she stared out the window.

"Excuse me?" He slid the key into the ignition.

"I'm sure you're thinking this is exactly what I deserve." She gnawed on her thumbnail. "What goes around comes around, right?"

Blake turned the key, an ache filling his chest. "Is that what you think?"

She kept staring out the window, sniffling. He leaned over and gently tucked her hair behind her ear. "Hey, look at me."

She turned away from the window and faced him. Her eyes were puffy and swollen.

"Listen. I have never wished for anything bad to happen to you. Even after you left. I wanted you to find whatever it is you were looking for. I want you to be happy, Lauren."

Her face crumpled and a fresh wave of tears came. He fumbled in the console for a tissue and handed it to her.

"You don't understand," she whispered, dabbing at her cheeks.

"Then why don't you explain it to me. What happened?"

"Holden and I aren't getting married."

He glanced at her left hand. His breath caught in his throat when he saw her bare finger. "You think I can't relate?" He huffed out a breath and dragged his hand through his hair. "I know a thing or two about having a broken heart."

She pulled his coat tighter around her body and shuddered. "I did something horrible after I left. Something unforgiveable. And I knew, somehow, I would have to pay."

An icy chill crept up his spine. He pressed his lips into a thin line and stared at her. "What are you talking about?"

She trapped her lower lip behind her front teeth. "Never mind. I can't do this. Please just take me home."

He clenched his jaw and shifted into drive. *Stubborn girl.* It had been nine years. What could she possibly have done that was still so horrible after all this time? He stole a glance at her profile, his pulse stuttering at her cute little upturned nose. He knew one thing: that Holden fella was an absolute fool to let her go. He looked out his window, partly to check for oncoming traffic but also to conceal the smile he felt playing at the corner of his mouth. Maybe he didn't have that coaching job nailed down yet, but he did have the only girl he'd ever loved riding next to him. This was his dream turned reality. An opportunity to show her how much he still cared. About her. About them.

CHAPTER NINE

L auren scraped the remnants of Sunday's breakfast into the disposal and slid the last plate into the dishwasher. Grabbing the spray bottle of vinegar and water from under the sink, she gave the counter a thorough cleaning. If she kept busy, maybe she wouldn't have to think about last night.

Still, Holden's words echoed in her head. *A little bit of trouble? Off the grid?* She envisioned him holed up in his parent's place at Sun Valley, prescribing painkillers to the neighbors. Ever since they met, she'd wrestled with revealing the truth about her past. Apparently she wasn't the only one living a lie.

"Maybe we deserve each other," she muttered, wiping the last of the vinegar from the counters. The reality of the situation was like an elephant parked on her chest. Everything she'd relied on was being yanked out from under her.

Shuffling a stack of papers, she glanced at the note her parents had left. They were at church and promised to save her a seat. She ignored the familiar pang of guilt over missing her brother's sermon and covered the last of the waffles and bacon with a sheet of foil. Seth might drag himself out of bed eventually and come looking for breakfast.

Her phone vibrated on the granite countertop. She glanced at the screen and sighed. Mrs. Putnam. She wrestled with letting the call go to voicemail but couldn't justify ignoring her. Grabbing the phone, she jabbed her finger at the screen then pressed the phone to her ear. "Hello?"

"Hello, my dear. Is this a good time?" Mrs. Putnam's voice was soothing and melodic. Lauren imagined her sipping hot tea in her breakfast nook, overlooking her husband's phenomenal rose garden.

"Yes, just working on the morning chores." Lauren switched the phone to her other ear as she tugged wet sheets from the washer.

"Oh, my. I thought you'd be having breakfast with that handsome fiancé of yours."

Lauren's heart lurched. "Not today. What's up, Mrs. P?" Although the older woman's manners were impeccable, she rarely made a phone call without a specific purpose.

"I wanted to call and see if you made it to Alaska? I know your parents must be thrilled to meet Holden. How's everything going?"

Lauren smiled. Doctor and Mrs. Putnam had found her stranded on the side of Highway 26, all her worldly possessions crammed in the trunk of her car. Eighteen years old with her last $50 stuffed inside her bra, they offered a job and a place to stay. Then they stood by and carried her through the darkest season of her young life. She didn't want to burden them with any more problems, but she couldn't mislead them, either.

"I'm here but Holden's not."

"Oh? Why? Did something come up?"

"You could say that. He dropped in just long enough to end our engagement." She swallowed the lump that clogged her throat. It still didn't seem real, even when she said the words out loud.

"Oh, dear. That's rather unexpected, isn't it?"

"Completely."

"I'm so sorry things aren't working out like you planned. I know you care deeply for Holden. But I can't tell you how excited I am that you finally decided to go home. Dwight and I have been praying that you would get an opportunity to go."

Lauren's chest tightened. Mrs. Putnam had a way of drawing a conversation back to God's will for her life. Although it was always a pithy bit of wisdom Lauren needed to hear, she didn't feel like going there today. What she really needed was some air. Slipping out the back door, she plunked down on the top step.

"I knew my family needed me, but it's worse than I thought. My Granny is losing her mind, if it isn't gone already. Then she fell and my mother has to care for her. That leaves me to run a floundering bed and breakfast. It's a bit much, quite frankly."

"I'm sorry about your grandmother," Mrs. Putnam said. "I know you treasure her so. I will pray for your time together, that it will be sweet and joyful."

"So far it's been anything but."

"Lauren, we both know why you are there."

"I can't tell them," she whispered.

"You have to stop running, sweetheart. This is eating you up. Tell them the truth."

"What if they're angry?" Lauren dabbed at the tears spilling onto her cheeks.

"What if they aren't?"

Lauren shook her head. *They'll be so disgusted.*

"I'll let you go now, dear. Dwight and I are praying for you. We leave for Morocco on Wednesday and we'll Skype you when we land in Casablanca. Doesn't that sound grand?"

"Have a safe trip, Mrs. P. Give Dr. Putnam a hug for me."

"Of course, dear. Bye now."

Mitchell's cold, wet snout nuzzled her bare arm. He dropped a scuffed tennis ball on the porch, tail wagging in eager anticipation. He sank low on his front paws then sprang back up, prancing on all fours.

"Pretty spry for an old guy, aren't you?" She scratched behind his ears and he reciprocated with a lick on her cheek.

"One time. That's it." She tossed the ball into the woods and Mitchell flew off the steps in hot pursuit. A squirrel chattered and Mitchell disappeared into the thick undergrowth. *I need to go for a long run.*

She went back in and climbed the stairs to the loft. Her favorite New Balance running shoes were still in one of her suitcases, pinned against the side by a stack of jeans. Slipping into black nylon shorts and one of her brother's old University of Washington shirts, she caught her reflection in the mirror over the dresser. *Good grief. Fix your hair.* After combing her fingers through the worst of the tangled mass, she gave up and tugged it all into a ponytail and dashed back down the stairs.

A cool breeze ruffled the tree branches. The rain fell in a gentle mist. She took a deep breath, exhaled slowly and stepped off the porch. Her shoes crunched against the gravel, keeping a steady rhythm as she jogged down the driveway. The tightness in her neck and shoulders uncoiled with every step. She pumped her arms, keeping her fists between her hips and her nose. If she focused on her technique then she wouldn't have to think about the hard truth Mrs. Putnam spoke.

A dull ache formed under one rib. She ignored it and ran faster. Telling her family the truth now seemed pointless. She handled the crisis all on her own, far from home where no one could know her secret. Squeaky clean reputations remained intact. Dredging it all up now was foolish. Their shock and disappointment would be too much to bear, especially now that she'd heard more about Mallory.

She had rehearsed the conversation numerous times, pacing around the living room. It was a monologue, really, because she couldn't bring herself to fully imagine her parents' responses. Good girls didn't do the things she'd done.

The shops on the edge of town came into view and she pressed forward, eager to escape her thoughts. At Main Street she turned toward the waterfront. Portland was a beautiful city but the view from Emerald Cove's harbor was unmatched. She longed to see it again.

A plume of smoke hovered above the marina. The cruise ship sounded two long blasts of its horn as it eased away from the dock. A small crowd had gathered to watch. Several passengers stood at the ship's railing, waving. They looked like dolls. The ship cut an impressive silhouette with its gleaming white hull towering several stories above the water.

Lauren jogged around the tourists as they meandered down the boardwalk. The smell of diesel fuel mixed with tangy salt water hung in the air. A young boy opened a cooler and cheered as the man next to him pulled out a silver fish. He tossed the fish on the make-shift counter designed for cleaning the day's catch. Lauren slowed to a walk as the man ruffled the boy's hair. The tender father-son moment hurt to watch. Time to go.

She turned away and collided with a firm, muscular chest clad in a mint-green button-down shirt. Hot liquid splashed on her hand.

"Ow!" She pulled her hand back, clutching it protectively.

"Whoa," Blake said, sucking his abdomen in and curling away from the coffee sloshing out of his cup. "Lauren, what are you doing?"

"I'm running." She dabbed at the burn on her hand with the cuff of her sleeve.

"Let me see." Blake reached for her hand but she shielded it from view.

"No. It's fine."

"At least let me put aloe on it. C'mon, Megan has some." He jerked his thumb over his shoulder.

"Megan?"

"My little sister. Remember her? She works right here in the coffee shop."

She glanced at the Copper Kettle Coffee Company sign on the wall behind him. The skin on her hand was starting to sting. Some aloe would probably help.

"Megan has a job?" The same little girl who bounced a basketball incessantly around the gym was old enough to work?

"Yep." Blake held the door open. "My baby sister is growing up."

The rumble of the espresso machine drowned out all conversation. A teenager with blond pigtails and wide-set blue eyes stood behind the counter, steaming milk. She raised one eyebrow at Blake and turned a dial on the machine.

"What's wrong?" she asked.

"I bumped into Lauren and spilled my coffee on her hand. Can I borrow your aloe?"

Megan's eyes flicked from Blake to Lauren and back to the silver frothing cup in her hand. She nodded.

"Megan? I can't believe it. How long have you worked here?" Lauren watched as Megan deftly poured milk into a paper cup, topped it with a dollop of foam and clicked the plastic lid in place.

"Just started two weeks ago. Here," Megan slid a tube across the granite counter. She turned to greet another customer. Blake opened the aloe.

"I can do it," Lauren said. The last thing she needed was Blake rubbing anything on her.

"Can I buy you some coffee?"

Lauren examined the angry red splotch on her hand before tentatively dabbing the gooey gel on it. He was just offering coffee. What could it hurt?

She nodded.

"Meg, hook this girl up. What's your pleasure?" Blake studied her.

"I'll have a grande non-fat sugar-free vanilla extra hot no whip latte. Please."

Megan narrowed her eyes and pursed her lips. "Okay. You want a refill, Blake?"

"Please."

Lauren watched Megan dump syrup into a shot glass and tamp coffee into the machine.

"That's quite the order," Blake said, his full lips curving into a wide smile.

A girl could get lost in those dimples.

"Thanks. What can I say? I know what I like."

The silence between them was deafening. She glanced up from her hand to see Blake's brows knitted together.

His eyes bore into her. "Is that right?"

She instantly regretted her words and wanted to bolt back out the door. But her feet felt glued to the black and white checkered linoleum, as if they didn't quite get the message.

She raised her chin and met his gaze. "I thought we were talking about coffee. You look nice. What's the occasion?"

He slipped his hands into the front pockets of his khakis and rocked back on his heels. "Thanks. Just came from church. I wanted to hear your brother preach. He did a great job."

Lauren felt her cheeks grow warm. "I'm sure he did."

"Coffee's up." Megan slipped cardboard sleeves around both cups. "Careful, they're extra hot."

Lauren ignored the sarcasm and took her drink off the counter.

Blake handed his sister some cash. "Keep the change."

Megan flashed him a smile. "Thanks."

"It looks like the rain has stopped. Want to take this conversation outside?" Blake tipped his head toward the door.

She nodded and followed him out to the white plastic table and chairs in front of the coffee shop. She glanced at the adjoining storefront with an orange-red kayak and a paddle propped in the window. Emerald Cove Rafting & Kayaking marched across the window in an edgy white font.

"Is this your new shop?" She studied the mannequin posed opposite the kayak in a deep purple and black wet suit.

"You like it?"

"It makes me want to jump in a kayak. Who helped you with the design?"

Blake feigned a wounded expression. "Who says I had help? You know, you're starting to give me a complex. First you can't believe it's me on the front of our brochure. Now you're implying that I don't know anything about marketing."

She ducked her head and twisted her coffee cup around inside its sleeve. A giggle escaped, despite her best intentions to stifle it.

"So Jeremy did the window?" she teased.

"No, I hired a friend from Anchorage." He concealed a smile with his coffee cup.

Lauren felt the unmistakable twinge of jealousy. Friend? What kind of friend?

"Oh." She took a long sip of her latte and pushed the image of Blake working closely with a beautiful woman from her mind. *Honestly. Get a grip.*

"Shannon recommended her, they were roommates freshman year. We could use somebody around here with an eye for aesthetics." Blake studied her. "What about you? Did you really leave town because you desperately wanted to be a nurse?"

"So we're back to this, are we?" She swiped her finger through the droplets of water that beaded on the surface of the table, avoiding Blake's gaze.

"You're stalling."

Go on. Lay it all out there. What have you got to lose?

"I'm only a medical assistant right now. Not quite the career I dreamed of, but that's how it worked out."

Blake arched one eyebrow, his blue eyes questioning. "So this is just a temporary thing then?"

"Not exactly." She shifted in her seat, crossed and uncrossed her legs. "Sort of. I wanted to be a graphic designer. But I never went to college. I'd pretty much have to start at Art 101. And the program's very competitive." She dipped her chin and shrugged. "My boss and his wife have been so good to me. They want me to go back to school. I guess I want to make them proud."

"I've never known you to shy away from competition. Have you applied?"

"No. Not yet. I could, but—" *But my former fiancé wouldn't approve.* She sighed. "I really don't know what I'm going to do now. After last night and everything. Plus, I'm officially unemployed."

Blake's eyes filled with empathy. "I'm sorry about your engagement. That has to be tough. And you lost your job, too? What in the world happened?"

"My boss closed his practice. He and his wife leave for a long-term medical mission in Morocco this week."

"You didn't want to go?"

"I tried. They wouldn't let me."

His eyes widened. "Huh. Why?" Blake's cell phone chimed and he picked it up, staring at the screen. "Shoot. Sorry. Tisha's texting me, we've got clients waiting."

The clingy blonde from the party.

"Oh. Okay. I'll see you around." She offered a weak smile.

He touched her arm and a jolt of electricity zinged through her. "I still have the pictures you drew for me. Every one. Your talent is incredible."

His hand lingered on her arm and Lauren swallowed hard, looking anywhere but at him. Then he was moving away, walking backward toward his truck. "I think there's more to the story, by the way. I want to hear the rest."

She pasted on a smile while her heart jumped in her throat. The rest of the story. Where to begin? It all started with him. One regrettable night and then a little stick with two pink lines.

CHAPTER TEN

Almost there. Her chest tightened and she sucked in another deep breath. Her quads burned and she still had to make the long, slow climb up the hill. Maybe four miles was a little much. All that coffee sloshing around in her stomach didn't help, either. She heard the hum of an engine and tires crunching on gravel behind her. She glanced over her shoulder. Jeremy Tully waved from the cab of his truck.

"Hey," he called through the open window, "that's a nice pace you've got going there."

She shrugged and jogged in place. "Thanks, I think. Have you been following me?"

Jeremy smiled. "Only since the hardware store when I saw you run by. Do much racing anymore?"

Lauren stopped jogging and studied him. "A few 5K's now and then. Why?"

"I'm recruiting for the Cove to Creek relay." He wiggled his eyebrows. "Thought you might like to defend your title."

Lauren smiled at the memory. She and Blake had run the Cove to Creek relay race with Shannon and Jess the summer before her senior year, winning easily. "I think a few others have claimed the title after me. That was almost ten years ago, Jeremy."

"But nobody's won with as much, how shall we say, 'flare' since."

Lauren glared. "If you're referring to the incident with Susannah, I didn't push her."

Jeremy threw his head back and laughed. "That's your story and you're sticking to it, right?"

"Absolutely."

"So can I persuade you to come out of retirement to join our team?"

Her stomach swirled with anticipation. It would be fun to race again. "Who's on your team?"

Jeremy lifted his Angels baseball cap and scratched his head. "Let's see. Me, Blake, Jess and Tisha so far."

"I don't know, Jer. My family needs a lot of help right now. I'm not sure I should commit to anything for Fourth of July yet." Not to mention being a third wheel. Tisha and Blake had looked quite intimate last night.

"Come on. Everybody gets excited about the Fourth around here. The whole town still shuts down for the festival and the race. I'm sure your folks will be watching. Besides, your entry fee benefits a great cause."

Lauren tipped her head. "Entry fee? I have to pay to run the Cove to Creek now?"

"Times have changed. For every person who enters the race, one of the cruise lines will match it. Dollar for dollar. The money goes toward new playground equipment for the park."

"What's the fee?"

"Only eight bucks. You know you want to." Jeremy winked and cracked open a can of Coke.

Lauren chewed her lip. It was one of her favorite traditions. The whole town came out for the relay race, stayed for the festival, then gathered for a dance later that evening.

The races in Portland just weren't the same. And he said it would benefit the town. When was the last time she'd done anything even remotely close to a service project, anyway?

She nodded slowly. "All right, I'm in. Can we settle up later? I don't have any cash on me."

"Sweet." Jeremy leaned out the window and gave her a fist bump. "Sure, you can register anytime. Thanks, Lo-lo. Can I give you a lift home?"

She waved him off. "No, I'm good. See ya."

Stopping to talk had killed her momentum so she decided to walk back up the hill to the Inn. When she was a few strides from the porch, the front door flew open.

"Aunt Lauren, watch this!" Joshua leaped off the top step, waving a gray plastic sword in one hand.

Lauren sucked in a breath, closing both eyes. The boy had no fear.

She opened one eye. Surprisingly, he had landed on his feet, crouched low to the ground. Just like a cat. Next he spun in circles, brandishing his weapon and barking orders.

"Hey, big guy. What's going on?"

"Nothin'. Mom said I had to wash my hands for lunch. But I came outside to check for bad guys. They're sneaky, you know."

"For sure. What's for lunch?" She scooped him up and spun in circles. He cackled with delight. Something stirred inside, a whisper of regret. Is this what little boys were like?

"There you are." Mom stood in the doorway, drying her hands on her faded polka dot apron. "Lunch is ready. Were you out for a run?"

Lauren nodded, setting Joshua down on the steps. "I'm sorry, I should've left a note."

"No worries, you're a big girl." Mom stepped aside and Lauren followed her nephew into the house.

"Well, looky here." Matthew came out of the kitchen, his tie tossed over one shoulder as he cradled Gavin in his arms. He leaned over and gave her a peck on the cheek. "Missed you this morning. We saved you a seat right up front, sorry you couldn't make it."

She elbowed him in the ribs. "Very funny. I heard you were preaching this morning. How did it go?"

"It was kind of a yawner." Dad piped up from the kitchen. He buckled Emmy and Ava into their booster seats. He winked at Lauren and handed a slice of bread to each girl.

"Yeah, I could hear you snoring from the pulpit, Dad." Matthew grinned and took a seat.

"Stop, you two." Mom scolded, plating generous helpings of lasagna.

"Where's Seth?" Lauren asked.

"He sent me a text, said he and Toby needed to get back to their claim." Dad shook his head. "We never know what that kid's up to."

"What's going on with him and Molly Simmons?" Angela passed Gavin to Matthew.

"He hasn't mentioned Molly, but I hear he and Toby have really found something incredible." Matthew tucked Gavin in the crook of his elbow and poured dressing on his salad with his free hand.

"He told me it was a killer claim." Lauren took a slice of French bread from the basket and passed it to Angela.

"I'm sure he and Toby have it all figured out. Mike, can you say grace?" Mom reached for her husband's hand. Before

Dad could say 'amen', the Emmy and Ava were wrestling over a carton of yogurt.

"Girls." Angela's fork clattered to her plate and she shoved back her chair with a heavy sigh. Lauren watched as she deftly pulled Emmy's chair away from Ava's and offered another carton of yogurt. Ava glared and threw it on the floor. The carton cracked open, squirting strawberry yogurt across the hardwood.

Plucking Ava from her chair, Angela whisked the toddler out of the room. Ava's howls of protest echoed down the hallway. Lauren raised her eyebrows and took a sip of her ice water. This parenting thing wasn't for sissies.

Matt reached for the salad bowl. "So tell me about this fiancé of yours."

Not now. Please.

"Matthew, let her eat lunch. There's plenty of time to catch up." Mom slid in between Joshua and Emmy.

"She can talk and eat." Matthew flashed a lop-sided grin, green eyes twinkling.

"What's his name? Harden?"

Lauren stared at her food. She missed eating her mother's lasagna. But she couldn't swallow another bite right now.

"Holden. Holden Kelly."

"That's right." Matthew stabbed at a cherry tomato. "So he's coming later?"

"He was here last night. Stopped by just long enough to break up with me."

Dad abruptly stopped chewing while Mom gasped and spilled her water. Matthew paused with his fork halfway to his mouth.

"Oh, sweetheart." Mom grabbed some towels from the counter and sopped up the water. "Why didn't you say something?"

"You didn't give me a chance."

"So he flew in, tracked you down, and dumped you?" Matthew shot a glance at Dad. "Sounds like he's quite a guy."

Lauren flinched, moving some food around on her plate.

"I'm sorry, honey. I know this must be difficult." Dad cleared his throat and reached for the bread basket.

You have no idea. She nodded and fought back the tears that threatened to fall.

"So what else is going on? Still working for that doctor?" Matthew shifted Gavin to his shoulder.

Lauren shook her head. "He closed the practice. Friday was my last day."

"So what will you do when you go back?" Dad shoveled more lasagna onto a hunk of bread and popped it in his mouth.

Lauren looked away. She'd have to find another job. And put her graphic design plans on hold. Again. "I haven't figured that out yet."

The phone rang, Gavin started to fuss and Angela came back in the kitchen with a very cranky Ava in her arms.

"Matt, we need to get going. She's falling apart." Angela stood behind Matt, her lips pressed into a thin line.

"What about Gavin? I think he's hungry."

"I'll feed him, but then we need to go." Angela slid Ava back into her chair then scooped Gavin from Matt's arms and disappeared into the living room.

Matt switched chairs and squeezed in between his girls, tugging his plate toward him. "Let's finish our lunch, okay?"

"That was Judy Maxwell." Mom set the phone down on the counter and came back to the table. "She wondered if I knew anyone who could put together a flyer for the relay and festival. Whoever she had lined up backed out last minute."

Lauren leaned forward in her seat. She could probably pull something together in a couple of hours. Good thing she'd brought her laptop.

"What does she need a flyer for? The same festival happens every year," Dad said.

"Apparently the cruise directors want someone on the dock promoting the festival." Mom passed the bread basket to Matt. "How about some more bread?"

Lauren pushed her plate aside, the buzz of a percolating project coursing through her veins. She twisted around in her chair and grabbed a pen and a discarded envelope off of the counter. The conversation turned to the new bridge project and a small development going up on the edge of town. New ramblers or something. She was only half-listening while Dad and Matt discussed the growing real estate market.

"What are you drawing, Aunt Lauren?" Josh leaned over her arm to examine her work.

"Just an idea I had for a flyer, that's all." She scribbled a tagline under a rough sketch of the mountains.

Conversation came to a halt. Silence encircled the table. She glanced up slowly to find her parents and Matt staring at her.

"What did you say?" Dad asked.

A flush began to creep up her neck. "I thought I'd help Mrs. Maxwell design that flyer." Butterflies danced in her stomach. She felt a little weird talking about her ideas out loud. It wasn't like she was a professional, or anything.

"You can do that sort of thing?"

She shrugged. "I've done a couple of projects back h—in Portland. Nothing big. It's kind of a hobby, I guess."

"There's a whole box of your artwork around here somewhere." Mom fed Emmy one last bite of lasagna then reached for a napkin. "You used to draw all the time. Let me wipe your face, Em."

Angela came back into the room, Gavin sound asleep in her arms. "He's out already. Let's go."

While Matt and Angela rounded up the kids, Lauren put her doodling aside and helped clear the table. Turning on the water at the kitchen sink, she added some dish soap and waited for the basin to fill. She reached for Granny's locket. *Do you see me, Lord? I'm washing dishes and doodling on napkins in the middle of nowhere. Are these the plans you have for me? Because this is not what I envisioned. Not at all.*

Joshua's laughter, echoing through the open front door, was all she heard. Of course. God's answer, if He even cared, would be drowned out by the sound of a happy child. She grabbed the sponge and scrubbed angrily at the marinara-encrusted pan in the sink. *Go ahead. Remind me again of my hideous mistakes. As if I'd forgotten.*

***

IT WAS ALL he could do to keep the raft upright in the river this afternoon. For once it wasn't the rapids or the crazy strong current fighting to take him down. Those tear-filled green eyes weighed heavily on his mind, distracting him from his customers, the email overflowing from his inbox— everything.

Blake tossed another log on the fire as Jess came out of the house and handed him a Coke.

"Thanks, man. I could get used to this." He leaned back in the lawn chair and smiled at his friend.

"You're welcome. I thought you might want to chill after all the excitement you had the other night." Jess gave him a knowing smile.

Blake pursed his lips and tilted his head. "What excitement would that be?"

"I see ya, playing it cool. That's fine." Jess tipped his Coke back and took a long pull.

"No, for real. What are you talking about?"

"We all watched you fighting off that hot blond. Then you swooped in and rescued the damsel in distress. Well played, my friend."

"Wait. Tish?" Blake groaned. "You think something's going on there?"

"No, not really. But I did think Lauren was going to come right out of her chair when Tisha put her hand on your leg."

Blake snorted. "Whatever. Lauren was a mess. I doubt she even noticed Tisha."

"What happened?"

Blake shook his head in disgust. "Guy blazed into town and broke her heart."

"Nice," Jess scoffed. "Sounds like a class act."

"That's what I thought but she was pretty upset."

"Well, I hope he took that ring with him. He's making us all look bad."

Blake couldn't help but laugh. "Don't worry. It's gone. Speaking of rings, why don't you propose to that woman of yours?"

"We'll get to me in a second. Where's the former fiancé now?"

"Who knows. Not here."

"Exactly."

I know where this is headed. "And your point is?"

Jess rolled his eyes. "Make your move, man. If he's dumb enough to leave her here alone all broken-hearted, then I say game on."

"This from the guy who's been stringing the same girl along for nearly a—oh, I don't know, let me think ... a decade. When are you going to step up?"

"I bought a ring last week, thank you very much. Don't worry about me, man. I'm a closer."

Blake tipped his head back against the chair. The fire popped and crackled, sending a ribbon of smoke into the pale blue evening sky. "A closer, huh?"

"Yep. Can't let this one get away."

"I can't imagine you or Shannon with anybody else, Jess."

Jess leaned forward in his chair and tossed a pebble into the fire. "That's exactly what me and Jeremy said last night about you and Lauren. Whatever made her leave doesn't matter now. She's back. You've got a second chance."

"Contrary to public opinion, I'm here to launch a business with my brother and get back in the classroom. Maybe replace Coach Hoffman if he ever decides to hang up his whistle. I didn't come home to reunite with my high school girlfriend."

"Ha. Could've fooled me."

Blake's chest ached. If only his heart believed his words. He didn't come home to fall in love with Lauren all over again. The truth was he never really stopped loving her. But their break up had nearly been his undoing. He'd rather be alone than scrape the pieces of his heart back together again. Yet he couldn't ignore the hope that ignited inside when he watched her fiancé—make that ex-fiancé—leave Jess's without her. Jess was right. This was a second chance. For both of them. He fully intended to win her heart once more.

CHAPTER ELEVEN

L ate the next morning, rain drops pattered the windshield as Lauren pulled into the parking lot of Emerald Cove's tiny library. The A-framed building with its rough-hewn logs and green metal roof hadn't changed much since she left. Vibrant purple and yellow pansies spilled from the flower boxes under the rectangular windows. A sculpture of a grizzly bear with a salmon in its mouth still stood near the front door.

She turned off the car and grabbed her purse. *Let's see what we can find.* The story of Mallory and her boyfriend dying in that accident and leaving behind a baby haunted her. It probably wasn't a matter of public record, but she desperately wanted to find her cousin. *Please tell me that such a tragic story had a happy ending.*

Jogging up the sidewalk, she side-stepped a woman and a gaggle of preschoolers coming out of the library. Lauren smiled. Story time was one of her and her brothers' favorite outings when they were little.

Once inside, she drew in a deep breath. Yep. Still smelled like she was standing in the middle of a wood pile. The woman sitting behind the front desk looked up from her computer and smiled politely over the rim of her glasses, tucking a strand of long blond hair behind her ear. Well, one thing had changed. Lauren didn't recognize her. Where was

Mrs. Woods? She'd worked at the library for as long as Lauren could remember.

"May I help you?" the woman asked with just a hint of a southern accent.

"I'm looking for Mrs. Woods. Is she working today?" Lauren craned her neck to see down the aisles of books that filled the rectangular room.

The woman's smile faded. "I'm sorry. She retired about five years ago. I'm Olivia Gilmore. Is there something I can do for you?"

Lauren's sighed. *Dang it.* Mrs. Woods knew everything there was to know about Emerald Cove. "I'm looking for some information about an adoption that occurred in the mid-eighties. Maybe 1986. Does the library keep any kind of public records?"

Mrs. Gilmore removed her glasses and set them on the desk. "Funny you should ask. We're in the process of converting all those files from microfiche to digital. A ginormous undertaking, if I do say so myself." She slid off her stool and came around the counter. "Follow me."

Her heart rate kicked up a notch as Lauren followed the petite woman in her lilac sweater set and gray pencil skirt into a small alcove not much bigger than a storage closet. File boxes were stacked from floor to ceiling, with dates scribbled in black marker on the ends. There was barely enough room for two people to stand among the towers. Wow. The entire history of Emerald Cove, shoved into a closet. *Wonder what other secrets these boxes could reveal.*

Mrs. Gilmore shoved a box aside with her low-heeled pump and reached around to flip the switch on the microfiche machine. It whirred to life and she dragged two old plastic milk cartons over, stacked them together and patted a bath towel serving as a makeshift cushion. "Not the best seat in the house, but it will have to do. Remember how to work one of these?"

Lauren bit her lip. "I think so." She glanced around. "Any idea where the eighties start?"

"Well, let me see." Mrs. Gilmore leaned over and lifted the lid on a box closest to the machine. "1980 through '88. I think this is what you need."

Dropping her purse on the floor, Lauren sat down on the milk carton and peered into the box. She carefully pulled out an envelope labeled '1985'. *Okay, Aunt Mallory. Show me how this all went down.*

"Let me know if you need anything." The librarian called over her shoulder as she returned to her post.

Lauren scoured the headlines of the Emerald Cove Gazette from 1985. She smiled, recognizing the birth announcements of kids a year ahead of her in school. It mentioned deaths, a couple of marriages, basketball scores, annual snowfall—the minutiae of daily life in a small town, but no details of any snowmobile accidents. *Must have the wrong year.* She popped the next floppy plastic sheet into the machine and frowned. 1988. Maybe these were out of order. Going back to the stack, she tried several of the sheets, quickly scanning each one. Nothing. It was like 1986 had never happened. *This is ridiculous.*

Lauren found the Mrs. Gilmore re-shelving picture books in the children's section. "Excuse me? One particular year seems to be missing. Can I look in a different box?"

Mrs. Gilmore frowned. "That's odd." She followed Lauren back to the alcove. "We rely on a handful of volunteers to help with the conversion process. The microfiche goes into a scanner, and then it turns into a PDF document."

"Where's the scanner?"

"At the museum. They have a bit more room and since the remodel, a temperature-controlled environment to store the converted films." She got down on her hands and knees and searched behind a stack of boxes and under the microfiche machine. "Golly, I hope it didn't get lost. That would be a shame."

"Any chance it was already converted? Maybe I could look at the PDF documents."

Mrs. Gilmore stood up, smoothing her skirt with french-manicured nails. "I suppose it's possible." She tilted her head toward the three computers stationed along the back wall. They were all occupied. "It looks like all of our computers with internet access are in use right now. But I could give you the website and you could look on your own."

Lauren sagged against the doorframe. What a wild goose chase. She should've known this wouldn't be easy. Her stomach growled, reminding her it was almost lunchtime. "Sure, I'd like to take a look. Thanks."

"Come out to the front desk."

Lauren slid the strap of her purse over her shoulder and followed Mrs. Gilmore back out front. She waited patiently while the librarian jotted the website on a yellow sticky note. She passed it over the counter to Lauren. "Here you go. I hope you find what you're looking for."

Lauren's smiled as she tucked the sticky note in her purse. "Thanks for your help. Have a nice day."

The rain had let up and she shielded her eyes against the bright sunlight streaming through the clouds. A thick layer of fog still clung to the base of the mountains and water splashed in the gutters as a car passed by on the street. A light breeze carried the aroma of french fries from the Fish House across the street. Her stomach rumbled again, more incessantly this time.   Unlocking the van, she lifted her laptop off the passenger seat and slammed the door. Maybe the Fish House offered free Wi-Fi. She could do a little more investigating while she waited for her lunch.

The restaurant was crowded, humming with conversation and punctuated by the cooks calling out orders in the kitchen. Weaving her way among the tables and chairs, she managed to score a small booth near the back of the restaurant. Lauren quickly claimed the table by sliding her laptop onto the orange Formica table.

Returning to the front of the restaurant, she took her place in line at the counter. She smiled at the giant collage of pictures still hanging on the wall in greasy frames. Reaching up, she straightened the one of her second grade t-ball team, all twelve of them drowning in their pale blue and white Fish House uniforms and requisite oversized caps. *We won every game that year.* Once they graduated from t-ball and moved onto basketball, they celebrated every home win with large chocolate milkshakes and bottomless baskets of fries. Even in Portland, she'd never tasted milkshakes that were as scrumptious as the ones served here.

"Hi." The teenage girl behind the register regarded her with a bored stare.

"I'd like the halibut and chips with a medium Diet Coke, please," Lauren said. "Do you have free Wi-Fi?"

"Yep. Password's scallop."

After swiping her debit card and collecting her number, Lauren went back to her booth and scooted onto the bench seat with her back to the door. She popped open her laptop and in a matter of minutes, she was online. Instead of pulling up the web address Mrs. Gilmore gave her, she couldn't resist surfing to her favorite blog. One post. That's all she'd read. Sometimes she just had to look. Glancing around the restaurant, she gnawed her lower lip. *Nobody in here knows me.* As the page loaded, she drummed her fingers on the table. In the most recent post, the toe-headed little boy with the adorable dimple mugged for the camera from the back of a pony. Her heart ached. *He's perfect.*

"Wow. He's cute. Who is he?"

Lauren squealed and slammed her laptop shut. She gulped and looked over her shoulder, heart hammering in her chest. "Shannon. You almost gave me a heart attack. What are you doing here?"

Shannon arched a curious eyebrow. "I'm getting lunch. What are you doing?"

"Nothing. Just waiting for my order." It was partially true, anyway.

Shannon tipped her head toward the empty seat across from Lauren. "Mind if I join you?"

"Please do." Lauren managed a weak smile. *Don't panic. She doesn't know.*

Shannon tossed her bag on the bench and sat down. "Are you a blogger?"

"No. I just like to lurk. How about you?"

Shannon's eyes sparkled. "I love to look at the home décor blogs. But I don't have time to start one of my own. Maybe someday."

Their numbers were called over the loudspeaker and they went to collect their orders. Shannon chattered the whole time, catching her up on the latest news, no doubt all of it gleaned from the other nurses at the hospital. As they settled back at their table, Shannon dunked a fry in a pool of ketchup and stared at Lauren. "So what else are you doing today?"

Lauren paused, a chunk of halibut halfway to her mouth. "I've started a little investigation."

"Taking after your dad, huh?"

"Not exactly. Did you know I had an aunt who died in a snowmobile accident?"

Shannon's brow wrinkled. "My grandmother told me about it one time. Why?"

"Did you know she had a baby before she died?"

"No way."

"True story. But somebody adopted her and I want to find out who. My mom says it was a couple that couldn't have children of their own."

"You think the baby grew up here in Emerald Cove?"

"It's possible."

"Wow." Shannon took a long sip of her drink. "We would totally know her. That's wild."

"You're telling me. I went to the library to look up any birth or adoption records, but a big chunk of the eighties is missing."

Shannon pulled her chin back, blue eyes cloudy with confusion. "What do you mean?"

Lauren shrugged. "The microfiche films from 1986 and 1987 are missing. As in gone. The librarian thinks maybe somebody lost or misplaced them during the conversion process."

Shannon narrowed her eyes and leaned forward. "Or somebody doesn't want you to find them."

Lauren laughed out loud. "You think somebody took them? That's crazy."

"Who knows. Nothing about this little town surprises me anymore."

"Do you think your grandmother might know who adopted the baby?"

Shannon tapped her index finger against her lip. "She might. She worked as a nurse in the orphanage for a while. She's on a Mediterranean cruise but when she gets home, you're welcome to stop by and visit. Sharp as a tack, that one."

The orphanage. Lauren recalled a few headlines about the orphanage in the old newspapers but hadn't bothered to read the articles. Maybe that was worth a second look. "I'm so curious. I just want to know what happened."

Shannon popped the last of her fish sandwich in her mouth and wiped her face on a napkin. "That's pretty scandalous information. I think I'd probably work pretty hard to keep that under wraps, too."

Lauren shoved her lunch aside and propped her chin on her fist. Who would go to such great lengths to conceal the details of an adoption that everyone would have known about anyway?

CHAPTER TWELVE

Lauren curled up on the window seat in the loft, her laptop open on the cushion next to her. A steady rain pelted the window and fog rolled in off the water. An incoming email caught her attention. It was from a friend of the Putnams, a physician who worked for a family practice in Portland.

Scrolling through the email, Lauren's pulse increased as she read the details. The practice was hiring experienced medical assistants and she'd received an 'impressive' recommendation from Dr. Putnam. The message indicated she should contact the business manager if she was interested.

Despite the townhouse age, its rent wasn't cheap. There was enough in her savings account to cover August, but after that things could get tricky. Not to mention a down payment on a different car if the Honda was, in fact, toast. Given the circumstances, she wasn't about to ask her parents for a loan.

Clicking the browser closed, Lauren sighed and stared out the window. A message like that couldn't be ignored indefinitely, but the thought of leaving her family right now sent a wave of anxiety coursing through her.

She eyed her suitcases still lined up against the wall. If they sat there much longer, she wouldn't have to unpack them. Maybe a hot bath would get her motivated. But the claw foot tub in her old bathroom downstairs was probably clean and awaiting guests. She would have to make do with a shower.

The bathroom had not received the same attention as the rest of the loft. Mom and Dad really needed to step up their game in here. The faded wall paper screamed 1987. Faint pink smudges of nail polish still stained the laminate countertop. While she waited for the water to warm up, she peeled off her sweaty clothes and dumped them in the hamper. Rummaging under the sink, she found a bottle of body wash. *Almond coconut vanilla.* Twisting off the top, she sniffed. *Not bad.*

A knock sounded on the door.

"Lauren?" Dad called.

"I'm in the shower, Dad."

"You have a phone call. It's Blake."

Her heart skipped a beat. Why would he call her?

"Can you take a message?"

Dad paused. "Sure."

His footsteps were heavy on the stairs. Although she planned to hang out and unpack, curiosity might drive her downstairs to get Blake's number. How ironic. After the hours they spent talking on the phone in high school, she still had his parents' number memorized. But he probably wasn't sitting at home with his parents. He had a business to run, maybe plans to grab dinner with that blond who draped herself all over him at Jess's.

"Stop it." She scolded, her voice echoing off the tiled wall. She gave up the right to know how Blake spent his evenings when she left town. His free time was no longer her concern.

Lathering shampoo in her hair, she replayed those last agonizing minutes before she headed for Oregon. Alone. Blake had come over at four in the morning and waited in the freezing rain. He'd begged her to stay, those amazing blue eyes brimming with tears. Other than the summer his dog died, she'd never seen Blake cry. Why had she been so stubborn?

Lauren shut her eyes against the incessant flashbacks and rinsed the shampoo from her hair. If only she could wash away the guilt and shame, too—wave goodbye to her unwanted companions as they swirled down the drain. Turning off the water, she brushed back the shower curtain. *Like it's that simple.* Cocooned in two fluffy brown towels, she went in search of clean clothes. The sundresses, skirts, and T-shirts she hastily packed were not going to cut it in this weather. Surely she'd packed more than one pair of jeans. She shivered and plunged her hands through the layers of clothing. Her fingertips grazed denim at the very bottom of the suitcase.

"Yes, perfect." She squeezed and tugged. The jeans came loose, spilling a stack of shirts and dresses onto the floor. Guess that means it's time to unpack.

After she was dressed, the contents of both suitcases found homes in the old dresser her grandfather built. Scooping up one last dress from the floor, her foot caught the edge of her tote bag and she stumbled forward.

The bag tipped over, releasing the carefully concealed white box from its hiding place. With trembling fingers, she unwrapped the blue T-shirt and glanced around the loft. This had to be hidden. Getting to her feet, she pulled open the closet door and found a large plastic bin on the top shelf.

Dragging a foot stool over, She stepped up on it and pulled the bin down. The opaque plastic prevented her from seeing the contents, but it wasn't heavy. Setting it on the carpet, she pried the lid off and the faint smell of lavender greeted her.

She smiled. The 'ugly' quilts. Granny had gone through a phase several years ago, insisting that her grandchildren each needed a quilt. They all watched as she tackled her new hobby with fierce determination, taking classes, toiling late into the night over each square. But her fabric selection left something to be desired and the end result was a mishmash of brown, lima bean green and burnt orange that defied description. Apparently the infamous quilts had found a home here in the loft.

Lauren tucked the box within the folds of the top quilt. There. No one would bother to open that bin. She hoisted the bin back on the closet shelf, climbed off the stool and shut the door.

A distraction, a project—anything—to occupy her mind. That's what she needed. Maybe her parents would listen to a few ideas she'd brainstormed for the Inn. Grabbing her laptop, she went back downstairs. The crack of a bat and distant roar of a crowd floated in from the living room. Dad must be watching a game on TV. Mom stood at the kitchen counter, swaying and humming "Twinkle Twinkle Little Star" with Gavin swaddled in her arms. Lauren's heart ached. If only Mom could have held her baby that way. No. Don't go there. She shoved back the bitter emotions, squared her shoulders, and breezed into the kitchen.

Mom turned around, a flicker of amusement in her eyes. "Did Dad tell you Blake called?"

Lauren nodded and sat down at the counter, casually flipping open her laptop and trying to pretend like she didn't care. "I'll call him later."

Mom shifted Gavin in her arms. "Well, you can call him whenever you want, but he indicated it was kind of important. Something about needing extra help on a kayak trip."

A kayak trip? "Maybe in a few minutes. I wanted to talk to you about a few ideas I have for the Inn before the guests get here."

Mom's eyebrows disappeared under her bangs. "What kind of ideas?"

"For one thing, your calendar method is so out of date. It would be much easier to generate a spreadsheet for reservations. I could add a column to track how the guests heard about the Inn. Then you could use that info to—"

Mom held up her hand. "Wait. I like my calendar. It's messy, but it gets the job done. And tracking? That sounds so--I don't know … intrusive. What brought this on?"

"Mom, let's face it. Business is slow this season. The Inn doesn't hold the same appeal it once did. What do you think about raffling off a free night's stay at the Cove to Creek festival this year?"

Mom frowned. "We attract a certain clientele. I can't tell you the number of repeat guests we have. It's astounding, really, that people would come back to stay again and again." Gavin fussed and Mom shifted him to her shoulder. She swayed and patted his backside.

"But if you kept more detailed records, you could see exactly who returned and how that relates to where you advertise." Lauren pulled up the website of another bed and breakfast in Seward. "See, look at what other B & B's have done with their websites—"

"Sweetheart, I appreciate your concern. I really do." Gavin began to cry louder and Mom raised her voice. "Trying something new mid-season is a bit of a stretch, with everything else we've got going on. But I'm willing to listen to your suggestions. Let me warm a bottle for Gavin and we'll talk some more."

Lauren pulled her laptop closer, the creative juices flowing now that she had Mom's blessing. Clicking her mouse to open a document, she glanced over the flyer she was working on for the festival. Mrs. Maxwell had come into the Fish House as Shannon and Lauren were leaving, and she'd gathered up her courage and offered her fledgling design services. They were meeting for coffee in the morning to go over the finished product before Lauren emailed it to the printer. It felt so good to be productive again.

Dad came in to the kitchen, frowning. "Dang Mariners. They can't get their act together this year." He tipped his head toward the phone. "Did you see Blake's number there? He wants you to call him."

"Good grief." Lauren snatched the Post-It note from the counter and studied the number.

Laughter bubbled from Mom's lips as she slipped a bottle into Gavin's mouth. "In case you hadn't heard."

Dad's gaze flitted between Lauren and Mom. "Did I miss something?"

"I was just reminding her that she needed to call him."

"You think he wants help with a kayaking trip? I haven't kayaked in years."

"You were quite a team once upon a time." Dad crossed his arms and leaned against the counter.

Lauren felt her cheeks grow warm. "Dad. Please. That's old news. We've both moved on." *Haven't we?*

"Just call him and see what he needs. You can always say no," Mom said.

Lauren sighed and reached for the phone. She dialed the number, every press of a button ratcheting up her anticipation.

The phone range once, then someone picked up. "Hello?"

No, her heart did not just flutter at the sound of his voice.

"Blake? It's me, Lauren."

"Hi. Thanks for returning my call. I know its short notice but we've got a big trip the day after tomorrow and I was wondering if you could help us out?"

"Me? What kind of a trip?"

"Half-day sea kayaking excursion out to Townsend glacier. Our clients are a family of nine, I would just feel better if we had one more guide."

Lauren twisted a ringlet of hair around her finger. Hardly did she qualify as a guide. "I don't know, Blake. I—"

"Look, I'm desperate. I've called everybody I can think of."

"Gee, thanks." Of course he wouldn't call her first.

"No, that's not what I meant." He sighed. "I feel bad asking you, with your Granny in the hospital and everything. But you'll be back right after lunch. I know you can make the trip. We used to go all the time."

She smiled at the memory of their families paddling out to the glacier together, lunch stowed in their packs. Those were the glory days, when the Tullys and the Carters were practically inseparable.

Maybe she could help him just this once. "What time?"

"That's the kicker. It's a 6:30 start."

"I should probably check with my parents, they might need me to—"

Both Mom and Dad shook their heads emphatically and waved her off. Funny, it's like they couldn't wait for her and Blake to spend time together.

"Um, sure. If you could let me know as soon as possible, I would appreciate it."

"I checked the calendar, it looks like we've only got two guests tomorrow night. I think my parents can handle it. What time should I be there?"

"Really? Wow, you're a lifesaver. I'll pick you up at six."

Ugh. Way too early. "See you then."

"So ... thanks. Yeah, I'll see you then."

She clicked off the phone and set it on the counter, avoiding her parents' curious stare. Well, this is definitely a distraction. Be careful what you wish for, right? Ideas for a booth at the festival and images of Blake in a kayak competed for attention in her mind. *Honestly. What are you thinking?* Even though she was single again, there was no sense rekindling a romance when she planned to be gone in less than a month.

He'd helped her out when they were in a tight spot. The least she could was return the favor. But that was it. They were two business owners in a small town looking out for each other. End of story.

CHAPTER THIRTEEN

Lauren wheeled the vacuum cleaner into the laundry room and stowed it in the corner. The timer on the dryer buzzed again, an irritating reminder that her battle against the daily chores raged on. *One more load and you'll be on your way.*

She opened the dryer and scooped the whole load into the waiting laundry basket. There was just enough time to fold everything before her lunch meeting with Mrs. Maxwell. It had required a few last-minute tweaks and a quick trip to Matt's office to borrow his printer, but the flyer for Cove to Creek days was ready to go. Hauling the load out into the living room, she dumped the sheets and towels onto the couch and grabbed her phone from the coffee table. Maybe a little music would make this mundane task more palatable and soothe the butterflies flitting around her stomach. *It's just a flyer. Relax.*

After a quick perusal of her music library, she selected one of her favorite Kenny Chesney songs and hit play. Reaching for a pillowcase, she heard the front door slam. Matt came in, shiny red tool box in hand.

"Good morning. What's up, sis?" He tried for a smile, but failed miserably.

"Good morning. Are you all right?"

He set his tool box down and dragged a hand over his face. "Rough night. I think Gavin cried for four hours straight."

Lauren winced. "I'm sorry. There's coffee in the kitchen."

"Thanks. I think I'll take you up on that. Is Mom around?"

"She should be back from the store soon." Lauren tipped her head toward the tool box. "Playing handyman today?"

Matt huffed out a breath and collapsed on the opposite couch. "Not because I want to. I've actually got a few appointments over at the church. But leaky pipes don't wait. When Seth's not around, it falls on me."

"I put a basin under the sink to catch the drips." Lauren made a neat stack of pillowcases along the back of the couch and started on the towels.

"I wish they'd just give in and call the plumber."

Lauren stopped the music and glanced at Matt. "Can I ask you something?"

He shrugged. "Sure."

"I've made some suggestions for improvements around here but when it comes to getting the ball rolling … any thoughts?"

A shadow flickered across Matt's face. "What do you mean?"

"Just some things they could do to make the place more appealing. S'mores around the fire pit, a hot chocolate bar— little changes to attract families with children."

"Mom wasn't real excited, was she?"

"Kind of lukewarm. I think I convinced her to try a computerized calendar and maybe participate in the festival this year, as long as I do most of the work."

Matt rubbed his fingers across his stubbly chin. "Those sound like great ideas … in theory. I think Mom's concern is what it would take to implement change. It's all she can do to make it through the day right now."

Lauren frowned. "But that's why I'm here."

Matt arched an eyebrow. "For how long? What about next week or next month? You can't just swoop in and fix everything, Lo. That never goes over well."

The towel she was folding slipped from her trembling fingers. "I'm just trying to help."

Matt stood and crossed over to where she sat. "I know. We appreciate it. I don't think this is the best time to delve into something new. I gotta get to work." He patted her shoulder, picked up his toolbox and headed for the kitchen.

Lauren cranked up the volume on her phone and tackled the last of the sheets, while Kenny sang about little umbrella drinks and the care-free island life. Although she hated to admit it, Matt was right. She didn't come home to shake things up, so maybe it was best if she quit trying so hard.

***

"HEY, LAUREN? YOUR phone's ringing," Matt called up the stairs.

Lauren snatched the flyer off her dresser, scooped up her wedges with her free hand, and flew down the stairs. She followed the sound of the ringtone to the couch. Grabbing the phone, she tapped the screen and pressed it to her ear. "Hello?"

"May I speak to Lauren Carter, please?" The voice was unfamiliar, professional.

"Speaking."

"Hello, Lauren. This is Tammy Austad. I'm the business manager for Hillsboro Family Practice. How are you today?"

She swallowed hard. The job Dr. Putnam had referred her to. Shoot. Why didn't she follow up on that last email?

"I-I'm fine, thanks. How are you?"

"I'm well, thank you. Do you have a few minutes?"

Lauren padded back into the kitchen and glanced down at Matt, who'd stuck his head back under the kitchen sink and started muttering to himself. "Yes, I'm available now."

"Wonderful. As I'm sure you're aware, you received a glowing recommendation from Dr. Dwight Putnam. We're looking for an experienced, dynamic medical assistant to fill an opening here at our clinic. I'm calling to check your availability for an interview."

Lauren's breath hitched, tapping the pen against the yellow notepad she'd pulled from a stack of Mom's stuff. "Wow. I'm flattered that you asked. Is there an initial phone screening or..."

"We like what we've heard so far from Dr. Putnam and at this time we'd love to set up a personal interview. How does next week sound?"

Next week. She hadn't changed her ticket yet, but since Holden abandoned their plans—not to mention their whole relationship—she'd dragged her feet on getting back to Portland. But this was a job. One she was capable of doing. One that paid the bills.

"I'm in Alaska visiting family right now. Is next Friday a possibility?"

She waited, biting the inside of her cheek, as Tammy checked the calendar.

"Absolutely. How does next Friday morning at ten o'clock sound?"

Lauren scrawled the info on the notepad. "Sounds great. Thank you for the call."

Tammy offered her phone number and Lauren made an additional note to look up directions later. Looks like Matt was right. What was the use in pushing Mom to make changes if she wasn't going to be around to help implement them?

***

BLAKE WALKED INTO The Fish House, his mouth already watering in anticipation. While the fish was plentiful in Tyonek and the natives had kept his freezer stocked, they weren't into deep-frying their catch. The sound of oil sizzling in the fryers filled the air and he licked his lips. He'd eat here every day if he could. Apparently it wasn't the Cove's best kept secret anymore, either, judging by the line at the front counter. While he waited his turn to order, he cast a curious glance around the dining room. His casual survey came to a halt when he saw Lauren sitting alone at a booth, her eyes on a single sheet of paper on the table in front of her. Huh. Wonder who she's with?

Lauren looked up and met his gaze, a smile turning up the corners of her pale pink lips. His heart stuttered, right on cue. He relinquished his place in line and walked over to her booth, drawn by the invisible pull of her eyes on his. He'd only stay for a minute. Long enough to see what she was up to.

"Hey, you." He stopped beside her and shoved his hands in the back pocket of his jeans. That sounded much cooler in his head. Dude. What is up with you?

She arched one eyebrow. "Hey, yourself. What's up?"

"Just grabbing lunch." He stole a peek at the paper on the table, some kind of announcement about Cove to Creek Days. "What's this?"

A faint blush colored her cheeks. She splayed her hand across the page. "Nothing."

Blake gently tugged at her fingers. "If it's nothing, why can't I see it?"

"It's a flyer, okay?" Impatience tinged her voice while her eyes flitted around the room.

"Did you make it?" He picked it up and studied it more closely.

"Yes."

"It looks great. Why are you embarrassed?"

She sighed, worry carving a crease in her forehead. "It's hard putting my work out there. Mrs. Maxwell gives the final approval. What if she hates it?"

"She'll love it. Don't sell yourself short. Who knows? It might be the first step in a booming new career for you."

Lauren looked at him like he'd sprouted three heads. "Easy, there. It's only a flyer."

Blake smiled. He'd always loved her witty comebacks. "You've got to start somewhere, right?"

"Right. Now scoot. Here she comes." Lauren snatched the flyer out of his hands and pressed it on the table, smoothing out a wrinkle he was certain didn't exist.

Blake raised both hands, palms up. "I'm out. See you tomorrow."

He turned back toward the front counter, stepping aside as a rather frazzled Mrs. Maxwell rushed past him. "Afternoon, Mrs. Maxwell."

She barely glanced up from her phone and offered a polite smile. "Hello, Blake."

He took his place in line once again, trying not to read too much into their brief exchange. Did the Maxwell's discuss school business over dinner? Debate the pros and cons of each job candidate before digging into dessert? As one of her former students, he hoped she'd cast a vote in his favor for replacing Coach Hoffman. But after all this time, maybe her allegiances were elsewhere. Pushing aside the doubt that nagged him, he quickly placed his order to go.

A few minutes later, Blake rapped his knuckles on the doorframe of Matt's office in the basement of the church, holding a paper bag and two drinks from the Fish House with his free hand.

"Hey, Blake. Come on in." Matt swept some papers off the corner of his desk and tossed them on the floor. He gestured to the empty folding chair in the corner. "Grab a seat. Thanks for bringing lunch."

Blake slid the bag onto the desk and pulled the chair up closer before settling in. "Thanks for seeing me today, I know you're a busy man these days."

Matt shook his head. "That's an understatement. It's all good stuff, though."

Unwrapping his fish sandwich, Blake glanced over Matt's shoulder at the photographs tacked to the bulletin board behind him. Matt had always lived life with the throttle wide open. Blake couldn't remember a time when Matt wasn't juggling three things at once. He'd shocked everyone when he married Angela immediately after high school, then blazed straight through college and seminary in California. While most guys his age were testing the waters of young adulthood, Matt had a family and now his first job as associate pastor at Emerald Cove's thriving community church.

"I saw a picture of Joshua on your Facebook wall. How many stitches?"

Matt chewed his cheeseburger, eyes closed, shaking his head in disbelief. "No stitches. Five staples."

"Ouch. Bet he won't run down the dock ramp again."

"Let's hope not. At least not in flip-flops."

Blake squeezed a packet of ketchup into the cardboard basket that housed his French fries and smiled. "He's all boy, isn't he?"

"Absolutely. Can't imagine where he gets it." Matt winked and reached for his Sprite.

"Ironic, isn't it? The legendary prankster becomes a pastor and spawns a passel of little pranksters."

"Ha. Angela knows all my tricks, anyway. Joshua will need to find some new material."

They ate in contented silence, Blake reflecting on the various pranks Matt had managed to pull off over the years. By far his favorite was the mysterious appearance of Coach Hoffman's truck hanging from the crane down at the boat launch.

"So." Matt inhaled the last of his burger and started in on his fries. "Give me a quick update on how things are going. Business is good, I hear?"

Dang, the dude could eat. Blake marveled at how quickly food disappeared around Matt. And where did it go? He probably weighed the same as he did back in high school.

"Business is great. Totally God's favor that this worked out for us."

"God's favor and a tremendous amount of hard work, I'm sure."

Blake nodded. "True. We're blown away by people's interest, though. Especially the kayaking. At this rate, we'll need another employee to finish out the season."

"And life outside of work? How's that?"

Blake hesitated. "Fine. Like I said, things are busy. I don't have a lot of free time, which is probably a good thing. But—"

"But?" Matt's eyes met his with a quizzical gaze.

Leaning back in his chair, Blake sighed. "I asked you to be my accountability partner because I knew you'd listen and give sound advice."

"Of course. What's on your mind?"

"I spoke to Mr. Maxwell about potentially coaching basketball if and when Mr. Hoffman retires. He didn't exactly give me a vote of confidence."

Matt wiped his mouth with a napkin. "What did he say?"

"It was more what he didn't say that got under my skin. Something about earning his trust—"

"Ah. The old 'prove to me you've changed' speech. I know you love that." Matt shook his head.

"Exactly. I feel like I've done my time, you know? Whatever happened to second chances?"

"I'm sorry he shot you down. Admittedly, addiction recovery is not something I've personally dealt with. But I know you've come so far. It would be a shame to let one naysayer derail your plans."

Blake pushed his food away, his appetite suddenly waning. "He's hardly just one naysayer. He's the superintendent. Kind of plays a major role in the decision-making process."

Matt rummaged in his desk drawer and came up with a package of Oreos. He pulled open the wrapper and pushed them toward Blake. "He is the top dog, but not necessarily the deciding factor. In case you've forgotten, word of mouth is a powerful weapon around here."

Blake waved off the Oreos. "That's what I'm afraid of."

"In this particular situation, I meant that as a good thing. Your family is loved and respected here, Blake. The community sees you moving back, building a business with your brother almost from scratch … that will carry you farther than you know."

"I just hope they have short memories and an extra measure of grace, you know?"

"Absolutely. Grace is a wonderful thing." Matt dusted the cookie crumbs from his fingers and reached for his Bible. "Let me read a few verses and then we'll pray, okay?"

Blake listened to the rustling of pages as Matt flipped through his Bible, stopping to scan a particular passage.

"Here it is. One of my favorite verses in the Old Testament: 'I will repay you for the years the locusts have eaten—'." Matt glanced up at Blake. "Some translations say 'restore' instead of 'repay'. I like that better. It offers hope that our struggles aren't for nothing, don't you think?"

Blake leaned forward, propped his elbows on his knees and let Matt's advice wash over him, replacing the lingering doubts he'd harbored when he first sat down. Matt was right. He couldn't let one negative comment take him down. The Lord had brought him this far. There was no reason to give up now. He'd keep moving forward, one day at a time.

CHAPTER FOURTEEN

Lauren waited on the top step of the porch, savoring the last of her coffee. The rain that pelted the roof for most of the night had finally stopped. Birds chirped and the fog parted to reveal patches of clear blue sky. All but the tops of the mountains were visible across the bay. Mitchell flopped down beside her, his muzzle finding a home on her leg.

"I know, old boy." She scratched behind his ears. "You can't come this time. Kayaks and dogs don't mix."

He whimpered and thrust one paw over her knee. She laughed and scratched him some more. His head popped up, ears perked as a truck came up the hill. Blake parked in front of the Inn and Mitchell was off the porch before Blake cut the engine.

Long legs clad in navy blue nylon wind pants and Adidas flip-flops slid from the driver's side. Her pulse quickened as he came around the front of the truck. His hair was only half-dry, curving over the edge of his Mariners visor. She caught a hint of soap and shampoo as he tossed the tennis ball Mitchell offered.

"Good morning." She raised her mug. "Need coffee?"

A sleepy smile spread across his face as he stretched his arms high overhead. She caught a glimpse of his chiseled abdomen as his T-shirt lifted. Lord, have mercy.

"I do need coffee. Megan is working on that for me right now. But thank you."

"That's a good deal you've got going there. Does she make your coffee every day?"

"Except Tuesdays. Jeremy can't convince her to get out of bed on her day off and fix us our mochas. Imagine that."

"Can't the Tuesday girl make mochas?"

Blake reached for her backpack. "Tried that. It's just not the same."

Lauren laughed. "Megan has found her calling. Let me put my cup inside and we'll go." She tip-toed back inside and set her cup in the sink. Guests were stirring and she didn't want to get caught in the kitchen.

She gave Mitchell one last pat on the head and Blake held the passenger door open for her. *Always the gentleman.* Their shoulders brushed before she climbed in the truck and the air crackled between them.

He went around and slid in the driver's seat. "I appreciate your help today," he said, turning the key in the ignition. "This is a big group excursion and we couldn't do it without you."

Heat warmed her cheeks under his gaze. "No problem. We only have two guests this morning. Mom can handle it and we certainly owe you."

"You don't owe me." He backed up and turned the truck toward town.

"Please." She rolled her eyes. "Melissa Baird would've skewered us in her review if you hadn't rescued me."

He laughed. A rich throaty laugh that made her tingle all over.

"How do you know I didn't sabotage the whole thing and give her a lousy tour?"

She narrowed her eyes. "You wouldn't."

"You'll just have to wait and see."

"You're right. Since she hasn't published the review yet. I can't imagine you sabotaging anything ever."

He pulled his buzzing cell phone from the console. "Jeremy and Tisha want to know where we are."

"It's only 6:15," she grumbled.

"They don't want to unload all the sea kayaks by themselves."

She would not let the idea of spending half the day with Tisha sour her good mood. Although she hadn't sea kayaked in years, she knew it would all come back as soon as she had the paddle in her hands. Maybe she'd even show Miss Minneapolis a thing or two.

"How did your meeting with Mrs. Maxwell go?" Blake tapped the brakes and the truck rolled to a stop at the bottom of the hill.

"Great. She loved the flyer. It goes to the printers this afternoon."

"See? Nothing to worry about. I told you it was awesome." His eyes lingered on hers. The warmth and encouragement there was enough to make her heart swell. He was proud of her. *If he only knew* ...

Enough. That line of thinking was a slow train to crazy town. Today was not about them.

"What's wrong?"

"Nothing."

"Whatever. You chew your lip when you're deep in thought. Always have."

She touched her fingers to her lips. Caught. Scrambling for an answer, she retreated to a safer topic. "Mrs. Maxwell asked me what the Inn was doing for the festival this year. I wish I could convince Mom to do something quick and easy. Like maybe—"

"A raffle."

"I'm sorry. A what?" She didn't even try to conceal her surprise.

Blake parked the truck in front of the shop, drumming his thumb on the steering wheel. "A raffle. Like a package deal. One night at the Inn and a half-day sea kayaking trip."

Her chin dropped. "Seriously?"

"Why not?"

"What's in it for you?"

He pulled his keys from the ignition. "It's great advertising. Pretty low cost. I think the community would totally go for it. What's not to like?"

She had to admit it was a brilliant plan. Not to mention easy to pull off. "I don't know what to say. Thank you. I'll talk to my parents and let you know."

"You're welcome." He tipped his head toward the Copper Kettle. "Are you sure I can't get you anything? Not even a quad venti half soy no whip sugar free extra hot mocha?"

She stuck out her tongue. "You're mocking me."

"I am."

"Are we meeting them here?"

Blake pointed behind her toward the harbor. "They're actually across the street at the put-in. See our van?"

She craned her neck to see a platinum blond ponytail bobbing about as a bright orange kayak was hauled out of the van. Dang it. There she is.

"Here." Blake passed her a set of keys. "Open up the shop. There's some gear with your name on it laying on the counter."

She looked down at her running tights layered under nylon shorts and frowned. "What's wrong with what I have on? You said wear layers."

"You need rain gear and a life jacket. On the off chance you get wet, I want you to stay warm." Blake jangled the keys in front of her.

She shivered at the thought of doing an Eskimo roll in the kayak. She reached for the keys.

"Bathroom's down the hall if you need it. I'll be there in a minute."

The key turned easily in the knob and she eased the door open. It smelled like pine trees and new shoes. She giggled when she saw the tree shaped air freshener dangling from the closet door nearby. Classic Blake. Efficient problem solver.

The counter was clean and the store quiet, except for the hum of a computer in hibernation. Black rain pants and a bright purple life jacket lay on the back counter. She dropped her backpack and found the bathroom. It was tiny, just enough room for a toilet and a pedestal sink. Posters of kayakers riding monstrous waves decorated the walls. She stripped off her hoodie and tugged on the rain pants. Pulling the bibs up to her chest, she buckled the shoulder straps over the thermal long underwear top she'd snatched from Mom's dresser. She studied her reflection in the small round mirror hanging over the sink. Hardly fashionable but today warmth trumped appearance.

The front door of the shop opened and closed. "Lauren?"

"Just a sec," she called. She cracked open the bathroom door and peeked out. Blake stood at the counter, unpacking a small cardboard box.

Padding toward him in her wool socks, she held up the life jacket with the attached spray skirt. "A little help here?"

His lips tipped up in a half-smile. "Sure." He stretched the life jacket open and she turned around and slipped her arms in, then gathered her hair in a ponytail at the nape of her neck.

"Thanks." She turned back around, smiling as she twisted her hair into a bun. The look in his eyes was familiar. Part tenderness, part longing. Her breath caught in her throat and her heart thrummed in anticipation.

He cleared his throat and took a step back. "Looks like you're all set," he said, his eyes dropping to the floor.

The distinct ache of disappointment knifed her heart. The moment was lost.

"Are those for me?" She nodded toward the gloves he clutched in his hands.

"Yes." He handed them over and tossed the plastic wrap back in the box. "I need to change."

"Right." She swallowed hard and took the gloves, careful not to let her fingers brush against his. *This is business, remember? Returning a favor and all that.*

Blake grabbed his wetsuit and went into the bathroom. Lauren pulled on rubber boots then went outside and stowed her backpack in Blake's truck. He came out a few minutes later, locking the shop behind him. He traded his wind pants for a wet suit, but the top half hung loose at his waist, meeting the hem of his T-shirt.

"Ready?" Without waiting for an answer, he hit the button on his key fob to lock the truck and started across the street.

She hustled after him, her spray skirt swaying and her boots clomping on the asphalt.

"How are those boots?" he asked, taking long strides down the ramp to the dock.

She kicked out her leg and stepped on the heel of his flip flop.

"Hey!" He stumbled and grabbed the handrail on the ramp. He glared at her over his shoulder.

"Oh, sorry." She smiled sweetly. "I'm a little clumsy today."

His irritation diminished and he laughed.

Down on the dock, Tisha turned at the sound of Blake's laugh and flashed a pearly white smile. When her eyes flickered to Lauren, the smile froze for an instant. She recovered and extended her hand.

"Good morning, I'm Tisha. You must be—"

"Lo-lo!" Jeremy called from the far end of the dock and let out a wolf whistle. "Nice ensemble."

Lauren waved and then shook Tisha's hand. "Lauren Carter. Nice to meet you."

"I didn't realize you were joining us this morning." Tisha shot Blake a questioning look.

Let's see you explain this one.

Blake dropped two life jackets on the dock and fixed his gaze on Tisha. "We're expecting a party of nine, five of them are minors. The youngest is barely eleven. Lauren will ride with her. It's a safety issue, Tisha."

Yeah, blondie. It's all about safety.

"Great." Tisha nodded. "Have you kayaked before?"

Lauren swallowed a snide reply.

"Tisha, help me out, will ya?" Jeremy moved between them and pointed toward the van and trailer. "We need one more kayak to get this party started."

Tisha turned on her heel and jogged up the ramp. Jeremy winked and nudged Lauren's shoulder as he passed by. Lauren couldn't hide her smile.

"What's so funny?" Blake locked eyes with her. His T-shirt lay discarded on the dock.

"Your girl's a little testy." She let her eyes slide down to his bare chest. Muscles rippled as he slipped his arms into a gray Quicksilver rash guard. *I think my morning just got a whole lot better.*

He pulled the rashguard over his head. "She's not my girl."

She raised one eyebrow. "You should tell her that."

He yanked the wetsuit up over his shoulders and zipped the sleeveless top, keeping his cool blue eyes locked on hers. A muscle in his jaw twitched. *Hmm. Sore subject.*

Jeremy and Tisha returned with another double kayak and a large family in tow. They were loud and boisterous, horsing around in their matching rain gear. The kids were all boys, except for one sullen, blue eyed girl with long raven black hair. She stood apart from the group, arms folded across her chest. Lauren assumed this was her partner for the day.

While Blake and Jeremy made introductions and reviewed the safety instructions, Lauren approached the grumpy tweener.

"Hey, I'm Lauren. We're going to ride together. Can I help you with your life jacket?"

The girl eyed the life jacket with utter disdain. She snapped and popped her bubble gum.

"I am not wearing that."

Lauren took a deep breath and embraced her inner cheerleader. "C'mon, orange is totally your color. Slip this on, you'll be the hottest thing around."

"Hannah, let's go," barked the male who most resembled the father figure in the group.

Hannah huffed out a breath, blew her bangs out of her eyes and snatched the life jacket from Lauren's hand.

Blake squatted and braced the first kayak against the dock. "Lauren, you get in first and show her how it's done."

Lauren glared daggers at him. Why did she have to be the guinea pig?

Blake's expression told her he meant business. She buckled her life jacket and jabbed one foot into the rear cockpit. The kayak rocked and her body swayed, forcing her to commit. She pulled her other leg in and slid into her seat. She forced a confident smile for Hannah's benefit.

The fear was evident on the young girl's face. Blake spoke softly, she nodded and tentatively climbed in. Lauren held her breath as Blake inched closer. He demonstrated how to adjust their spray skirts to keep the cockpit dry but she wasn't listening. She studied his hands, moving deftly to secure a dry bag to the webbing on the kayak. Those same hands once held her, toyed with her hair, carried her books to class...

He touched her shoulder and she snapped back to reality. "I'm sorry, what?"

He held her gaze for a moment. "I asked if you had any questions?"

Heat climbed up her neck. *Dang it. Pay attention.* "No, we're all good."

She grabbed a paddle and glanced at the back of Hannah's head. "We're going to push off in three, Hannah. Three, two, one and here we go."

The bow of the orange kayak slid forward in the blue-green water as Blake gave them a gentle shove. She dipped the blade in the water, first on the left then tipped the shaft and touched the water on the right. Hannah sat motionless, her shoulders hunched. The paddle lay across the kayak, blades still dry.

We're off to a roaring good start. "Hannah, this will be a lot more fun if you paddle, too."

The girl mumbled something unintelligible and one blade slanted lazily toward the water.

Lauren racked her brain for some way to motivate the young girl to participate. Although she hit the gym almost daily in Portland, she lacked the endurance to paddle for both of them on a four hour tour. Maybe they should turn back.

"What's the matter, Hannah-banana?" Two of her brothers eased alongside, their paddles moving in tandem as their bright yellow kayak sliced through the water. "Are ya chicken?"

"Shut up." Hannah smacked the water with the blade of her paddle. Droplets of water splashed in their faces, which only provoked more teasing.

"Bwak, bwak, bwak," they cackled like chickens and pulled ahead. Lauren's blood boiled and she looked back toward Blake. Tisha maneuvered her kayak next to his and as she spoke, he threw back his head and laughed. *Perfect.*

"Try to relax your torso," Jeremy instructed, paddling up on their right side. "Most of your power will come from your legs and torso, believe it or not. Arms just carry the power to the paddle."

Hannah's shoulders slid a fraction of an inch away from her ears. A gangly boy with dark black hair peeking from his Red Sox hat rode with Jeremy. He seemed more interested in following Jeremy's instruction than taunting Hannah.

Lauren breathed easier as she watched Hannah respond to Jeremy. Maybe a little encouragement was all she needed.

"Stomach in, shoulders back. That's it. Nicely done!" Jeremy cheered.

They glided out of the harbor and into the bay. Gray, soupy fog clung to the mountains that rimmed the bay. Lauren prayed the rain held off. Blake and Tisha led them away from the choppy wakes of the larger boats motoring out of the harbor. As the kayaks glided into smooth water, Lauren basked in the serenity that surrounded them. Hannah's father pointed to a raft of sea otters swimming nearby.

"Look, Hannah," Lauren whispered. "Some of the otters have babies."

Hannah's head snapped up, her eyes widened. A wet furry face appeared off the bow of their kayak, a tiny pup parked on her stomach.

"Adorable!" Hannah produced a cell phone and snapped several pictures.

As the morning progressed, Hannah's brothers kept a safe distance and the girls found their rhythm. Lauren shoulders ached from the exertion and she hoped Hannah stepped up her game on the way home.

Jeremy announced they would beach the kayaks in a few minutes to have a snack and enjoy the view of Townsend Glacier. Lauren could see Hannah practically hyperventilate.

"No worries, girl," Lauren said. "We've got this."

"Maybe I can eat my snack in the kayak," Hannah said.

"Don't be ridiculous." Hannah's mother materialized beside them, perfectly manicured nails gripping the shaft of her paddle. "You don't want to miss the view, do you?"

"C'mon, where's your sense of adventure?" Hannah's father asked.

Lauren bristled at their insensitive comments. Hannah wilted under their criticism, dropping her chin to her life jacket. Blake and Tisha were already out of their kayaks, rubber boots sloshing through the water lapping at the rocky shoreline. Hopefully Jeremy could offer some pointers on exiting the kayak properly. She opened her mouth to call his name when the kayak began to rock and roll. Hannah had stood up, her body weight shifting way over the midline of the kayak. They were still in at least six feet of water.

"No!" Lauren yelled. That was the last thing she heard before she found herself upside down in icy cold water, trapped under the kayak.

CHAPTER FIFTEEN

The murky water enveloped her. The rocky floor of the ocean was barely visible above her head. Icy fingers of fear snaked through her gut. *Come on, think!*

Lauren fumbled for the edge of the cockpit. There was no way she could roll the kayak. She needed to get out. Now. Her lungs screamed in protest. Water filled her rain pants, dragging her down. The spray skirt came loose with one desperate tug. She kicked free and the kayak rolled right side up. She swam toward the light. Jeremy's instructions to never let go of the paddle echoed in her head. She had no idea where her paddle went. Perhaps her mistake could be overlooked given the circumstances.

Breaking through the surface of the water, she gasped for air.

"There she is!" Jeremy and his partner in the Red Sox hat were beside her in an instant. She clawed at the stern of his kayak, her teeth chattering. Hannah was nowhere in sight.

"You're freezing. We gotta get you out of the water." He cupped his hands around his mouth. "Hey! Blake! We need a water taxi!"

"A what?" She could feel her fingers slipping. They were numb. She must have left her gloves back on the dock. Blake was going to be mad.

"We need a boat to pick you up and take you back."

"That's crazy. I-I-I can p-paddle b-b-back," she chattered.

"You can't paddle home soaking wet." Jeremy extended his paddle. "Come on. I'll tow you in closer so you don't have to float."

"I'm fine. Where's Hannah?" She could see the adults huddled around a figure on the beach. The boys were gathering sticks and throwing them into a big pile.

"Hannah's on the beach. We need to get her warmed up, too."

"I'll warm up as soon as I start paddling again," she grumbled.

Jeremy narrowed his eyes. "You are so stubborn, you know that?" He turned to the raven-haired boy in the front of his kayak. "Ross, I need you to paddle while I help Lauren get back in her kayak."

Wide-eyed, Ross lifted his Red Sox hat and scratched his head.

"I'm not getting back in that thing. It's full of water!" Lauren cried.

"We have a pump."

"I can swim." Lauren let go of the kayak and flipped on her back. She couldn't remember ever feeling this cold. Somehow she had lost her rubber boots and the water-logged wool socks made her feet feel like they weighed fifty pounds. Arms flailing, she made a very weak attempt at swimming the backstroke.

A lean muscular arm wrapped around her chest and she squealed. "What are you doing?" She twisted to see Blake behind her, water lapping at his chin.

"I'm trying to help you," he said, tightening his grip and swimming toward the beach.

"I'm f-f-fine," she protested, trying to break free. Her feet didn't quite touch bottom.

"Really? Is that why your lips are blue? We have to get you warm."

She gave up resisting and let him tow her into the shallow water. Struggling to walk on her own, she found her legs weren't responding to her brain's instructions.

"I've got you." Blake scooped her up and sloshed through the breakers to the narrow strip of gray sand. The boys had a fire going and Hannah sat propped up against a log, staring into the flames. Lauren wanted to ask her what in the world she was thinking, standing up like that but the expression on the girl's face was alarmingly detached.

Blake lowered her gently to the ground and fumbled with the buckles on her life jacket. She studied the lines on his forehead, the muscle twitching in his jaw. His breath warmed her face.

"I'll call Jason Cavanaugh on my cell. Hopefully he can pick you up." He avoided her gaze as he pulled off her life jacket then fumbled for his cell phone.

"There's a name I haven't heard in years. Pick me up how?" She shivered and yanked off the rain pants.

"In his boat. He's my emergency water taxi when he happens to be fishing nearby."

"Is this really an emergency? We just got a little wet. Why don't we—"

Blake pressed a finger to her lips and leaned in. Anger flashed in his eyes. "This is a potentially dangerous situation. Hypothermia is still a possibility. You're going. No arguments." He dropped his hand and she sat back in stunned silence. Her lip tingled from his touch. Why was he angry? Did he think she did this on purpose?

Blake stood up and trudged over to Hannah and her parents. He squatted next to the fire. Lauren couldn't hear their conversation but she could tell by his animated hand gestures and the ramrod straight posture of Hannah's mother that things were not going well. As their voices grew louder, Tisha glanced up from an impromptu game of tag she was playing with the teenagers. Her eyes met Lauren's. A trace of annoyance flickered across her face before she turned away and huddled with Hannah's brothers. Whatever. *This is so not my fault.*

The unmistakable rumble of a boat engine captured everyone's attention. Lauren looked up and saw the white bow with kelly green trim and the name *Ellie Mae* painted on the side. Jeremy and Ross paddled their kayak out to meet the boat. Blake walked back toward her, glancing at his phone.

"Jason will have to drop anchor," Blake said.

"What? Why?"

"He can't come in here, it's too shallow. We'll have to paddle out to him." Blake's fingers danced over the screen on his phone.

Lauren glanced at Hannah. She hadn't moved. Her parents sat on either side, like sentries standing guard. *There's no way she'll get back in a kayak.*

"Ross and Jeremy will row in with Jason's raft and pick you up."

Lauren wrapped her arms around her torso. "Why don't we all ride back with Jason?"

Blake stared at her, impatience flickered across his face. "Jason can't haul us and our kayaks."

"Why not b-b-beach the kayaks and c-c-come back for them later?" Her teeth chattered again and she rubbed her arms vigorously.

Blake sighed. "You're kidding, right? High tide could easily wash them all out to sea. That's thousands of dollars in equipment. Here," he offered her a hand up. "Why don't you scoot closer to the fire?"

She shook her head. "I don't want to speak to Hannah right now." *Or be anywhere near her at the moment.*

Blake dropped his hand. "Suit yourself. But you're going to have to ride back with her."

Lauren scowled and huddled against the log. Jeremy and Ross were in the raft, each had an oar in hand. Jason had somehow pulled their kayak on board the *Ellie Mae*.

By the time Jeremy and Ross came ashore with the gunmetal gray raft, Lauren was certain she'd never feel warm again. She stood slowly, dusted the gritty sand from her backside and moved toward them. The water and sand squished through her soggy wool socks and she grimaced. Gross.

Jeremy frowned. "Where are your boots?"

She shrugged. "I lost them when I rolled."

He shook his head. "Good grief. This gets worse by the minute. We have got to get you warm."

"Yeah, you mentioned that." She couldn't stop shivering. The sunshine eluded them. Her head felt as thick as the fog that blocked their view of the glacier.

"You need to put your life jacket back on." Blake appeared at her elbow. Hannah and her father stood behind him. A look of sheer panic filled Hannah's features as she eyed the raft.

Lauren shrugged back into the life jacket while Blake and Jeremy conferred on the logistics of ferrying people and kayaks out to Jason. Blake insisted he row the raft back out and escort Lauren, Hannah and Hannah's father back to town. She was in no mood to argue. Visions of a warm bed and a hot cup of coffee danced in her head as she tried to climb into the raft. Her foot slipped and Ross's hand shot out to steady her.

"Thanks," she mumbled, too tired to even think about being embarrassed.

Hannah refused to get in the raft and her father lost his temper. Lauren's eyes widened as he let a string of profanity rip and all but dumped her in the raft. She whimpered as he snapped the buckles on her life jacket closed.

The air was fraught with tension as Blake climbed in. A vein bulged in his forehead and his ears were bright red. Blake and Hannah's father rowed in silence. Lauren prayed they would make it back to town in one piece.

Jason greeted them with a smile. Lauren hadn't seen him since they graduated from high school. He was short and muscular, barrel chested with a crew cut and wide-set hazel eyes. He winked and leaned over the stern. "Miss Lauren. Aren't you a sight for sore eyes?"

Lauren offered a weak smile. Blake tossed Jason a line and he pulled the raft against the *Ellie Mae*.

"Go on, Lauren," Blake instructed.

She didn't know if she had the strength to climb the swim ladder. She slung her leg over the side of the raft, a fresh wave of anxiety washing over her.

Jason extended both arms and lifted her off the last rung and into the boat. He squeezed her shoulder. "Good to see you, sorry it's under these circumstances."

"Thanks for the ride. You're a lifesaver."

He shrugged. "This is what friends do. We gotta stick together out here."

As the others climbed aboard, Lauren felt her legs quivering. She sank onto the giant cooler Jason kept lashed to the boat. Blake saw her and raised his eyebrows. "You okay?"

She nodded, her teeth still chattering.

Blake turned to Jason. "Do you have dry clothes and blankets? Any hot drinks on board?"

"Sure thing," Jason nodded and gave Lauren the once-over. "My wife keeps extra clothes down below and I fired up the coffee pot while I was waiting. Christi wouldn't mind if you borrowed her stuff."

Lauren shook her head. She opened her mouth to protest but the words wouldn't come.

Blake slid onto the cooler next to her, his blue eyes dark with concern. "Listen, these wet clothes have to come off. You go change into Christi's stuff and I'll fix you some coffee."

She stood up and made her way through the sliding glass door into the galley. The smell of coffee greeted her and she glanced longingly at the carafe waiting on the counter. Moving into the forward cabin, she saw a large zip top bag with clothes inside laying on the bed. She sank onto the cushions and pulled a pillow under her head. She clutched the bag to her chest and closed her eyes. If she could just rest for a few minutes.

"Lauren, wake up." Blake jostled her arm.

"Hmmm?"

"You need to change your clothes." Blake nudged her again.

She batted his hand away. "Just let me rest for a minute."

"I can't. You might have a head injury or hypothermia. C'mon." Blake shoveled his arms under her back and propped her up. "You need to stay awake and get warm."

He tugged on the cuff of her shirt sleeve. Her eyes popped open and she gripped his forearm. "What are you doing?"

"You have to get out of these wet clothes."

She scooted away and crossed her arms over her chest. "I'm not changing in front of you."

He sighed and rolled his eyes. "It's not like I haven't seen it before."

She gasped and her jaw dropped. "I can't believe you just said that." She picked up a pillow and whacked him in the arm. *Even if it is true.*

A gleam of mischief glinted in his eyes. "Don't start something you can't finish."

"Oh, I'll finish it."

He cocked an eyebrow and tilted his head. "I'd like to see you try." His voice was husky and she couldn't tear herself away from those incredible dimples. Warning bells sounded in her head. *Down, girl.*

She cleared her throat. "I'll get changed."

He nodded and disappeared through the galley.

Christi Cavanaugh had several pairs of sweats and long sleeved shirts to choose from. Lauren left the smallest sizes for Hannah. She settled on gray sweatpants and an old navy blue ECHS wrestling shirt. The sleeves were way too long and the legs of the sweats pooled around her ankles. It felt so good to be dry. I owe you one, Christi. She put the extra clothes on the bed for Hannah and jammed her wet stuff in the bag. The galley floor was freezing cold on her bare feet. She went back to the bed and rummaged until she found a pair of men's gym socks. Better than nothing.

Back on deck, Blake handed her a cup of coffee.

"Thanks." She smiled and wrapped her hands around the steaming mug.

"Hannah, there are extra clothes down below if you want to change," Blake said.

Hannah's father nudged her arm. "You need dry clothes, sweetie." The young girl hesitated, then stood and shuffled inside.

"Once we're underway, you need to sit inside out of the wind. Would you like a sweatshirt?" Blake offered a hoodie.

"Hannah can have it." Lauren sipped the coffee slowly, letting the warm liquid slide down her throat. "I'm getting warmer."

"Yeah, you look positively toasty. Let's borrow some blankets from Jason."

Jason appeared and assessed Lauren from head to toe. "Never thought I'd see the day when Lauren Carter wore my clothes. You look good, girl." She pretended to glare at him over the rim of her coffee cup.

"Blake, I stowed the kayak. I'm ready to go. There are blankets under the bench seat in the galley." Jason fist-bumped Blake and headed for the fly bridge.

Lauren stepped into the galley and set her coffee on the counter. Hannah sat at the little table, eyes downcast. Lauren opened the bench seat cushion and pulled out two blankets. She offered one to Hannah but the girl remained motionless. *Fine. Have it your way.*

"Would you like something to drink, Hannah?" Blake asked.

Lauren turned and saw him leaning against the doorway. She glanced back at Hannah. The girl gave the slightest shrug of her slender shoulders and stared at the table. *Ungrateful little thing, aren't you?*

Blake took the blanket from Lauren's hands and draped it over her shoulders. She looked up as he squeezed her shoulder. "Sit." Something stirred inside when she saw the tenderness lingering in his eyes.

She sank onto the cushion opposite Hannah. The engine rumbled and Hannah clutched the table as the boat picked up speed.

"How about some Russian tea?" Blake opened a plastic container next to the sink and scooped some rust-colored powder into a mug.

"What's that?" Hannah asked, her voice soft and timid.

Lauren stared. *She speaks.*

"Oh, you haven't lived until you've tried Cavanaugh's special blend of Russian tea. Did your parents ever let you drink Tang?"

Hannah shook her head. "We aren't allowed to have a lot of sugar."

Blake leaned closer to the table. "Then you probably shouldn't tell them about this. It's loaded with sugar." He set the mug in front of Hannah. "This will be our little secret."

A smile threatened to break through her sullen features. Blake sat down beside Lauren and slung his arm casually across the back of the bench seat behind her. Lauren sipped her coffee and pretended not to notice. It would be so easy to scoot closer, reclaim her spot in his arms. *Stop it.*

The trip back to town went quickly. Lauren finally stopped shivering. Hannah slurped down her Russian tea and asked for a refill. Blake kept Hannah entertained with stories from his teaching days in Tyonek. She laughed and asked lots of questions, the dramatic events of the day already forgotten. Lauren watched the two of them interact and something stirred deep within her. He was so good with kids. But it wasn't her place to feel proud of him. He wasn't hers.

When the boat passed the buoys marking the harbor entrance, Blake stepped out on deck to help Jason tie off the lines. Lauren suspected he needed to speak with Hannah's father, too.

"I'm sorry," Hannah said.

"For what?" Lauren turned from the window and stared at the young girl. She had her chin propped on her fist, hair hanging in straggly knots around her face.

"I caused a lot of trouble here today." Hannah's eyes darted up to Lauren's face then back to the table.

You got that right. "Why did you jump?"

Hannah twisted her mug in circles. "My brothers are always teasing me, calling me a chicken. I thought it would be cool if I did something totally crazy. I really didn't think about how cold it would be if I tried to swim. I'm so sorry you tipped over." Tears pooled in Hannah's eyes.

Lauren softened. Poor girl. She reached over and squeezed Hannah's hand. "It's okay. I'm fine. Don't worry about it."

Hannah nodded and dried her eyes on the sleeve of her shirt. Lauren turned once more and looked out the window. A familiar figure stood at the end of the dock, watching the *Ellie Mae* cruise into the harbor.

"I know all about annoying brothers. There's one of mine." Lauren pointed out the window. Matt waved to Jason and Blake.

"Why is he here?" Hannah asked.

"Good question. I better go see what he's up to." They cleaned up the galley and went out on the back deck. Jason maneuvered the boat into its slip. Blake tossed the lines to Matt and he tied them off at the cleat.

"Matthew, what brings you by today? Trolling for lost souls?" Jason teased.

Matt grinned. "Not today. I'm just looking for Lauren."

She narrowed her eyes. "Why?"

Matt scratched his head. "It's probably better if we speak privately."

Lauren took his outstretched hand and stepped onto the dock. A shadow crept across his features and her gut twisted in a knot. "What's going on?"

Matt turned his back to the boat and leaned in close. "I want to give you fair warning that we have unexpected company at the Inn."

Lauren knitted her brow together. A fleeting image of Holden flashed through her mind. Surely he wouldn't come back again. Was someone looking for him? "Who?"

"Aunt Jane. She showed up about an hour ago."

She winced. Poor Mom. "But she's a day early."

"I don't know about that, but I think you better come with me. Mom is a wreck."

CHAPTER SIXTEEN

L auren nibbled on her thumbnail as Matt drove them back to the Inn. Aunt Jane was back in town. Did she come to see Granny? Would Mom tell Jane about Granny's dementia? This was not good.

"Did you get a chance to talk to her?"

Matt shook his head. "Not really. Mom sent me to find you. I can't believe we've never met her."

"Well, I think you'll get your chance to hang out. Apparently she's staying at the Inn."

Matt shot her a look of disbelief. "No."

"True story."

"I hope that changes. Mom is super stressed. You can almost feel the tension between them."

An icy tingle raced up her spine and Lauren shivered.

Matt glanced over and flipped on the heater. "Are you cold? And why are you wearing Jason's old clothes? "

"I helped Blake and Jeremy with a sea kayaking trip. The girl I was with panicked and jumped out of the kayak. Jason gave us a ride back."

"What happened?"

"Let's just say my Eskimo roll is a little rusty." Lauren warmed her hands over the vents.

"Seriously? You went in the water? Do you need to see Dr. Wheeler?" Matt's eyes widened.

Lauren smiled. "Why, Matthew, you seem genuinely concerned about your big sister."

"Of course I'm concerned. That water is freezing cold."

"I feel a lot better with dry clothes on. I'm okay." Besides, they needed to get home.

Matthew parked the minivan in front of the Inn. They sat in silence for a moment and stared at the front door.

"Let's do this thing," he said, extending a fist toward Lauren. She bumped his fist with her own and drew in a ragged breath. How bad could it be?

Matt led the way up the steps and through the front door. An older woman in dark washed jeans and a pale blue cashmere sweater sat on the couch in the living room. She flipped through a magazine, one leg crossed over the other and a silver ballet flat dangling from her foot. A Coach purse sat propped against the couch. *Whoa. Nice purse.* When the front door clicked shut, the woman looked up and dropped the magazine in her lap. She stood, tucking one side of her silver blunt-cut bob behind her ear. A mixture of emotions flashed across her impeccably groomed features.

"Hello again, Matthew. And you must be Lauren." She stepped around the coffee table and moved toward them with her arms outstretched. She was taller than Lauren expected. Must have gotten Pop's height. "I'm your Aunt Jane."

"Hi." Lauren stiffened as Jane attempted an awkward hug. She smelled like she'd fallen in a vat of expensive perfume. Matt sneezed.

"Bless you," Jane said, pulling back and giving him a pat on the arm.

"Thanks." Matt cleared his throat.

"Just look at you." She turned her green eyes on Lauren and a thin smile stretched across her face. "My, that's an interesting outfit."

Lauren squirmed under Jane's piercing gaze. "I went for an unexpected swim."

"Oh, well. I see." She shook her head. "I still remember the day you were born. You—"

"Oh, Lauren and Matt, I didn't realize you were back." Mom came in from the kitchen with a cup of coffee. "Lauren, did you meet your Aunt Jane?"

Lauren nodded. Mom passed the coffee to Jane. "Here you are, lots of cream and sugar in there." She laughed nervously.

"Thank you, Debbie. I was just telling Lauren I remember the day she was born. It seems like yesterday." Jane lifted the coffee cup to her lips.

Mom's eyes flitted from Jane to Lauren and back to Jane. Her face paled. "Oh?"

Mom's hand trembled as she brushed her bangs out of her eyes. What was going on here? She hadn't seen her mother this worked up since Seth disappeared on a fishing trip back in high school.

"You made a very dramatic entrance and oh, that red hair." Jane laughed. "We were all so surprised."

Matt cleared his throat. "Aunt Jane, why don't we sit down and you can tell us what brings you to Emerald Cove."

She glared at Matt. *Zip it.*

"Why don't we have lunch first?" Mom asked. "Lauren, come help me make the sandwiches."

Jane shrugged. "I would love some lunch."

The front door flew open and they were nearly trampled by Matt's children.

"Daddy!" Joshua yelled, careening toward Matt at top speed and wrapping his arms around Matt's legs. Emmie and Ava toddled in wearing matching purple dresses sprinkled with pink polka dots. They clapped their hands and giggled as Matt scooped Joshua up and swung him around in a circle.

A look of complete relief washed over Mom's face. Whatever Jane planned on telling them would have to wait.

Lauren left Matt and his children with Aunt Jane and followed her mother into the kitchen.

"What's going on?" she whispered.

"What do you mean?" Mom called as she disappeared behind the pantry door. Lauren slid onto a stool and waited. Mom brought peanut butter, bananas, and a loaf of bread to the counter. She avoided Lauren's gaze.

"Come on, Mom. You were shaking in your boots out there. Why does Aunt Jane make you so nervous?" Lauren reached for a knife and slathered peanut butter on a slice of bread.

"She's up to something. I can sense it." Mom's knife clacked against the cutting board as she sliced a banana into coins.

"Anything I can do to help?" Angela wandered into the kitchen with Gavin nestled in the crook of her arm like a football. Lauren grimaced at the spit-up oozing down Angela's shoulder.

Mom turned and offered a weak smile. "Hi, Ang. Oh, do you need a towel?"

"What? Why?" Angela glanced down at her shoulder. "Oops, yeah, I guess I do." She grabbed the dish cloth draped over the edge of the sink and dabbed at her worn T-shirt with her free hand. "Is that woman on the couch really your sister?"

Mom nodded. "Could you get the egg salad out of the fridge, please?"

Angela tossed the dish cloth in the sink and pulled open the refrigerator door. She bumped Gavin's head on the door as she reached in and he began to cry. "Oh, sorry little buddy." The helpless cry of the newborn caused the hair on Lauren's arms to stand at attention. An old familiar ache welled up within her. Angela produced a pacifier and popped it in his mouth.

"Here." Mom passed her three sippy cups from the drying rack. "Fill these with milk, please."

Lauren got up to get the milk and the shrill ring of the phone startled her. The cup slipped from her hand, bounced off the counter and rolled under the table.

"I'll get it, Mom." Lauren reached for the cordless phone lying in the middle of the counter. "Hello? Inn at the Cove."

"Debbie?" The woman's voice sounded vaguely familiar.

"No, this is Lauren. May I help you?" She crouched down and crawled under the table in pursuit of the errant cup.

The woman hesitated. "Hello, Lauren. This is Sandra Tully. Is your mom around?"

Lauren sucked in a breath. Of course she wouldn't ask how she was doing. She probably hated her for breaking Blake's heart.

"My mom is here, but we have company." The kitchen filled with voices and activity as Matt, Aunt Jane and the children came in. The little girls clamored to get into their booster seats. Lauren stood up, set the cup on the counter and pressed her hand to her ear to block out the racket. "May I take a message?"

"Yes, it sounds like you have a house full. When I finished my shift this morning, your grandmother was extremely agitated. That's unusual for her. She's most anxious late at night. Please tell your mother she needs to drop by and visit today."

This was getting complicated. She glanced over her shoulder. Mom had stopped making sandwiches and stood at the counter with her eyebrows raised expectantly. Lauren panicked. "I'll be sure to let her know. Thanks. Bye." She clicked the phone off and set it on the counter. Probably didn't win any bonus points for hanging up on her, either.

"Who was that?" Mom asked.

Lauren felt Aunt Jane's curious stare. A slow heat crawled up her neck. Joshua tugged on Aunt Jane's sweater. "Sit by me, sit by me," he begged. But Lauren could tell she was most interested in hearing about the phone call.

"Sandra Tully wants you to stop by the hospital today," Lauren mumbled quickly.

Mom stiffened. A fork full of egg salad hung suspended over a slice of bread.

Aunt Jane zeroed right in. "Anything you want to share with me, Deb?"

Mom slowly shook her head. The egg salad glopped onto the bread. "No. Not particularly."

Jane's berry-red lips hung open. Her green eyes flashed. "I see. When were you planning to tell me about Mother?"

Here we go. Lauren shot a glance at her brother. He had taken over her task of pouring milk into his kids' cups. He stood with the cap off the milk, eyes darting between Mom and Aunt Jane.

Mom pressed her lips into a thin line. She slapped the sandwich together and sliced it in half.

Aunt Jane closed the gap between them in two quick strides. "Debbie?" She pressed her French-manicured fingers against her sister's arm. "I asked you a question."

Lauren glared at her brother. Do something. He shrugged helplessly.

Mom set the knife on the cutting board and turned to face Aunt Jane. Her eyes glistened with tears. "Honestly, Jane, I didn't know you cared."

Jane gasped. "That is not fair."

"Fair? You want to talk about fair?" Mom's voice went up an octave. The children munched on their sandwiches in silence, eyes round as saucers.

"Mom—" Matt interrupted.

Mom pulled her shoulders back and lifted her chin. "You've done nothing for twenty-seven years but mail souvenir postcards and brag about your husband's money. You didn't even come back for Dad's funeral. I don't want to hear one word from you about fair."

Jane cut her eyes toward Lauren and then back to Debbie. "You know exactly why I left. When you're ready to talk about that, let me know. I'll be at the hospital." She turned on her heel and stormed out of the kitchen. A moment later the front door slammed.

Mom sagged against the counter, dropped her chin to her chest, and began to cry.

CHAPTER SEVENTEEN

L auren grabbed a tissue from the box on the counter and passed it to Mom. "Here."

"Thank you." Mom dabbed at her cheeks. "I didn't want it to come to this."

Lauren put the knife in the sink and rinsed the cutting board. Now what? Someone needed to stop Jane before she got to Granny. Lauren tried to catch Matt's eye while she twisted the lid back on the jar of peanut butter. He leaned against the fridge, arms crossed and brow furrowed. Maybe Matt could run interference.

Angela slipped her arm around Mom's shoulders, resting her head against Mom's. "I'm sorry you're upset."

Mom patted Angela's hand. "Thanks. I'm sorry you had to hear that."

"We're all adults here, Mom. I think we can handle it," Lauren said.

Mom shook her head. "You don't know the half of it."

Gavin spit out his pacifier and it landed with a plop at Angela's feet. "Tell us. Maybe we can help."

Lauren scooped it up and passed it back, glancing at the clock. "I think somebody should go after her."

Matt nodded. "I agree. If Granny had a rough morning, she won't be able to handle a surprise visit from Aunt Jane."

Mom took a deep breath, exhaled slowly and shuddered. She shook her head. "I can't even go there right now."

Matt and Lauren exchanged worried glances. She couldn't go to the hospital or she couldn't deal with the situation? Cries erupted from the table as a tug-of-war broke out between the twins over a sandwich crust and Joshua whined for cookies. Angela moved to intervene. Gavin began to cry and Angela scurried between the children as each one became increasingly more agitated.

"Matt," she said. "We need to get home for naps."

Lauren sighed. "Well, I guess that leaves me."

Mom's face blanched white and she stared at Lauren. "No."

"I'm not going to sit here and give Aunt Jane unrestricted access to Granny. If she's up to something, I want to know what's going on. Did Seth fix the van?" She rifled through the basket for the keys.

Mom pressed her lips into a thin line and closed her eyes. "I don't think you should chase her down."

Lauren grabbed the keys and whirled around. "I'm not chasing anybody down. I'm going to visit Granny. If she happens to have an unwanted guest, I'll be there to help out."

"Aren't you going to change first?" Angela gave her a disdainful once-over.

Lauren glanced down at her sweats. Oh, yeah. She hadn't bothered to change out of Jason and Christi Cavanaugh's old clothes. She shrugged. "That would give Jane too much of a head start. I'll be back as soon as I can." She planted a kiss on her mother's cheek and waved goodbye to Matt and his family. She padded toward the front door. Shoes would probably be a good idea. The hall closet provided few options.

She snagged a pair of her mother's old hiking boots and jammed her feet inside. A little snug but they would have to do for now.

She opened the front door and Mitchell greeted her on the front porch. His tail thumped against the porch rail. "I'm sorry, Mitchell. Not today." She jogged to her mother's minivan and hopped inside. Dang. Her wallet and cell phone were still in her backpack inside Blake's truck. She would lose too much time trying to track him down. Maybe he would bring them by when he finished with his clients. Her heart fluttered in hopeful expectation and she chided herself. *Broken engagement, remember? Isn't there a period of mourning or something?*

The van smelled faintly of Italian food. Mom must have delivered a meal to someone from church. Lauren glanced back up at the house. Mom stood in the kitchen window watching. Lauren's chest tightened. Aunt Jane had really gotten to her. She needed to get to the hospital before things got worse.

She turned the key in the ignition. Nothing. "C'mon, I don't have time for this." She banged on the steering wheel with the palm of her hand. Matt and Angela could drop her off at the hospital. Then again, she would rather run all the way there before she climbed inside a van full of cranky children. She took a deep breath and turned the key once more. The engine coughed and sputtered before it roared to life. She kissed her fingertips and touched them to the visor overhead. *Thank you.*

Gravel pelted the underside of the van as she careened down the hill. She barely tapped the brake at the stop sign, pulling out onto Hillside Drive without looking. Thank goodness the road was deserted. Maybe she was driving a little fast. Jane was going to get to the hospital first, anyway. Lauren's stomach twisted in a knot. How would Granny react to seeing her daughter again? Aunt Jane had spent more than half of her life separated from her family. A lump formed in her throat. The memory of a baby in a pink and blue knit hat, swaddled quickly and whisked away, flashed through her mind. *Not now. Stay focused.*

A half-dozen cars sat waiting at the intersection with Main Street. Not a single car was moving in either direction. A gaggle of silver-haired ladies stood in the middle of the street, staring and pointing out toward the water. Lauren blew out a breath. She couldn't see what they were pointing at but she needed them to move, pronto. Somebody blasted their horn and the women startled. Then they all scurried to the sidewalk as fast as their legs could carry them.

Once she turned onto Main Street, traffic picked up and Lauren cut through on a side street. The hospital parking lot was nearly empty. She parked, turned off the car, and ran toward the sliding glass doors.

The waiting room was deserted. Someone had tuned the television to the Golf channel and polite applause erupted as Lauren raced to the nurse's station. Shannon stood at behind the counter, head bent over a chart. She glanced up as Lauren's boots squeaked across the linoleum floor. Worry clouded her blue eyes. "I've been trying to get a hold of you. I can't find anybody who has your cell number. There's a lady here who claims to be your aunt but——"

"Tall? Light blue sweater? Silver hair to about here?" Lauren sliced her fingertips at her jawline.

Shannon's eyes widened. "Yes. How did you know?"

"She showed up at the Inn. She and my mom had words a few minutes ago so I followed her over here." Lauren glanced around the empty waiting room. "Where is she?"

"I told her she needed to hang out until your grandmother was awake. Maybe she went down to the cafeteria?"

Lauren's pulse kicked up a notch and she turned on her heel and started toward Granny's room.

Shannon closed the chart and rounded the counter. "Wait. Where are you going?"

"Something tells me Aunt Jane isn't just hanging out in the cafeteria. I bet she found a way into Granny's room." Lauren ignored the employees only sign posted on the double doors and pulled them open. Shannon grabbed the door before it could swing shut.

"That's crazy. She can't just waltz in there when I asked her to wait."

Lauren glanced over her shoulder. "Like I'm doing now?"

Shannon scowled. "We need some kind of security around here. This is ridiculous."

Lauren slowed as she approached Granny's room. Muffled voices floated out the open door. Before Shannon could go in, Lauren grabbed her arm. "Stop. Listen."

They stood in the hallway outside, pressed their backs against the wall and leaned toward the door.

"You remind me of someone. Are you new?" Granny asked.

Lauren glanced at Shannon. She stood with her head cocked to one side, brow furrowed.

"Do you remember my name?" Jane's voice was even and cool.

"No, but give me a minute. Are we going to do some exercises today?"

"I suppose you could call it exercising." Jane's voice grew louder as she moved about the room. The girls shrank back against the wall. Lauren's heart pounded in her ears. "I hope you're nicer than the other girl that comes in here."

"What do you mean?"

Granny cleared her throat. "It hurts. The exercises."

"I'm not going to hurt you. I want to jog your memory, so to speak."

Lauren sucked in a breath. What was Jane up to?

Shannon elbowed her in the ribs. "What is she talking about?" She whispered.

Lauren shrugged and pressed a finger to her lips.

Granny chortled. "Good luck. I'm not as sharp as I used to be."

Lauren pressed her lips together to keep a laugh from escaping.

"I want to ask you a few questions, that's all."

"Well, we'll see about that. I'm tired. Maybe we could do this another time."

"I just got here. Let's have a short little visit."

"Well, I'm not going anywhere. One more day won't kill you. Goodbye now."

"I can sit right here and wait until you wake up."

Shannon stepped around Lauren and entered Granny's room. "What do you think you're doing?"

Lauren crept in behind her and hovered in the doorway.

Jane's eyes flashed with anger. "Excuse me?"

Shannon positioned herself at Granny's bedside, blocking Jane's access. "I told you to wait until I gave you permission to come in here. I won't have you aggravating my patients. Mrs. Watson has asked you to leave. Now go before I call security."

Jane smirked. "Security? Really? That's probably my brother-in-law, Mike. He doesn't intimidate me one bit. Never has." Her eyes flickered to Lauren.

Although a snide retort was on the tip of her tongue, Lauren restrained herself and forced a nonchalant expression.

"You may come back tomorrow during regular visiting hours." Shannon pointed toward the door.

Jane huffed out a breath, gathered her purse and walked slowly toward the door. Lauren touched Jane's arm as she passed. "What do you want from us, Jane?"

Jane gave Lauren's hand a look of disdain and sniffed. "I want to make amends for my past. Is that so wrong?"

Jane brushed past her without another word. Goosebumps pebbled her flesh and she sank into a chair. Now that was just weird. She raised her eyes to meet Shannon's. Shannon tipped her head toward Granny and smiled. Lauren glanced at Granny. Her head rested against the pillow, eyes already closed.

Lauren rubbed her fingers across her forehead. Was Granny that far gone that she didn't recognize her own daughter? And why didn't Jane reveal her identity? One thing's for sure, after watching Mom and Jane tangle in the kitchen, it was clear this was going to get downright ugly.

Lauren tipped her head back against the wall and closed her eyes. *Oh, Aunt Jane. Why are you really here?*

CHAPTER EIGHTEEN

Blake shut down the computer and taped the next day's schedule to the counter where it wouldn't be missed. Jeremy and Tisha came in the front door trading stories from their afternoon adventures.

"You should've seen the look on her face when I told her there weren't any restrooms." Jeremy laughed and shook his head in disbelief.

"And I had to listen to her complain all the way back to town." Tisha punched him in the shoulder. "Thanks a lot."

"Good trips today?" Blake slipped his arms into his fleece jacket, wincing as his shoulders protested.

"Minus this morning. What was up with that?" Tisha rolled her eyes.

Blake grimaced. "Yeah, that was kind of a mess. In the future, I think we need to be extra cautious with our younger customers. Hannah will be fine, thank God, but that was too close for comfort."

"What about Lauren?" Jeremy flashed him a lopsided grin. "Is she all right?"

Blake's chest tightened. He couldn't stop thinking about the look of absolute panic on her face when she popped out from under her kayak. If anything had happened to her or one of their customers, he wouldn't be able to live with himself. "Matt picked her up. I haven't heard from her."

"Maybe you should go check on her." Jeremy wiggled his eyebrows. "Make sure she's warmed up."

Blake's face grew hot under Jeremy and Tisha's curious stares. "Yeah, maybe I'll do that. Can you lock up?"

"Sure thing. Get some rest, bro. See you tomorrow."

"Good night." Blake barely glanced at them before dragging himself out the door to his truck. Every muscle in his upper body hurt. He might not be able to lift his arms tomorrow. That was way too much paddling. They needed to hire more help, instead of relying on random friends to fill in. There was no way they could sustain this pace for the rest of the summer. He opened the door of his truck and slid behind the wheel. He tipped his head back and stared at the ceiling. It felt so good just to sit still.

Katy Perry's "Firework" started to play and he leaned forward and glanced around. His eyes landed on Lauren's backpack lying on the passenger side floor mat. He smiled. Of course. The perfect excuse to drop by the Inn. He had to return her phone. Poor girl probably couldn't live without it.

He turned the key in the ignition, shifted into reverse and eased the truck out of the parking space. There was Mr. Maxwell holding a car door open in front of the Italian restaurant across the street. Blake managed a smile through gritted teeth and waved. Mr. Maxwell waved back and took his wife's hand, helping her from the car. Blake had heard more rumblings that Coach Hoffman had bought a condo at a retirement place in Arizona. He frowned. It would be nice if somebody would confirm that. Surely there would be a decision about the coaching position soon. He'd learned a lot teaching in Tyonek and–let's be honest—the pay was fantastic. But he'd jumped at the chance to come back home.

This is where he belonged. If he could take over the basketball program from his mentor, that would make all those lonely nights away from his friends and family worth it.

Traffic on Main Street crawled. He rolled his window down and propped his elbow on the edge as he waited for an indecisive tourist to either speed up or turn. The line at the new Thai place was out the door and wrapped around the building. His mouth watered and his stomach growled. He'd forgotten all about dinner. Maybe he would drop by his parents' place and forage in their cupboards.

He turned onto Hillside Drive. The evening sun sat on the edge of the mountains, ready to dip below the craggy peaks. The waters of the cove shimmered and the hillside was bathed in golden light. He turned up the hill toward the Inn. Mike's patrol car was the only one parked out front. Maybe Lauren wasn't even home. He had to at least knock on the door. He needed to know she was okay.

He fished her backpack off the floor, turned off the truck and shoved the door open. It was all he could do to put one foot in front of the other. He knocked softly on the door, his pulse thrumming. The knob turned, the door swung open. Lauren stood on the other side. Her hair fell down her back in crazy curls that he just wanted to tunnel his fingers through one more time. The hem of her white T-shirt peeked out from under a dark blue sweatshirt and she had ditched Cavanaugh's sweats for a pair of faded jeans. He swallowed hard. Dang it if she didn't slay him.

Those luscious lips formed a half smile and her eyes met his. "Hey, this is a nice surprise."

Warmth spread through his chest. "You left your backpack in my truck."

"Oh, thanks." She reached for it. He handed it over, careful not to let their fingers touch.

"Want to come in for a minute? I was just finishing dinner."

He held up both hands. "I don't want to interrupt."

"You're not. I'm waiting for some guests to arrive." Blake hesitated.

"C'mon. You look exhausted and I bet you haven't eaten yet." She stepped aside and pulled the door open wider.

He couldn't resist. A fire crackled in the fireplace and those leather couches looked very comfortable. She picked up the TV remote and muted the Mariners game. A Styrofoam container sat on the coffee table next to a plate of Thai food. His eyes widened. "Is that pad Thai?"

She smiled. "Would you like some?"

"I don't want to take your food."

"Yes you do. It's written all over your face. Lucky for you, there's extra." She pointed to the couch. "Sit. I'll fix you a plate."

He unzipped his jacket and tossed it on the back of the couch. Then he sank into the corner closest to the fire. She wouldn't get any argument from him. Some rookie he didn't recognize was batting in Ichiro's spot. Bases loaded in the bottom of the sixth inning. Man, the Mariners just weren't the same without Ichiro.

Lauren returned with a steaming plate and a tall glass of iced tea. She set them both down on the coffee table and passed him silverware wrapped in a napkin. He grimaced and pushed himself up to an upright position.

She froze. "What's wrong?"

"Nothing. Hard day. My back and my shoulders are sore."

"Want something for the pain?"

He wrinkled his nose and shook his head. "I don't like to take anything." He bowed his head and blessed the food. When he opened his eyes, she was still staring.

"I would be glad to take a look at your shoulder when you're finished eating."

He paused, a loaded fork halfway to his mouth. "So sports medicine's your thing?"

She reached for her plate and settled back on the couch. "The doctor I worked for, Dr. Putnam, he tried to teach me as much as he could. He made sure I shadowed a lot of other physicians, too. I've spent a lot of time with an orthopedic surgeon."

Blake savored the first bite of the noodles and spicy chicken. "Mmm, this is incredible. Thanks for sharing your dinner."

"You're welcome. I might be able to find some dessert if my nephew didn't eat it all."

He tipped his head toward the television. "How's the game?"

"Not that great. Mariners pretty much stink this season."

Blake laughed. "Tell me how you really feel."

"It's true. Look. When you knocked on the door the bases were loaded. Now the inning is over and they're still scoreless heading into the seventh. Ridiculous."

He smiled. He forgot how much she loved baseball. Her cheeks held the slightest tinge of pink and her eyes were bright with enthusiasm. There was one stubborn ringlet that bounced against her temple as she talked. It was all he could do to keep from reaching over and tucking it behind her ear.

She caught him watching her. "What?"

Busted. His neck grew warm. He tried to play it off. "Nothing. I think it's great you like baseball, that's all."

"I've missed watching the games with my Dad since I left."

Blake looked around. "Where are your parents, by the way?"

"They went over to the hospital to check on my grandmother."

"How's she doing?"

Lauren sighed and her shoulders sagged. "She's about the same. We are trying to figure out where to move her. She can't stay at the hospital indefinitely. My Aunt Jane turned up today and now everybody's super stressed."

Blake glanced at her. "I'd forgotten all about your Aunt Jane. What's she doing here?"

Lauren chewed on her lower lip, brow furrowed. "She mentioned something about making the past right. I don't know."

"Where's she been?"

Lauren shrugged and reached for his empty plate. "San Diego, I think. Would you like something else? I was kidding about my nephew eating all the dessert. There's chocolate chip cookies on the kitchen counter."

"Your mom's chocolate chip cookies?"

"Those are the ones."

Blake moaned and fell back against the cushions. Debbie Carter's chocolate chip cookies were legendary. She used to send dozens on basketball road trips. There was never even a crumb left by the time they got back home.

Lauren disappeared into the kitchen and returned with a platter of cookies. She took one and passed the rest to him. "How long has your shoulder bothered you?"

The cookies tasted better than he imagined. He rotated his shoulder forward and backward. After a day like today it was hard to remember a time when it didn't hurt. "I think it's all the overhead movement I've been doing. Moving kayaks and rafts, combined with a lot of paddling. It's killing me tonight."

Lauren nodded and moved around the coffee table toward him. His pulse ratcheted up a notch with every step she took. "Mind if I take a look?"

He shook his head, thankful his mouth was packed full of cookie. His voice couldn't be trusted at this point. She slipped her fingers under the sleeve of his T-shirt. A stirring awakened in his belly and warmth flooded his chest. He tried to focus on the game. She gently prodded the muscles on his upper arm.

"Here?" she asked, her fingers sliding up over the top of his shoulder.

He cleared his throat. "Um, no, mostly the front."

She pressed harder on the front of his shoulder and he sucked in a breath. "Ow."

"Sorry. I'm almost finished." She stepped in front of him and moved his iced tea. Then she shoved the coffee table out of the way. "Stand up. I want to see something."

He complied. She circled his wrist with her slender fingers and he prayed she couldn't feel his pulse pounding. Her other hand grasped his elbow. "Now I want you to hold your elbow against your side and try to push your arm out, like you're opening a sliding glass door. Except I'm going to resist you."

He stared down at her. Determined green eyes stared right back. He imagined her flying across the living room. Probably ought to take it easy.

He made a fist and pushed against her hand. She gritted her teeth and pushed back. "Harder."

He pushed again and a sharp pain shot up his bicep. "Ah, hey, I think that might be it." He clutched his shoulder with his other hand and sank back down on the couch.

"I knew it." She sat down next to him and tucked her knees under her chin. "You have biceps tendonitis."

He rubbed his shoulder and studied her. "What?"

"I think the tendon that connects your biceps muscle to your shoulder is irritated."

"Wonderful. What's your recommendation, doc?"

"Ibuprofen and an ice massage."

He wiggled his eyebrows. "Massage, huh? I like the sound of that."

She narrowed her eyes. "You missed the operative word: ice. Freeze water in a paper cup, then peel back the paper and rub the ice on the front of your shoulder. It's more effective than an ice bag. You might consider giving your shoulders some rest."

He puffed his cheeks and blew out a long breath. Rest. Like that was going to happen. "Any other suggestions?"

She frowned. "You aren't going to listen to me, are you?"

He hesitated. "I don't think rest is an option right now. We have more clients than we can handle, which is a blessing. I can't leave Jeremy hanging. I'll rest in September."

"I see." She stood and tugged the coffee table back where it belonged and began clearing the remnants of dinner. "Want some ice while you watch the rest of the game?"

He glanced at the television. What could it hurt to ice his shoulder and watch the last couple of innings? "Sure. Thanks."

Her lips curved into a satisfied smile. "I'll be right back."

He grabbed the remote, propped his feet up on the coffee table and turned up the volume so he could hear the commentary. Lauren moved about in the kitchen, scraping plates and loading the dishwasher. A pang of guilt struck him. He should get up and help her. But he couldn't muster the energy.

She returned with a bag of frozen peas and a blanket. "This will do for now."

"Vegetables cure tendonitis? Who knew?"

She rolled her eyes. "No, it's just easier to keep in place than a bag full of ice. I'm going to shove this under your shirt so it stays. Is that okay?"

"I guess." He flinched as the cold bag touched his skin. She leaned in to re-adjust the bag of peas and her hair tumbled forward, brushing his cheek.

He sat perfectly still, soaking in the scent of her. She smelled like vanilla, with a hint of coconut. Feelings long dormant began to stir. *She's right there.* He reached up, eyes riveted on hers. She met his gaze, one eyebrow arched as she tilted her head. *Go for it.* He brushed her hair back with his hand, cupped his fingers around the nape of her neck, and pulled her in. Gently at first, his lips brushed against hers. Then he deepened the kiss, showing her how much he'd missed her. How much he needed her. She responded to his touch with a soft moan and pressed her fingers to his cheek.

CHAPTER NINETEEN

Those confident hands tangled in her hair, his lips moving over her mouth, her neck—she was breathless. Her heart pounded and desire coursed through her extremities. A knock sounded on the front door and Lauren planted her hand on Blake's chest and pushed away. She pressed her fingers to her lips and stared at him. "What have we done?" she whispered.

He rubbed his hand across his jaw. "I think it's called kissing."

"You have to go."

His eyebrows shot up. "Now?"

"Yes," she hissed and grabbed his coat.

The knock sounded again, louder this time. "Don't you want to see who's at the door?"

"No. Yes." She tossed his jacket at him and smoothed her hand over her curls. Heart still hammering, she took a few steps on jittery legs toward the door. How did this happen? One minute she was handing him a bag of peas, the next she was on his lap.

She paused and checked her reflection in the hall mirror. Her cheeks were flushed, no doubt from the stubble on his jaw grazing her skin. She glanced back at the couch. Blake hadn't moved. His eyes met hers and he winked. Another delicious wave of excitement washed over her. She'd forgotten how much she missed his touch. Wait. The door—

Muted conversation came through the door and she reached for the knob. Her palms were sweaty and it took two tries to unlock the deadbolt and open the front door. A well-dressed couple stood on the porch, clutching the handles of their suitcases.

"Hi, I'm Lauren. May I help you?"

"Yes, we're the Sullivans. I believe we have a reservation tonight." The man stared at her over the top of his wire rimmed glasses. His salt and pepper hair was neatly combed and he wore a navy blazer over a plaid button down. His khaki pants were heavily starched with a crisp seam down the middle of each leg. The woman stood behind him in wool slacks and a black sweater, staring over his shoulder.

"Please come in." Lauren stepped back.

They pulled their suitcases over the threshold into the hallway. The woman paused when she saw the guestbook. "Look, Frank. Another couple from Chicago was here."

A bat cracked and applause rang out, drawing Frank into the living room. Lauren groaned inwardly. She heard Blake introduce himself and launch into a quick recap of the inning. *So much for getting him out of here.*

"What brings you to Alaska?"

Mrs. Sullivan set down the pen and smiled. "This is our fortieth wedding anniversary gift to each other."

"Happy anniversary," Lauren said. Disappointment jabbed her in the gut. This is the kind of information Mom should be collecting for reservations. If she had known it was a special occasion, they could have placed fresh flowers in the Sullivan's room or arranged for a romantic dinner out. Guests needed to know the Inn would go the extra mile to make their trip memorable.

"My, you have a lovely place here." Mrs. Sullivan followed the conversation into the living room, glancing around as she walked. Her eyes landed on Blake. "Oh, hello. Are you Lauren's husband?"

An awkward silence ensued. Lauren rubbed her neck. "No, we're not ... together." She refused to look at Blake.

Mrs. Sullivan's eyes bounced between Lauren and Blake. "Oh, excuse me. Two young people in such a romantic setting, I just thought—I'm sorry."

Lauren folded her arms across her chest, heat flooding her cheeks once again. She swallowed hard. "This is Blake Tully, a friend of the family."

Blake waved, his lips curved in a half smile. Oh, how that infernal dimple taunted her. She had to get him out of there.

"May I show you to your room, Mrs. Sullivan?"

The woman returned to her luggage. "Absolutely. Frank," she called over her shoulder, "let's go see our room."

Mr. Sullivan turned around, a look of annoyance flashed across his face. "The bases are loaded, Pam. Just a minute."

Lauren shifted from one foot to the other. Before she could explain the procedures for breakfast, the front door opened. Mom and Dad came in, engrossed in conversation. They stopped and smiled at the strangers in their living room. Mom walked right over and extended her hand. "You must be Pam Sullivan. I'm Debbie Carter. Welcome to the Inn at the Cove." The introductions continued and Lauren's heart sank as Dad greeted Blake with a hearty handshake and a slap on the back.

"Let's make some coffee. Who wants pie?" Mom's eyes twinkled as she tugged on Lauren's sleeve and pulled her into the kitchen. Mrs. Sullivan followed, her heels clicking on the hardwood.

Lauren grabbed the half and half from the fridge and a clean pitcher from the cabinet.

Pam Sullivan perched on a bar stool at the counter. "How long have you lived here?"

"Always." Mom pulled the foil off of two pies and selected a knife from the block beside the sink. "My parents built this house before I was born."

"Has it always been a bed and breakfast?"

"No," Mom said. "It was originally a place for unwed mothers to deliver their babies."

The forks slipped from Lauren's hand and clattered to the floor. Mrs. Sullivan flinched. "I'm sorry." Lauren picked up the forks and set them in the sink. Her heart sped up. A home for unwed mothers? Maybe that's why Granny was confused.

"I can't imagine giving birth way out here in the boondocks," Mrs. Sullivan said.

Lauren grimaced. *Me either.*

"Well, it was kind of the only option until the hospital was open." Mom glanced at Lauren. "Would you mind getting the coffee started?"

Lauren nodded and rifled in the cabinet for a clean filter.

"So how did you decide to start a bed and breakfast?"

Mom went into her usual spiel about the Inn. Lauren measured coffee into the filter and moved to the sink to fill the carafe with water. When she turned back to the coffee maker, she collided with Blake and water sloshed out of the carafe onto his shirt. She gasped and he clutched her to him. Great. Their eyes met and she was certain he could hear her heart pounding. His Adam's apple bobbed in his throat as he swallowed hard and slowly removed his hand from her waist.

"Sorry," he murmured and held up the bag of peas. "I didn't mean to sneak up on you. I, um, thought these should go back in the freezer." He brushed past her and opened the freezer.

Lauren parted her lips to speak but nothing came out. She managed a nod. *What was I doing?* She looked down at her shaky hand, still holding the carafe. Coffee. Right. She moved back to the coffeemaker, poured the water in and clicked the 'brew' button. Her other hand fluttered to her neck. It was on fire. How did he do that? She couldn't let her mother see how flustered she was. *Deep breaths. Not a big deal.*

"Are you hungry, Blake?" Mom asked. "I have pecan pie and also strawberry rhubarb."

No. No pie. Lauren willed him to decline the offer. *You have got to go.*

Blake groaned and rubbed his stomach. Lauren pretended to be mesmerized by the coffee brewing. "I better not. Lauren already let me have some of your fantastic cookies. I need to get going."

"Next time, then." Mom waved. "Good night."

Lauren took a deep breath and turned toward him. "I'll walk you out."

Blake smiled at Mrs. Sullivan. "Nice to meet you. Happy anniversary."

"Thank you."

Lauren led the way out of the kitchen. "What a charming young man," she heard Mrs. Sullivan say. Blake grinned. Lauren rolled her eyes.

Dad and Mr. Sullivan stood in front of the fireplace, deep in conversation. Blake said goodnight and grabbed his jacket off the couch. Lauren stood by the front door, arms crossed.

"Did you hear that?" Blake nudged her with his shoulder as he walked by. "She thinks I'm charming."

Lauren tried her best to look annoyed. "She just met you. Give it time."

He laughed a deep throaty laugh and zipped up his jacket. He looked into her eyes and amusement was replaced with smoldering desire. Lauren panicked. He wasn't going to kiss her again, was he? Her eyes darted to the fireplace. Not in front of her parents and their guests.

"Thanks for bringing my stuff by." She reached past him and opened the door with a flourish. He hesitated, studying her for a minute. He dipped his chin to his chest and moved out onto the porch. She slipped out behind him and pulled the door shut. It was chilly once the sun slid behind the mountain and she shivered.

Please. Go.

He stepped down one step and turned to face her, his hand resting on the porch railing. "Lauren, about tonight—"

She put up one hand. "You don't have to say it. I understand."

He raised his eyebrows. "You do?"

"Of course. It was a mistake. You don't have to apologize."

She wished it was dark so she didn't have to see the anger flash in his eyes.

"Is that all I am to you? A mistake?" His voice was rough.

She chewed her lip. Silence hung heavy between them. Her heart ached. *I can't do this.* "Blake, I—"

He shook his head and stepped down one more step, his posture stiff. "Goodnight, Lauren. Thanks for dinner."

"Sure." She watched him walk to his truck. Every step was like a dagger in her heart. He climbed in and drove away without looking back.

She slid down the door and sat huddled on the porch. Tears threatened to fall and she drew a ragged breath. The wall she'd carefully constructed was starting to crumble. A few minutes in his arms and she was falling for him all over again. Blake squealed his tires at the bottom of the hill. Her stomach twisted. This was a one way ticket to heartbreak. For both of them. If he knew the truth, there's no way he would ever forgive her. When was she ever going to learn?

CHAPTER TWENTY

L auren tossed and turned all night. As the first light of a new day dawned, she threw back the quilt and stared at the ceiling. The memory of Blake's soft lips on hers flashed in her mind. And she'd kissed him back. Didn't even have the good sense to protest.

It was just a kiss. *Lighten up.* It didn't mean anything.

But the expression on his face last night told her it meant something to him. Blake. Her first love. The minute his hand touched the nape of her neck, it all came rushing back. They'd parked out at Jess's cabin, wrapped in sleeping bags in the bed of his old truck underneath a canopy of stars—no.

She sat straight up and flung her feet over the side of the bed. *We're not doing this today.*

Shoving her feet into her slippers, she stood up and her phone fell on the floor.

"Good grief." Must have fallen asleep surfing the net. The battery icon on the screen blinked its warning. She'd have to find her charger. Two missed texts and a voicemail waited. She touched the screen tentatively and read the texts. Both were from Holden, asking her to call him. The voicemail was more of the same. He said it was urgent. *Whatever.*

She tossed her phone on the bed then padded toward the bathroom. The mirror reflected puffy eyes shrouded in dark circles. A hot shower did little to erase her fatigue. Voices floated up the stairs. The Sullivans were already up and ready to start their day. She dressed quickly and twisted her hair into a bun. If she could get breakfast going, maybe her parents could catch a few extra minutes of sleep. She pasted on a smile and went downstairs.

Aunt Jane hovered in front of the coffeemaker, humming softly as hot coffee trickled into the carafe. Mom stood at the counter, whisking eggs in a mixing bowl, brow furrowed. A dense layer of fog still hung low over the bay while sunshine streamed in the window, bathing the kitchen in a soft yellow light.

"Good morning," Lauren said.

Aunt Jane turned, the bangles on her wrist jangling. She was already dressed in white pants that emphasized her long legs and a coral pink sweater set that must have cost a fortune. "Good morning, dear. My, you look exhausted. Up late?"

Gee, thanks. "Just have a lot on my mind, that's all." Lauren went to the dishwasher and opened it, pulling out three clean mugs. She set them on the counter then slid onto one of the bar stools across from Mom.

"Good morning, sweetheart." Mom slowed the whisk and studied her. "Anything you want to talk about?"

"I know this isn't the best time." She cast a meaningful glance in the direction of Aunt Jane. "But Blake made a great suggestion yesterday that I think we should consider."

"Oh?" Mom opened a package of ham and started dicing.

"What if we host a raffle at our booth during the festival? We could give away a free night's stay. He said we could combine it with a sea kayaking trip. It could be a fun date or a romantic getaway…"

"Are they still carrying on with that silly festival?" Jane brought the coffee carafe over to the counter and filled the mugs. "Honestly. You think they'd come up with some fresh ideas after all these years."

Uh-oh. Mom pressed her lips into a thin line. An awkward silence hovered over them.

"The festival actually draws a pretty big crowd. Blake might be on to something," Mom said.

"Deb, you can't be serious." Jane tipped a spoonful of sugar into her mug, shaking her head. "Total waste of time."

Lauren opened her mouth to object, then clamped it shut and went to the fridge for some half and half instead. This conflict between Mom and Aunt Jane probably wasn't about the festival, anyway. There was definitely something deeper going on here.

"I'd like to hear more before I make a decision, Jane."

Lauren returned to her stool, poured half and half into her coffee and avoided making eye contact with Aunt Jane. "I know this is all very last minute. But other than the tickets and a little bit of advertising, it wouldn't cost much to pull this off."

"Is food included?" Jane blew on her coffee. "That costs something."

"I think it's a wonderful idea. That's generous of Blake to include us." Mom dumped the chopped ham into a bowl and handed a block of cheese to Lauren. "Would you mind grating some cheese for the omelets?"

"Sure." Lauren got up and stepped around Aunt Jane, then rummaged through a drawer for the grater.

"And who do you suppose is going to buy one of these tickets?" Jane plucked a bite of ham from the bowl and popped it in her mouth.

Seriously. Back off. "Anybody can participate. I can't speak for Blake, but we have immediate availability here. Tickets will be cheap, anyway." Lauren talked through the details while she opened the cheese.

"How cheap? If you have to split the proceeds with this Blake fellow you need to think about that."

Lauren winced. She and Blake hadn't bothered to discuss dollars and cents. And after last night, she didn't exactly relish the thought of speaking with him anytime soon. "I don't know. Maybe a dollar a ticket?"

"A dollar? That's only—"

"Jane." Mom set the knife down and gripped the edge of the counter with both hands, eyes downcast. "That's enough."

"I know what I'm talking about, Deb. I've spent the last fifteen years running a successful business in San Diego."

Mom let go of the counter and turned to face her sister, cheeks flushed. "This isn't San Diego and I didn't ask for your opinion. Feel free to stay for breakfast, but this discussion is over."

Whoa. Score one for Mom. Jane's eyes narrowed, her fingers tightened around her mug.

Before she had a chance to respond Mrs. Sullivan breezed into the kitchen, with Mr. Sullivan not far behind. "Good morning. Wow, that coffee smells delightful. May I have some?" Her eyes flitted from Lauren to Mom and then stopped on Aunt Jane. Her brow arched. "Am I interrupting something?"

"Of course not." Mom pasted on a smile and tipped her head toward Jane. "We're just taking care of some family business. This is my sister, Jane. Jane, Pam Sullivan and her husband, Frank."

"Oh, I didn't realize you had a sister. My, what a lovely blouse." Mrs. Sullivan extended her hand to Jane.

"Jane Watson Merrill Montgomery." Aunt Jane accepted Mrs. Sullivan's hand and gave her a cool appraisal. "Thank you. It's part of Cabi's spring selection. Are you familiar with Cabi?"

This should be interesting. Lauren busied herself with serving breakfast while Aunt Jane steered the conversation in a direction that suited her. It quickly became apparent that Mr. Sullivan was eager to get going but his wife lingered at the table. She and Aunt Jane traded stories of their many shopping experiences in Paris. As Lauren washed the mixing bowl, her breath hitched at the mention of France. She wanted to see Paris. *Just once.* Since Holden had broken their engagement, that dream was gone, too. Holden. She'd left her phone upstairs on purpose. What could he possibly want with his repeated calls and texts?

***

BLAKE SAT IN the driver's seat of his truck with the window rolled down. He drained his insulated mug of the last remnants of coffee and nested it back in the console. He should get out and act like he cared about their customers. But after last night, he couldn't get excited about much of anything. Guilt hung over him like a dark cloud. He shouldn't have kissed her. For once he'd acted spontaneously and look where it got him. *A mistake.* That's what he was to her.

Maybe she was right. He really had no business kissing her like that after she'd just been dumped.

Jeremy waved at him and Blake reached for his helmet on the passenger seat. With a heavy sigh, he got out of the truck and headed toward the yellow rafts anchored on the rocky shore. A family of eight stood at the edge of the river and donned their rain gear while Jeremy gave the safety instructions. They were discussing how to divide up and fill both rafts.

"Age before beauty," commented the oldest male and probably the father as he planted one foot inside Blake's raft.

"How about boys against girls?" Suggested a petite brunette, winking as she sidled up to Jeremy.

Jeremy nodded and blessed her with a lazy grin. "I think I want to be on your team."

After more discussion and good-natured ribbing, the sons followed their dad into the first raft and the women huddled around Jeremy. Blake shook his head as his brother beamed at yet another opportunity to be the center of attention. *He is a chick magnet.*

The father jumped out of the raft and dashed over to kiss his wife and the mother of his children. She giggled like a school girl and waved with a gleam in her eye before stepping into Jeremy's raft with the rest of the women. Blake wilted just a little as he watched this exchange. He wanted that; playful, silly, yet still crazy in love with a boatful of children to share it with. *You are a one man pity party.* He picked up his oars and took his seat on a bench in the raft. He couldn't stand there all morning wanting what he couldn't have. He had a job to do. It was time to let the river wash his heartache away.

***

LAUREN DIDN'T RECOGNIZE the nurses who greeted her when she walked into the hospital. "Are you here to see your grandmother?" The older one shifted uncomfortably in her chair, brows furrowed as she stared at her computer screen.

The hair on Lauren's arms stood up and her chest tightened. "Yes. Is there a problem?"

"No." The nurse exchanged glances with her co-worker. "Mrs. Watson has had a busy morning, we just don't want her to overdue it."

Lauren looked around the waiting room and half-expected Aunt Jane to look up from the pages of the magazine. But only a handful of people sat in the orange vinyl chairs and none of them resembled Jane. "What kind of busy?"

"Dr. Wheeler stopped in to check on her, followed by physical therapy and now she's probably finishing her lunch." The nurse looked up at the clock on the wall. "She typically takes a nap now."

Lauren sighed. She longed for a few minutes with Granny. Only a short visit to ease the hollow ache inside. "I won't stay long, I promise."

The nurse hesitated. "I suppose that would be fine. Thirty minutes is plenty, though."

Lauren smiled. "Thirty minutes. Got it." She breezed through the double-doors before the nurse could change her mind. Her flip-flops smacked against the linoleum as she made her way to Granny's room. Her pulse quickened and she breathed a prayer that Granny would still be awake and alone.

She peeked in and found Granny sitting up in her hospital bed, head bowed over the open Bible on the table in front of her. Lauren leaned against the doorframe and watched Granny's lips move in silent prayer. It was such a comfort to see Granny still able to do at least one thing that she loved.

Lauren cleared her throat. "Granny?"

The old woman raised her head slowly and a smile spread across her face. "Hello, my dear. What a nice surprise." She stretched out her arm and Lauren moved toward the bed.

"How are you today?" Lauren squeezed Granny's hand and planted a kiss on her upturned cheek. "The nurse told me you had a busy morning."

Granny's brow puckered and Lauren regretted her comment. What if she confused Granny by mentioning past events?

"Oh, the doctor and that woman who wants me to do all those ridiculous exercises stopped by. I keep telling them I'd be more comfortable in my own bed if they would just let me go back home." She sighed and shook her head. "But they don't want to listen to this old bird."

Lauren laughed. "We want you to be well before you come back home."

Granny huffed out a breath. "That's too long to wait. Why don't you take me home this afternoon? I bet there's a wheelchair around here somewhere we could borrow." Granny craned her neck to see around Lauren.

A wave of sadness washed over her. Granny had cared for her every need when she was a little girl. It seemed only fair that she would return the favor and grant this one request. She shook her head. "I'm sorry, Granny. I wish I could. How about if I sit with you for a little while and you can tell me what you're reading today?"

Granny glanced down and her eyes scanned the page. "Oh, I'm reading one of my favorite passages in all of the New Testament: Luke chapter fifteen, the story of the prodigal son. Do you remember that one?"

"Of course. Why is it your favorite?"

"I had a dream last night that my daughter Jane came back and nobody cared. Wouldn't that be awful?" Granny lifted her eyes from the Bible and stared at Lauren. The sorrow lingering there was like a fist in Lauren's gut. She sucked in a breath. *She already forgot what happened yesterday?*

"Granny, I—"

"I love the part where the father sees his son coming from far off." Granny kept talking as if she didn't hear Lauren. She turned and stared out the window. "I wonder what that felt like?"

Lauren bit the inside of her cheek. "Do you want to see Jane, Granny?"

Granny turned back to face Lauren and slowly nodded her head. "Yes, I believe I do."

Lauren cleared her throat and stared at the floor. "Here's the thing I always wondered. What if the prodigal son wasn't sorry for what he'd done? That part of the story always bothered me a little bit." Obviously Jane didn't show a whole lot of remorse. She definitely wasn't clothed in humility or asking forgiveness.

Granny shifted in her bed, cradling her casted arm close to her body. "I suppose that would be a much different story, wouldn't it?" She tipped her head back against the pillows and looked at the ceiling. A few moments later, her eyelids fluttered closed.

Lauren sighed and sank back in the chair. She'd come to spend a few quiet moments with Granny and now she felt more conflicted than when she arrived. Maybe Jane shouldn't be allowed to visit Granny at all. On the other hand, if her dementia was so advanced she didn't recognize Jane then why did it matter? Lauren couldn't even be sure Granny knew who she was. She had yet to greet her by anything other than Mallory.

***

BLAKE STEPPED OUT of his rain gear and threw it in the back of the truck. A horn honked and he waved as their clients pulled away in a rented SUV. They were a lot of fun to ride with. No complaining, just happy to be on an adventure together. Those were the best kind of customers. He grabbed a bottle of Gatorade and a power bar and sat on the tailgate. Jeremy sidled over, the top of his wet suit peeled down to his waist. He grinned and popped the top open on a can of Red Bull.

"Great run today, man."

Blake nodded. "Wasn't bad."

Jeremy took a bite of a Snickers bar and furrowed his brow. "What's eating you? Those rapids were epic."

"Tired, I guess."

"Why don't you go home and take it easy. We've got a big week ahead. The festival's tomorrow and then you need to be well-rested for Cove to Creek."

Blake groaned. "I don't think I can make it."

Jeremy rapped his knuckles on Blake's head. "Hello? This whole thing was your idea. You can't bail on me now."

"You won't even miss me. It's just a race."

"Not cool, man. We're in this together. Besides, we need you and Lauren so we can win. You can't skip the race. Where's the fun in that?"

His heart sank. "Lauren?"

Jeremy tipped his head back and slurped the rest of the energy drink from the can. "Yeah, didn't I tell you she's taking Shannon's place?"

"No," Blake growled.

Jeremy shrugged. "Must have forgot." He stood up and clapped a hand on Blake's shoulder. "Lighten up, dude. It's gonna be a good time. You go on home, I'll finish up here."

"Deal." Blake watched the river gurgle and churn against the bank, his offer to partner with the Inn echoing in his head. After last night, that was going to be awkward at best. He'd have to delegate that one to Mom and Megan. Now the race— that was one of his favorite events. He'd definitely missed not being a part of it when he lived in Tyonek. But spending so much time in close proximity to Lauren wasn't going to be easy. She didn't want to be with him. He slid off the tailgate and then tossed the Gatorade bottle in the back of the truck. Maybe it was time to move on.

CHAPTER TWENTY ONE

L auren jogged up the hill towards the Inn, a light rain falling as she willed her legs to carry her home. Most running experts advised a short, easy run the day before a race. But she wasn't most people. Granny's health problems, Jane's arrival and the job in Portland—not to mention the memory of Blake's kiss—all swirled into a messy cocktail that kept her from sleeping well. She'd finally given up and climbed out of bed, eager to feel the pavement under her feet.

Chest heaving, she slowed to a walk and circled Matt and Angela's minivan a few times to cool down. They were up early. Maybe Mom was watching the little girls today. That could be a problem. There was so much to do if they were going to pull off a booth at the festival. She'd tried to catch Blake at the shop last night, but Jeremy said he'd sent Blake home to rest up. Whatever. She couldn't put this project together by herself. Maybe she was expecting too much given all that was going on right now. Climbing the steps, she reached for the doorknob but someone beat her to it. The door opened to reveal Matt standing on the other side.

"Good morning, sis," Matt said. "Did you have a nice run?"

"It was okay. What are you up to?"

"Come in and see for yourself." He winked and stepped aside.

Angela waved from the couch, where she was busy feeding Gavin. Lauren waved back and followed Matt into the kitchen. "What's going on?"

"Oh, good. You're back. Hand her the coffee, Matthew." Mom sat at the kitchen table, a proud smile on her face.

Matt lifted a paper cup from a cardboard tray on the counter. The Copper Kettle's logo was stamped on the outside and two pink straws protruded from the black plastic lid. "For you," Matt said, bowing slightly as he passed her the coffee.

Lauren cupped her chilled hands around the drink. "Wow. Thanks. What's this about?" She tipped her head toward the table, which held several bags of Hershey's kisses, a giant roll of red tickets, and a very large empty bowl. The little girls were in their chairs, munching on cheerios, while Joshua sat at the counter, laboring over a coloring book.

"Dad and I thought your suggestion for the giveaway at the festival was exactly what we needed." Mom reached for the scissors and a bag of chocolate. "It turns out Sandy Tully is in charge of setting up the booths. When I called her, she said Blake had already given her the details but hadn't had a chance to follow through. I know he's extremely busy right now."

Lauren sipped her coffee and avoided Mom's curious gaze. Busy. Of course he'd use his work as an excuse to avoid her. After the way she'd treated him, why wouldn't he?

Angela came into the kitchen, Gavin pressed against her shoulder and a smile on her face. With her free hand, she passed a gift bag to Lauren. "A little something for you."

Lauren took the bag and peeked inside. A water bottle, trail mix, Gatorade and a new pair of socks were all tucked inside. "Oh, you guys." Lauren splayed her hand across her chest. "You didn't have to do this. I don't know what to say."

"It's the least we could do, after all you've done for us," Mom said.

"Stop. It was nothing." Lauren pulled out a chair and sat down at the table.

"Don't be silly," Mom said. "We couldn't have survived all this craziness without you."

"If you aren't careful, you'll earn yourself a full-time position as innkeeper." Matt winked and slipped an arm around Angela's shoulders.

Lauren's last sip of coffee lodged in her throat and she leaned forward, sputtering. Angela came alongside and whacked her on the back. Lauren continued to cough, the warm liquid stinging her throat. What could she say to that?

"Well." Matthew pulled up a stool next to Joshua. "I guess we know how you feel about that idea."

Lauren coughed one last time and looked around at the expectant stares. The concern evident in Mom's eyes did not go unnoticed. "I suppose now would be a good time to tell you I have an interview in Portland next Friday."

"Oh, no." Mom dropped the bag of chocolate, spilling silver-wrapped kisses onto the floor around her chair.

Angela brought her a glass of ice water. "What kind of an interview?"

"Thanks." Lauren took a long drink, the cool water soothing her throat but doing little to ease the ache in her chest. Maybe this wasn't good timing, after all. "It's with a family practice in a suburb of Portland. They need a medical assistant and my old boss recommended me."

"Have you thought about looking for something around here?" Mom poured the chocolates into the bowl.

Lauren winced. "I never said I was staying. My original plan was only a week, remember?"

"Plans have a way of changing," Matt said.

Lauren thought about the stack of *Modern Bride* magazines on the floor next to her bed back in Portland. Or the proliferation of wedding-themed pins on her Pinterest board. Yes, plans definitely had a way of changing.

"I hate to wish for things to go poorly for you, but I was really looking forward to the hot chocolate bar and the S'mores you talked about," Angela said.

Lauren smiled. "Thanks, Ange." Maybe things were thawing between them and there was hope for a relationship after all.

"Well. No sense crying over spilled milk. We've got a festival booth to set up." Mom stood and gathered her supplies. "Who's with me?"

***

Blake slid the folding chair off the stack and arranged it next to the others behind the long table. This was a task he could handle. Mindless and repetitive. More importantly, he could work in the opposite direction of Lauren and her mother, who were busy putting the finishing touches on their booth. He'd managed a casual wave when they first arrived, then volunteered to help some of the older ladies set up for their quilt display. While his shoulder protested about the extra activity, he was determined to remain occupied and away from Lauren.

"Yoohoo, Blake?" Tisha interrupted his thoughts. "Can you take a look at this?" She gestured over her shoulder toward the booth. His mother, Lauren and Mrs. Carter stood in front of their table, brows furrowed as they pointed and fussed.

He groaned inwardly. "I'm sure it's fine. Whatever you ladies think is best."

"Please? Your opinion counts, too." She touched his arm, her eyelashes flitting rapidly against her cheek.

Blake glanced at her hand and set down the last folding chair. "I'll be there in a minute." He took his time, weaving through the people who'd gathered to get ready for the festival. If he waited long enough, maybe Tisha would forget she'd asked. He stopped near Jess, who stood in a huddle of high school boys, obviously engrossed in delegating responsibilities. After Jess finished talking, they all piled in and gave a hearty cheer that sounded an awful lot like, "Hoosegow!"

"Oh, no." Blake watched them disperse, jawing with one another as they headed down the street. He folded his arms across his chest and glanced at Jess. "What's that all about?"

Jess flashed a mischievous smile. "We're bringing the hoosegow back."

"Really? I thought that went the way of the VHS tape and other relics from the 90's."

"Very funny. It's part of our history, man. We gotta do it."

Blake shook his head. "I don't know. I heard Shannon's grandmother threw such a fit the last time ... I didn't think that thing would ever see the light of day again."

"Good thing she's still on that cruise, isn't it?" Jess clapped him on the shoulder. "Relax, we're here to have a fun."

A shrill whistle interrupted their conversation. Blake turned toward the booths and saw Tisha waving him over. He sighed. "I guess I'd better see what the ladies are up to."

Lauren had her back to him, adjusting some red, white and blue bunting they'd hung across the front of the table. She wore that same yellow dress—the one she'd worn her first day back in town——and dang if it didn't have the same effect the second time around. He averted his eyes from admiring her shapely calves peeking out from under her skirt and intentionally stood by Mrs. Carter.

"Good morning, ladies. How are things?"

Mrs. Carter balanced a framed photograph against a tall vase of flowers and stepped back. "There you are. What do you think?"

Blake surveyed all they'd done: fresh flowers, a bowl of chocolates and—that photograph—he felt his mouth drop open. "Where did you get this?" He leaned down for a closer look. A young couple in a double-kayak paddled through the water, dwarfed by a massive blue iceberg in the background. Blake swallowed hard and glanced at Lauren. "That's us. Our last trip to Townsend before I left for college."

A faint blush colored her cheeks. "It was still hanging on the wall in my old room. Mom said we could borrow it." She tipped her head toward the table. "Do you like what we've done with the place?"

Blindsided by the memories that photograph provoked, Blake struggled to shift back to the present. Did she still think about that trip? Huddled around the camp fire long after their families had crawled into their tents, he'd slipped his class ring on her finger and asked her to wait for him …

"Is it the flowers?" Mrs. Carter pointed to the vase. "If it's too much, we can move them. Shannon brought those by, I thought that was sweet."

Blake shook his head to clear away the memories. "No, no. Everything's great. The flowers are fine. Thanks for doing this."

"No, thank you. Mike and I appreciate everything you and Lauren have done. The Inn wouldn't have survived this season without you."

Blake waved a dismissive hand. "Happy to help. We've got to stick together, right?" He tried to catch Lauren's eye, but she was engrossed in conversation with a group of tourists who'd strolled up to their booth. He watched her for a minute, the pink bow of her lips turning into a persuasive smile when they hesitated to buy a raffle ticket. Someone cracked a joke and the sound of her laughter made his pulse speed up. He bit his lip. Resistance was futile where she was concerned.

"C'mon." Tisha linked her arm through his. "I need a partner for the three-legged race."

He shifted his weight from one foot to the other. She'd probably caught him staring at Lauren and figured he'd needed a diversion. You know what? She was right. "I haven't done a three-legged race in ages. Let's see if I've still got it."

"You two have fun. We've got this covered," Mrs. Carter said.

***

Lauren sagged in the folding chair and drew a long sip of the Diet Coke Shannon had brought with their lunch. Slipping off her shoe, she rubbed her aching foot. Again, the peep-toe wedges were a bad decision. She set down her drink and reached for the bowl of red tickets, twisting it in a circle.

She'd stopped counting after Mom sold the two hundredth raffle ticket. Some lucky couple would receive their prize package at the dance tomorrow night.

A cheer went up from the crowd gathered around the main stage. Lauren turned in her seat to see Jeremy pumping his fist in the air, while Blake stood beside him, whipped cream smeared across his jaw. Thoughts of their moments together at the Inn, her own fingers caressing that very jaw—familiar feelings stirred deep within. What if the Sullivan's hadn't knocked on the door? *Stop. You. Are. Ridiculous.* While Jeremy basked in the applause, Blake lifted another pie from the table and planted it squarely in Jeremy's face. The crowd roared with laughter. Lauren shook her head. Boys.

"He's adorable, isn't he? Even with whip cream all over his face."

Lauren whipped back around to find Shannon standing next to her, a satisfied smile stretching from ear to ear. "Shannon. You sure know how to sneak up on a girl."

"If you weren't so busy admiring the scenery, you would've heard me coming, right?"

Lauren squirmed under Shannon's knowing gaze. "I wasn't admiring anything."

"Of course not. I'm sure you—"

A loud ragtime piano tune drowned out their conversation. "What in the world?" Lauren stood up and craned her neck to see what was going on. The crowd parted to allow a black pick-up truck towing a mobile jail to roll down Main Street. Women in costumes reminiscent of those once worn by Emerald Cove's many saloon girls posed in the bed of the truck. At least four more ladies were inside the trailer, waving through the metal bars and blowing kisses.

"You cannot be serious." Shannon shook her head in disbelief. "If my grandmother was here, she'd throw an absolute fit."

"Well, she better not find out who's in the driver's seat," Lauren pointed to the truck.

"What?" Shannon followed Lauren's finger to Jess sitting behind the wheel. She narrowed her eyes. "He's in so much trouble."

Jess stopped the truck and the music faded. The mayor climbed out of the passenger seat, dressed in a vintage police officer's uniform. He adjusted his wide-brimmed hat and surveyed the crowd. When his eyes rested on Lauren, he spoke to Jess and then made his way towards her.

"Oh, no." Her heart lodged in her throat. "I think he's coming for me."

"That's crazy. What would he want with you?"

"Are you Lauren Carter?" The mayor stopped in front of her, his bushy moustache emphasizing his exaggerated frown.

Lauren swallowed hard and nodded.

"Mr. Thompson, what's going on? Of course she's Lauren Carter." Shannon wedged herself between the mayor and Lauren.

"I've an outstanding warrant for your arrest." He unfolded a crumpled piece of paper and pretended to read it. "Says here you were responsible for another's demise and never paid your dues. We've come to extract justice."

Lauren's vision blurred. Was this somebody's idea of a joke? The hoosegow used to be all in a good fun, a humorous tribute to the town's once-lawless ways during the historic gold rush. But the mayor's proclamation hit dangerously close to home. *Another's demise?*

"Can't she buy her way out?" Shannon asked. "I thought all proceeds benefitted the playground fund."

"She can." The mayor nodded. "One hundred dollars is the going rate."

Lauren didn't even bother to hide her surprised laughter. She didn't have a hundred bucks and her purse was back at the Inn. "Well, that settles it, then. I guess I'm going for a ride." Face flaming with embarrassment at the hoots and catcalls coming from the onlookers, Lauren followed the mayor to the back of the trailer. The obnoxious music began playing from the mounted speakers and the door opened. Two young 'saloon girls' smiled and beckoned her inside. She climbed into the makeshift cell, accepted the pink feather boa they draped around her shoulders and looked around for a place to sit.

Blake sat on the wooden bench seat mounted in the middle of the hoosegow, wearing a royal blue feather boa. He met her gaze, eyes dancing with amusement, and patted the empty spot next to him. "Welcome to the party."

CHAPTER TWENTY TWO

B lake watched Lauren walk toward him, cheeks flushed and her eyes flashing. The set of her jaw told him everything he needed to know. She sank onto the bench seat next to him, and stared out at the crowd lining Main Street. He nudged her shoulder. "This is supposed to be fun, you know."

She refused to look at him. "Is this your idea of a good time?"

"Trapped in this sweet ride, wearing my own feather boa, and surrounded by beautiful ladies … what's not to like?"

Her lower lip quivered before she trapped it behind her teeth. *Uh-oh.* She was getting upset. He was going to clobber Jess when this was all over. "Cough up a Benjamin and you'll be outta here."

She scuffed her shoe against the gritty floor of the hoosegow, gripping the bench with both hands as they started to roll forward. "Believe me, I would if I could. The mayor said I was in here because I caused another's demise."

He tugged on one end of her boa. "He's messing with you. I'm sure somebody told him about your incident with Susannah."

She shook her head. "This has nothing to do with Susannah."

He clenched his teeth. These mysterious references to her past were getting old. "Is this some kind of a game? If your deep, dark secret is that much of a burden, why don't you just spill it?" There. He'd said it.

Her spine went rigid. She lifted her chin and stared at him. A tumultuous cloud of surprise, anger and frustration flashed in her eyes. "Do you really want to talk about this now?"

Warning bells chimed in his head. The dam that held his emotions in check started to fissure, slowly at first. Then the words began to tumble out before he could inspect them. "I know you thought you came here to parade that fiancé of yours around town and plan your dream wedding—"

"That was before he dumped me. Thanks for rubbing salt in that wound."

"Did you stop to consider maybe it was for your own good?"

She pressed her lips into a thin line and shook her head. "I can't believe this. Are you going to give me the come to Jesus talk?"

"Do you need it?" He reached out and tucked a wild curl behind her ear, then let his hand rest on her shoulder. She closed her eyes but didn't move out of reach. Heart pounding in his chest, he decided to go for broke. "I've loved you a long time, Lauren Carter, and you can't fool me. Whatever it is, the gig is up. You need to let it go."

Lauren's eyes opened, two green pools of hurt and despair, moist with fresh tears. His heart ached. He longed to pull her into his arms but everything about her warned him not to close the distance between them. Mayor Thompson's voice boomed through the loudspeaker as he identified his next prisoners, superintendent Maxwell and his wife. Blake groaned and dropped his chin to his chest. *Please. No.* Of all the people to pile in the hoosegow at a time like this.

He raised his head and prayed they'd buy their way out. The couple stood at the ring toss game, cheering as their grandson tried to win a prize. The color drained from Mrs. Maxwell's face when the hoosegow stopped and the mayor called her name a second time. Mr. Maxwell made a big show of opening his wallet and extracting several bills. The mayor climbed out of the truck, bull horn in hand. He offered generous praise for the donation to the playground fund and shook Mr. Maxwell's hand. The crowd cheered and then the obnoxious piano music began to play again.

Lauren jumped up from the bench, swiped angrily at the dampness on her cheeks. "Do you have your phone?"

Blake pulled his smartphone from his pocket. "Yes. Why?"

"Text Jess. Tell him I need out. Now."

"Are you okay?" One of the high school girls riding with them must have noticed the tears. Her eyes were wide with concern, false eyelashes batting against her cheek as she touched Lauren's arm. Blake fired off a quick text to Jess. They needed to get her out of there before she made a scene.

"No." Lauren brushed past her and went to the tailgate, kicking against it with the sole of her shoe.

"Lauren, hang on." Blake shoved his phone in his pocket and went after her. "Wait a minute, we'll get you out."

He wasn't sure getting between her and that door was the best idea but her emotions were escalating and the harder she pounded on the plywood with her fist, the more people in the crowd were starting to notice. He wrapped his arms around her from behind, pulling her against him. She writhed and twisted, fighting to break free.

"Let me go," she hissed.

"I'll let you go when he opens the door and not a minute sooner. You've got to calm down, people are watching." He spoke into her ear, forcing a firm and soothing tone, masking the panic that shredded his insides. What in the world just happened here?

Jess was out of the cab and heading toward the back of the hoosegow, a mischievous gleam in his eye. He opened his mouth, no doubt to fire off a smart remark. Blake gave him his most pointed stare and shook his head slightly. *Don't.*

Jess clamped his lips shut and lowered the tailgate, a bewildered expression on his face when he noticed the tears. "Come on out. Party's over," he mumbled.

Blake released his hold and Lauren was out of the hoosegow, curls and boa bouncing against her yellow dress like a fiery comet.

"Whoa." Jess watched her go. "She is *ticked.* What did you do?"

"I told her I'd loved her a long time. Apparently that was not what she wanted to hear." He squeezed Jess's shoulder. "Say a prayer for me. I'm going in." Blake followed Lauren through the crowd and down to the waterfront. Most of the people milling about wore the navy and white outerwear that signified they were passengers on the *Columbia Princess*, the current cruise ship in port. At least that lessened the chances of someone they knew well interrupting his pursuit.

He kept his distance, since that dress and hair were easy to spot. When she ran out of sidewalk, Lauren simply sank onto the nearest bench overlooking the water and wrapped her arms around her torso. His chest tightened. *Lord, give me wisdom and patience because I'm lacking in both.* Drawing a deep breath and exhaling slowly, he walked up to the bench and sat down near her. A breeze was blowing off the water, carrying a tangy cocktail of diesel fuel and fish from the boats returning with another day's catch. A feather in her boa came loose, floating gently toward the ground. "Talk to me. What's got you so rattled?"

She reached for the locket around her neck, zinging it back and forth on its chain. A wan smile stretched across her face. Somehow he knew her words would be anything but funny. He steeled himself for whatever came next. "Most girls dream of finding a guy like you. First you're helping my family out, then you kiss me like—like I haven't been kissed in a very long time— now you tell me you've loved me forever and all I can think about is how horribly selfish I've been."

"Love covers a multitude of wrongs. Doesn't it?"

"Don't you see?" She turned and faced him, brow furrowed. "It's too much. I don't deserve you."

"Believe me, I've said the same thing about a million times. If only my heart would listen." He dragged his palms down the legs of his jeans. "I crashed and burned after you left. Wasted every night of the week, hanging out with people who were going nowhere fast—"

"That explains why you never called me."

Anger and resentment bubbled up inside. "Believe it or not, calling the girl who ripped your heart out and stomped on it is frowned upon when you're in detox."

She flinched. "What did you say?"

"I did ninety days of in-patient rehab, missed a semester of school. Then I had to beg to get my basketball scholarship back. It's only by the grace of God that I've stayed sober … eight years this October."

She pressed her knuckles to her lips, tears brimming in her eyes yet again.

Blake tipped his head back and stared at the sky, his knee bouncing as he slung one arm along the back of the bench. "You're probably wondering why I'm telling you all this."

She shook her head. "No. I—I need to hear it."

"This isn't a guilt trip. I just—" He raked his fingers through his hair. "From the minute I touched you at baggage claim, I knew. I knew I was going to fall all over again." He turned toward her, his heart in his throat.

"What are you trying to say?"

"I need to know how you feel. About me. About us. You can't kiss me like that, then tell me it was a mistake. I won't be your rebound guy. I need to know you aren't going to run as soon as life throws a curveball."

She stared out at the water. "But running's what I do best, don't you think?"

He closed his eyes, shaking his head slowly. "Please. Just put me out of my misery, okay? I'm dying here."

"You're right. I shouldn't have led you on. My life is one hot mess right now and you need someone who can commit. I get it." She paused and he opened his eyes, hoping this was the moment she'd finally break free of the burden she carried. "I've got an interview in Portland next week. If they make an offer, I plan to accept it. I'm sorry, Blake. I can't be what you need."

Blake pressed his lips into a thin line and stared straight ahead, his vision blurring. Her words broke over him like a rogue wave, dousing any embers of hope he'd clung to. He wouldn't give her the satisfaction of watching him fall apart. Pushing up from the bench, he forced himself to look her in the eye. "Well, I guess I know where we stand. See you around." He stormed off, knuckling away a tear. At least his shop was across the street and he could hide out until he pulled himself together.

CHAPTER TWENTY THREE

The morning of the race dawned cool and bright. Lauren whispered a prayer of thanks. This day was going to be hard enough. Although rain and dense fog matched her mood, it wasn't ideal for a relay race. She'd spent another night sleeping fitfully, waking often with yesterday's conversation stuck on repeat in her mind. What a disaster. If Blake found out the truth now, he'd never forgive her. That stupid hoosegow rolled up and she'd lost her mind. He'd been so tender and honest, while she'd done nothing but wound him. All over again.

Swinging her legs over the side of the bed, she slipped out of her pajamas and pulled on her running tights and the oldest T-shirt she could find. The trail up the hill to the water tower would be a muddy, slippery mess. She glanced at the faded letters on her shirt. Look at that. Her lucky shirt. Huh. Wasn't she wearing it the last time she won the race? Well, a good luck charm never hurt. She'd need all the help she could get today. She twisted her hair into a long braid and splashed water on her face. The aroma of bacon and cinnamon rolls wooed her downstairs.

"There's our girl." Dad smiled as she dropped her running shoes at the bottom of the stairs and headed for the coffee maker.

"Morning." She stood on tiptoe and planted a kiss on his rough cheek.

"Are you ready for the race?" Mom stood at the oven with the door open, mitts on both hands as she lifted a pan of cinnamon rolls onto a trivet.

Butterflies fluttered in her stomach, mixing with the shame and guilt she already housed. "I'm a little anxious."

Dad patted her shoulder. "You'll be great. Just have fun."

"Can I fix you a plate?" Mom offered.

Lauren splashed half and half in her coffee. "I'll get it. I don't want to eat too much." She couldn't stand running on a full stomach.

"I can give you a ride down to the starting line when you're ready," Dad said.

"Thanks. Let me pound this coffee and I'll be ready to go."

Mom slid a cinnamon roll onto her plate. Lauren wrinkled her nose. "Mom, I can't eat that before a race."

"It's carbohydrates. Besides, this is Cove to Creek, not the state championship."

Lauren ducked her head and loaded her fork with scrambled eggs. It was too early to argue.

Footsteps in the hallway interrupted their conversation and Lauren turned to watch Mr. and Mrs. Sullivan as they strolled into the kitchen. Lauren struggled to hide her amusement. He was dressed for an expedition in the Arctic while Mrs. Sullivan looked like she stepped off the pages of Vogue.

Dad caught her eye and hid his smile behind his coffee cup.

"Good morning." Mom hugged them both and offered coffee.

"I'm ready to go," Lauren whispered before sliding out of her chair. She was too anxious to eat anything else. Besides, Aunt Jane would wander in soon and Lauren didn't want to hear her critical commentary of the Cove to Creek. She'd heard enough last night when they'd spent a couple of hours sorting through Granny's things. Aunt Jane hadn't said one kind word about Emerald Cove since she'd arrived. Maybe that meant she wouldn't stay much longer.

Dad grabbed his jacket, jangling his car keys.

"Where are you off to this morning?" Mrs. Sullivan's berry red lips curved in a curious smile.

"Big day today. The annual Cove to Creek relay race," Dad said.

"Oh? Well, have a good time." Mrs. Sullivan waved and turned back to stirring her coffee.

Mom wrapped her arms around Lauren and kissed her cheek. She pulled back and smiled. "Good luck, hon. I'll see you at the finish line."

"Thanks, Mom."

Lauren followed Dad outside. She stopped when he unlocked the door of his patrol car. "Dad, you can't be serious. I don't want to show up in that."

"Would you prefer the old, unreliable minivan?"

Lauren frowned. "No."

He gestured to the passenger side. "Get in. You can ride up front today."

She climbed in reluctantly. The interior smelled of leather and spearmint gum. Dad turned the key and the engine purred. She had fond memories of racing Seth out the front door to see who could greet Dad first when he came home. The winner always got to sit behind the wheel and play with the CB radio. The loser was confined to the passenger seat. Seth almost always got there first.

A few wispy clouds floated across a brilliant blue sky. The water was especially green and rather calm. "Beautiful day to win a race," Dad said.

Lauren glanced his way and smiled. "Yes, it is."

"You've been gone a long time, sweetheart. We've missed you. It's been nice having you back under our roof again."

Lauren licked her lips. "I couldn't stand it when I heard about Granny. I had to see her."

"Is that the only reason you're here?"

Holden's chiseled features flashed in her memory, a lock of dark hair falling over his forehead. "What do you mean?"

"I'm just concerned, that's all. Seems like your situation with, uh, Holden caught you unaware."

Lauren's throat tightened. She swallowed hard. "Unaware of what?"

"Is there anything I need to know? Are you in some kind of trouble?"

How did he know? "I've made a mess of things, Dad. It's … complicated."

Dad gave her a questioning glance. "If there's anything I can do, just say the word."

"Thanks."

Dad pulled into the empty parking lot behind the bank and turned off the engine. He reached across the seat and squeezed her hand. "Have fun today." He let go of her hand and got out of the car, striking up a conversation with another police officer lingering nearby.

The butterflies had multiplied. Maybe she should've eaten a little more. Jeremy's black truck slid into the parking space next to theirs. He looked through the window and grinned. She waved but her hand froze in mid-air when Blake climbed out of the passenger side, then flipped the seat forward so Tisha could join him. *You can do this.* She pushed the door open and Jeremy greeted her.

"Mornin', sunshine." He winked and stretched his arms high over his head. "I see you're riding in style."

"Very funny." She narrowed her eyes and punched his shoulder.

"Careful, wouldn't want you to hurt your hand." His eyes twinkled as he flexed his muscles.

Laughter bubbled up in her throat. She could never stay mad at Jeremy. Shoes scuffled on the pavement and she stole a glance at Blake. Their eyes met and the heavy ache of regret weighed her down. He was never good at concealing his emotions. Dark circles ringed his eyes and a pillow mark creased his cheek. This was a very bad idea.

"Hey," he said, his eyes flitting from hers to Jeremy's and then toward the ground.

"Good morning." She managed a small smile and a polite nod in Tisha's general direction. Tisha wiggled her fingers before pulling them back in the sleeves of her long sleeve gray T-shirt. Her sleek platinum blond ponytail bobbed on her shoulder as she jogged up and down in her fancy trail runners. *At least she came ready to race.*

"Sleep well, big brother?" Jeremy reached out and rubbed Blake's cheek.

Blake frowned and knocked his hand away. "Not really. Why?"

Jeremy shrugged. "No reason. Tisha, what do you think? Ready to win this thing?"

She smiled and her sparkling white teeth gleamed in the sunlight. "You know it."

A shrill whistle rang out and they looked up to see Jess and Shannon waving from the registration table.

"Let's go check in." Jeremy led the way across the parking lot. Lauren fell in step behind Blake and Tisha, who was chattering non-stop. Groups of people huddled around the registration table, talking and pinning numbers on each other's shirts.

"Wow." Lauren looked at a woman's number as she passed by. "This looks pretty official."

"Yep, things have changed a little since your last race, Lo-lo." Jeremy said.

Tisha shot her a look. "You've raced before?"

"It's been a long time."

"Don't let her fool you." Jeremy glanced back over his shoulder. "Lauren won this race back in the day."

Tisha's mouth fell open.

"We were a team. And that was a long time ago," Lauren said, averting her eyes from Tisha's gaping mouth.

"Hey." Shannon grinned and handed her a piece of paper with black numbers and fancy logo printed on it. "Are you excited?"

Lauren looked at her number. 252. Sounded good. "I'm getting there. Big turn out?"

"Almost three hundred entries. I don't know where they all came from."

Lauren scooped up a handful of safety pins from the bowl. She turned away and bumped right into Tisha. Not exactly the person she hoped would pin her number on for her.

"Would you like some help?" Jeremy held out his hand for the pins.

He stood behind her and tucked the pins between his lips. "I'm glad you're racing today. I know you wish you were somewhere else right now."

Lauren raised her chin. She was glad he couldn't see her face. "This race is one of my favorite things about Emerald Cove. I wouldn't miss it."

"My brother's in a mood today. Don't pay any attention to him."

Lauren stiffened. "That's sort of a tall order, don't you think?"

"That's true. You two never could stay away from each other." He patted her on the shoulder. "You're all set."

Her cheeks warmed under his bold declaration.

A whistle blew and a man with a megaphone bellowed instructions for the racers to line up by age group. The runners moved toward the starting area in a large pack. Lauren recognized many of the people lining the course with lawn chairs, staking their claim on any chunk of vacant sidewalk they could find.

The hum of conversation escalated as the runners fanned out and started to stretch their legs. Lauren stood next to Jess and leaned over to touch her toes, feeling the tug in her hamstrings. When she straightened, a familiar laugh rang out nearby. Lauren glanced at Blake in time to see Tisha smiling as she grasped his shoulder and stretched her quadriceps. Whatever. But she couldn't look away. His sleeveless shirt emphasized his ripped biceps and broad chest. He hadn't bothered to shave and the stubble on his cheeks sent her mind wandering back to their encounter at the Inn.

"Enjoying the view?" Jess nudged her with his elbow.

Her cheeks flamed and she averted her eyes. "Not really."

"Aunt Lauren!" A little boy's voice floated over the crowd and Lauren turned toward the sidewalk. Perfect timing. Joshua stood next to his parents, waving enthusiastically and holding a big piece of poster board with her name printed in block letters with red marker. She waved back.

"I'll be right back, Jess." She weaved through the racers until she stood in front of her family. "Hi, Joshua. That's an awesome sign, buddy."

"Yep." He grinned from ear to ear and wiggled the sign in the air.

Lauren glanced at Angela and Matt, who were busy dispensing snacks to the little girls in their double stroller. Angela wore Gavin in a baby carrier, his little legs in tiny footed pajamas dangling from the openings. She bit her lip and focused on Joshua. Admiring a newborn would be enough to send her over the edge today.

Matt looked up from the stroller and smiled. "Hey, it's our favorite racer. Good luck, Aunt Lauren."

Lauren shivered, jogging in place to warm up. "Thanks. Are you saving a seat for Mom?"

Angela nodded. "She's at the hospital picking Granny up."

Lauren stared. "What?" Granny wasn't ready for an outing. She puffed her cheeks and blew out a breath.

"Don't worry about it, Lo-lo. We'll take care of Granny. Go race." Matt patted her arm.

Lauren pinched her bottom lip behind her teeth. It was hard not to worry. An air horn sounded and she jumped.

"Relay teams," a man called through a megaphone. "To the starting line. Race begins in three minutes."

Lauren's heart sped up. "I better go. See you guys." She waved and turned back into the crowd, bumping shoulders and hips and trying not to step on toes. This had to be a record turnout for the relay race. Blake and Jeremy stood huddled with Tisha and Jess near the starting line. Blake caught her eye as she moved closer, but his expression was unreadable. She glanced away. Maybe he would run the first leg and she could avoid talking to him until after the race.

"Runners, listen up." Megaphone man piped up again. "Some part of your body must touch the tower. The hill is muddy and wet. No hitting, tripping, shoving. We're watching you."

"When did they add all these new rules?" Lauren asked. "He is such a killjoy."

"I think somebody complained after a certain incident with a girl named Susannah," Jess nudged her.

Lauren huffed out a breath. "That's ridiculous. She totally tripped."

"First racers to the starting line."

"Wait. Who's going first?" Lauren glanced from Jess to Jeremy.

"We thought you could run anchor. Tisha will start us out," Jeremy said.

Great. That meant a lot of standing around. Waiting. With Blake. She'd have to take a warm up lap around a parking lot. Anything to ease the tension between them.

"Here we go." Tisha bounced up and down like a pogo stick as the first wave of runners took their places along the white line spray painted on the asphalt on Main Street.

Lauren checked her shoe laces, stretched one last time and took a deep breath. The crowd began clapping and cheering. A shot rang out and the runners surged forward. The crowd erupted in more shouts and someone banged on a cowbell.

Lauren couldn't help but smile. Their enthusiasm was contagious.

"Well, well, well. What do we have here?" A strong hand clapped her shoulder and Lauren turned to see Mr. Peters, her old math teacher, grinning from ear to ear. "Decided to come home and defend your title?"

"Hi, Mr. Peters. No, I—"

"Blake, nice to see you again." Mr. Peters turned away before she could answer and shook Blake's hand. "I hear this rafting thing is really taking off. How about that?"

"It's going well so far, Mr. Peters."

"Glad to hear it. Well, guess I better find my team." Mr. Peters turned away then came back and leaned in close. "Oh, Lauren. I hear Susannah Farmer is running this year. Better watch your back." He chuckled and disappeared into the crowd.

Lauren cringed and shook her head. *Never going to live that down.*

Blake met her gaze and quirked a curious eyebrow.

"I didn't push her. Seriously." He was there. Didn't he remember?

"I know, I know. She totally tripped."

Lauren swallowed hard and looked around. "Do you really think she's here?"

Blake shrugged. "It's possible. I heard she was back in town for her class reunion."

Lauren craned her neck to check out the other runners, but none fit the image of Susannah she carried in her memory. Of course the girl wouldn't look the same as she had ten years ago. Instead of worn out tennis shoes and faded shirts that were once the trademarks of the race, the runners lined up nearby wore expensive nylon shorts and form-fitting tops. She looked back at Blake. "Things have really changed around here, haven't they?"

A muscle in Blake's jaw tightened. "In more ways than one."

For a moment, the race and the other runners, the spectators—all of it—faded into the background. His eyes held hers and she longed to tell him that her feelings for him hadn't changed. Time and distance had muddled everything. Guilt had nearly snuffed out any chance at happiness. But deep down, she was still that same girl he'd fallen in love with when they were teenagers. Not now. She shook her head, breaking eye contact. "I—I need to warm up some more. I'll be over here."

Before Blake could answer, she'd slipped through the crowd and headed for the bank parking lot, her stomach twisted in knots. Mrs. Putnam had told her a dozen times that concealing the truth would eventually consume her. That running away didn't solve her problems. Lauren jogged in a slow circle. How ironic. The opportunity to break free stood right in front of her and she'd turned tail and run. Only a few more days. Then she'd be on her way back to Portland. The reality of her situation socked her in the stomach and she stopped jogging. Could she really leave again and not tell Blake the truth?

CHAPTER TWENTY FOUR

A smattering of applause broke out as Blake came down the hill and rounded the corner. Lauren waited at the starting line, poised for him to tag her. His side ached as he sprinted down Main Street. At least this was one time she couldn't run away. Jeremy stood between Tisha and Jess, hands cupped around his mouth. "C'mon, bro!" His brother's words of encouragement spurred him forward, neck in neck with another runner. He crossed the line first and touched Lauren's outstretched hand.

Lauren took off with a slight lead over the other teams and he doubled over, hands on knees, gasping for breath. His legs were splattered with mud.

"Great run, man. How do you feel?" Jeremy asked.

Blake stood up, chest heaving, and reached for the cup of water Jeremy offered. "That hill's crazy steep."

"You're telling me. I almost bit it a couple of times."

Blake's breathing slowed and he accepted another cup of water from Tisha.

"You looked amazing out there." She let her fingers brush against his before she let go of the cup.

Good grief. "Thanks. You too." He finished the water and tossed both empty cups in the trash. "Let's jog down by the hill and cheer for Lauren."

Jeremy arched one eyebrow. "For real?"

"Why not? She's got the toughest leg of the race. Besides, I saw Susannah Farmer waiting to run anchor for the guy who was right behind me." It was also the only discreet way he could think of to avoid Tisha's not so subtle advances.

Jeremy rubbed his hands together. "Ladies and gentlemen, it looks like we've got ourselves a race."

"I'll come with you," Jess said.

They jogged through the crowd, Blake's legs protesting with every step. But he knew if he didn't cool down, he'd be in bad shape tomorrow. He watched Lauren up ahead, weaving in and out of the slower runners. A little boy held out his hand and she gave him a high five as she ran by. The front runners left the pavement of neighborhood streets and turned onto the trail. Lauren had managed to hang on to the lead, but a lean, long-legged girl wearing orange and black was gaining ground.

"Let's go, Lauren!" Jess yelled.

Lauren swung her arms faster to propel her body forward. A flash of orange surged toward the front of the pack. Susannah.

"She's going to catch her," Blake said.

"Maybe not. Lauren hates to lose," Jeremy said.

Rocks and chunks of gravel trickled down the hill, giving way under the runners' feet. Susannah made short work of the hill, while Lauren struggled to gain a foothold. *Don't give up.*

Blake kept his eyes on the water tower that stood at the top of the hill, a fresh coat of green paint blotting out the years of graffiti applied by exuberant graduates.

Somebody let out a whoop as they smacked the water tower with their hand. Blake watched Susannah make her way back down the hill. She smiled sweetly and said something to Lauren as she ran by. Blake couldn't help but laugh. He'd give anything to have heard that little exchange. So it was a rematch after all.

"Is she talking trash?" Jeremy asked.

"Looks like it. I bet Lauren loved that."

Blake watched Lauren start her decent down the hill. As the runners jostled for position, Lauren caught her toe on a rock and stumbled forward. Blake's heart stuttered. Panic surfaced. Sliding down the steep muddy hill face-first would mean the end of the race. She regained her balance after a few awkward strides. Blake exhaled the breath he'd held.

Susannah was already at the bottom of the hill and headed back toward town. When Lauren followed a minute later, discomfort marred her features. "You've got this," Blake jogged along the edge of the course, calling out encouragement because he knew her body protested.

"Let's go, Lauren. Don't let her win this race," Jeremy yelled, clapping loudly.

While she didn't acknowledge them, it must have helped because the creases in her brow relaxed and she kicked harder. The distance between Lauren and Susannah diminished. Did Lauren have enough reserves to pass her?

The finish line came into view and the crowd lining the street began to cheer. Blake spotted Granny sitting in a wheelchair on the sidewalk in front of the church. She looked regal, with her silver hair pinned up in a twist and a beautiful blue quilt wrapped around her legs. The rest of the family surrounded her, clapping and cheering as Lauren approached. A faint smile crossed Granny's lips and she lifted her hand and waved. Even Emmy and Ava were excited. They sat in their stroller, smiling and waving rainbow-colored pinwheels.

"Whoa. Check that out." Jeremy pointed. Blake looked down Main Street. Susannah had slowed to a jog. She was just a few strides ahead of Lauren and noticeably limping. *Here's your chance.* Susannah stole a quick glance over her shoulder and winced.

Blake could see Shannon holding one end of a long yellow ribbon that marked the finish line. Susannah cried out in pain and fell to the pavement, clutching her calf muscle. Lauren hesitated for half a step and then blew past her. The ribbon curled around her abdomen and she thrust both arms in the air.

Blake turned to Jeremy. "Unbelievable."

Jeremy grinned. "I knew she could do it."

They jogged down the edge of the street, eager to celebrate their win. Shannon was clapping and jumping up and down when the rest of the team surrounded Lauren.

"Great race!" Shannon squeezed Lauren's shoulder. "I'm proud of you."

Lauren hugged her back, smiling as she tried to catch her breath. "Thanks." She panted and looked back at Susannah.

"Don't worry about her," Shannon said, following her gaze. Susannah had grasped the hands offered and stood. "She'll be fine."

Jeremy pumped his fist in the air. "Nicely done, Lo-lo. Way to take out your opponent."

Lauren cringed. "I didn't take her out. I think she cramped up."

A lop-sided grin spread across his face. "You know I'm kidding."

"Great race, girl." Jess gave Lauren a high five and then bumped fists with Blake. "Nice work out there, dude."

"Thanks," Blake said. "We were quite a team today." He stared at Lauren while she took a long sip of water from the bottle Shannon offered. She lowered the bottle, wiping the sweat from her brow with the sleeve of her shirt. She turned to him and smiled. His pulse surged in response.

"Thank you for cheering for me. I wanted to give up and you kept me going."

Their friends stared expectantly, watching this brief interaction with great interest. While he cheered for her in hopes that she might win the race, they obviously had loftier expectations. *Take it easy, guys.* Blake cleared his throat. "Happy to help."

"I'm taking my girl out for lunch. Anybody want to join us? We can celebrate, just like the glory days." Jess slung his arm around Shannon's shoulders. Blake waited for Lauren to respond first. She glanced in the direction of her family. "I don't think so. I'd like to spend some time with my Granny this afternoon."

Shannon nodded. "Of course. It's so great to see her out here today."

"I'll take a rain check, too. There's stuff to do at the shop," Blake said. Jeremy had convinced him to close down for the festival and the race. While his shoulder appreciated the rest, he was afraid to see what lurked in his inbox and voicemail.

"Catch you all at the dance tonight, then." Jess said. "You're going, right, Lauren?"

Lauren hesitated. "Maybe. Why?"

"You have to. The winning team always makes an appearance. It's tradition." Jeremy and Shannon exchanged glances. "Besides, Blake needs somebody to dance with."

Lauren tipped her head, green eyes dancing as she studied him. "I'm sure he'll have plenty of willing partners."

"You know there's only one he wants," Blake said, enjoying the blush that crept over her cheeks at his bold statement. He hoped he didn't run her off. She'd made her feelings crystal clear. But if she was going to look at him like that, he wasn't going to pass up a chance to tell her how he felt.

"Whew." Shannon fanned her face with her hand. "Is it getting warm out here or what?"

"This is one dance I don't want to miss, I can tell you that." Jeremy pointed at his eyes then at Blake's, a knowing smile on his face.

"Stop." Blake slid his arm around Jeremy's head and tugged him into a headlock, rubbing his knuckles against Jeremy's sweaty scalp. Just what he needed, another smart remark to make the situation even more awkward.

They all laughed, easing the tension.

"I need to speak to my family." Lauren waved. "Thanks for including me on your team. It was fun."

Jeremy freed himself from Blake's grip and scooted away. "See ya later, bro."

Jess and Shannon stood beside him, watching him watch Lauren walk away.

"I'm proud of you, Blake," Shannon said. "I knew you wouldn't give up on her."

Blake shook his head, still staring after her. "I couldn't if I tried, Shan."

Several former teachers and a few classmates stopped to congratulate Lauren. She shook their hands and smiled, making her way slowly through the crowd. Granny was surrounded by a cluster of well-wishers and Lauren waited patiently for people to step aside so she could get to her family, three generations of Carters celebrating their hometown. His heart ached. Anyone could see this was exactly where she belonged. What would it take to convince her?

CHAPTER TWENTY FIVE

L auren sat in the middle seat of Matt and Angela's minivan, wedged between Joshua and Gavin's car seats. She stared out the window as they drove toward the Inn, her stomach swirling with the same butterflies she carried when she left this morning. What had she agreed to back there? She'd all but promised a dance with Blake. She shook her head. Not a good idea.

Matt met her eyes in the rearview mirror. "Everything okay?"

"Yeah, I'm fine. Thinking about the race, that's all."

"That was fun to watch. You all made a great team." Matt turned up the driveway into the Inn.

"Are you expecting early guests today?" Angela pointed to a sleek sedan parked out front.

"Uh-oh." The hair on Lauren's arms stood up. "I think that's Aunt Jane's rental car."

"That's interesting. I wonder why she's here by herself?" Matt shifted the van into park.

Joshua tugged his thumb out of his mouth. "What's wrong, Mommy?"

Angela glanced over her shoulder and feigned a reassuring smile. "Nothing, honey. We're surprised Aunt Jane wasn't at the race, that's all."

"She had boxes to pack," Joshua said.

Lauren's heart thudded in her chest. "What are you talking about?"

"She told me. She wanted to pack Granny's stuff in boxes." Joshua shoved his thumb back in his mouth.

"Oh, boy." Matt opened his door. "I think we'd better get in there."

Emmy and Ava started babbling from their car seats in the third row. Gavin's eyes popped open. He pushed his pacifier out of his mouth and began to cry.

"Do you want help unbuckling the girls?" She tried to give Gavin his pacifier back but he responded with a louder cry.?"

Angela shook her head. "It's too hard to get them all back in their car seats. You go ahead."

"I wanna go." Joshua fussed as Lauren crawled over him and opened the minivan's sliding door. Lauren hopped out and turned back to speak to Angela. "I can watch him."

Lauren could see the tension in the Angela's rigid shoulders as she sat silently in the front seat, staring out the windshield. Then she nodded. "That would be great. Thank you, Lauren. Be a good listener, Joshua."

"Yahoo," Joshua cheered and popped out of his car seat before anyone could change their mind. Lauren grabbed his hand and helped him jump out of the van. "Come on, let's go find Mitchell."

They set off across the sloping front lawn toward the water. Lauren whistled and Joshua called for him but the only sound they heard was the water lapping against the rocky shoreline.

"Let's look behind the house." They circled around the back of the house, tramping through the bushes and yelled for Mitchell one more time. Lauren longed to go inside and see what Aunt Jane had done in their absence. But it was probably better if Matt handled things.

The rumble of motors and tires crunching on gravel brought them back around to the driveway. Dad climbed out of his patrol car while two men Lauren didn't recognize slammed the doors on their Ford Escape. Lauren gripped Joshua's hand in her own. He rattled off questions faster than she could formulate answers.

"Who are those guys? Can we see Mitchell now? Where's Grandma? What's Grandpa doing? Is Aunt Jane here?" Joshua's little hand squeezed Lauren's tighter and his body hummed with anticipation.

Lauren smothered a smile behind her free hand. Mitchell came out of the Inn with Matt, bounded down the stairs and proceeded to bark with wild abandon at the strangers in the driveway.

Joshua fussed and tried to climb up Lauren's legs. Matt shook his head and rolled his eyes heavenward. "Joshua, come here, buddy." Mat reached for his son and scooped him up in his arms. "Everything is going to be okay. It looks like Grandpa has a couple of friends with him today."

Joshua wrapped his arms around Matt's neck and clung to him. Lauren glanced toward the Inn. "What's she up to in there?"

Matt shifted Joshua in his arms and frowned. "I didn't speak to her. There are boxes all over the living room floor, labeled like she plans to pack them with Granny's stuff. Does Mom know about this?"

Lauren nodded. "We sorted some stuff out last night. I assumed she had Mom's blessing to keep going. I'm a little concerned she was here by herself, though."

"I wonder—"

"Lauren?" Dad motioned for her to join them. "Matt, will you excuse us for a minute?" Her stomach tightened. She looked at Matt and shrugged. What was this about?

"I think we'll head home. See you later." Matt took a very agitated Joshua back to the car. Lauren walked across the grass and met Dad and the two men in front of the porch. They were young, clean-shaven and wearing jeans and North Face fleece jackets. When they pulled their wallets from their pockets and flashed their badges, she stopped walking. "What's going on?"

"I'm Detective Clark, this is Detective Holmes. We're from the Portland PD and we'd like to ask you a few questions."

She swallowed hard. "Okay."

"Are you Monique Warren's roommate?"

Lauren's scalp prickled. "Yes. What happened?"

"We picked her up for selling narcotics to an undercover officer. She won't say where she's getting the medication. We thought maybe you could help us figure that out." The detective's piercing blue eyes bore into her. Lauren trembled. *Oh, Holden. What have you done?*

Dad cleared his throat. "Answer their questions, sweetheart. Do you know where your roommate got the drugs?"

"Monique had surgery last year. Her orthopedic surgeon prescribed painkillers throughout her recovery."

"Did you ever see this surgeon prescribe the medication you're referring to?" The other detective scribbled notes on a small pad he'd pulled from the chest pocket of his jacket.

"Yes."

"Do you know this surgeon's name?"

Lauren hesitated. "Yes. Holden Kelly. He was my fiancé."

The detectives exchanged glances. "Was?"

"Yes. He recently broke off the engagement."

"Because he was dispensing medication illegally or is there another reason?"

A surge of irritation coursed through her veins. "I didn't say—"

"Boys, that's it for today." Dad held up his hand. "You've got enough info there to proceed with your investigation."

Detective Holmes pressed his lips into a thin line. He glanced at his partner then at Lauren. "We're not finished, Ms. Carter. You can expect a subpoena when this case goes to trial."

An icy ball of apprehension settled in her stomach. "I—I'll be back in Portland next week."

"We'll be in touch. Thanks for your time." They shook Dad's hand and returned to their rental car.

"Have a safe trip home," Dad said. Once the detectives started the car, Dad leaned down and kissed her forehead. "I'm sorry about that. The chief told me they were coming but I didn't want to interrupt your race to tell you."

"I've half-expected someone to start asking questions." She watched the car until it disappeared from sight down the hill. "What will happen to Holden?"

"Hard to say. They will conduct a thorough investigation, I'm sure."

Lauren swallowed against the lump that formed in her throat. She never imagined her relationship with Holden would come to this. "I need to shower," she mumbled.

"I need to go pick up your mom. I'll be back," Dad said.

She nodded and climbed the steps, her legs trembling. Turning the knob, she opened the door and went in, closing it quietly behind her. She leaned against it and looked around. Several cardboard boxes were lined up in front of the fireplace, each partially filled with Granny's possessions. Aunt Jane wasn't in the living room and Lauren sank onto the couch, her gut twisting in an anxious knot. Monique. Arrested. Where was Holden in all of this? Did she need an attorney? She dropped her head in her hands and groaned. What a mess.

Lifting her head, three framed photographs stacked on the coffee table caught her attention. She picked up the top one and blew off the dust that had accumulated on the frame. It was a favorite picture of her with Matt and Seth. Pop had taken them fishing in his boat. They were each grinning and proudly holding up silver Salmon on the end of their fishing lines. She couldn't help but smile. At the time, the fish seemed huge. Seth had talked about that fishing trip for weeks afterward. *Miss you, Pop.*

"You can keep it if you want."

Lauren squealed and jumped up, her heart pounding. She whirled around. Aunt Jane stood halfway between the kitchen and the couch, holding another cardboard box. "Aunt Jane, you scared me to death. Where did you come from?"

"I didn't mean to scare you. I was up in the loft."

Goosebumps shot down her arms. She moved around the couch, gripping the frame so tightly that the wooden edges jabbed against her palms. "You were what?"

"In the loft, looking for more of Mother's things to pack up." Aunt Jane arched one perfectly penciled eyebrow. "I hope you don't mind."

"Um, actually, I do mind. I'd rather you not go snooping around when no one else is here. What exactly are you doing with all of these boxes?"

"What I should've done a long time ago." Aunt Jane squared her shoulders. "I'm taking Mother back to San Diego with me. It's obvious you all lack the means to provide for her care."

"That is absolutely not true. My parents would move heaven and earth to take care of Granny. Unlike you, who—"

Aunt Jane snorted, holding up one hand to silence her. "Spare me the tired lecture of how irresponsible I was, running off when things got tough." She fixed her with an icy stare. "How's that saying go? 'People who live in glass houses shouldn't throw stones'? You are the last person who should be doling out criticism, Lauren."

CHAPTER TWENTY SIX

The first notes of Lady Antebellum's "Dancing Away With My Heart" spilled from the speakers. Several couples strolled hand in hand onto the dance floor. Lauren surveyed the crowd inside the community center. Wow. Packed house. Almost all of Emerald Cove had turned out for the Cove to Creek dance, including one particular blond-haired blue-eyed paddler. She watched him, talking to one of his old buddies. The mirrored disco ball sprayed confetti flecks of light across his broad shoulders. Her eyes lingered, enjoying the way his dark red T-shirt hugged his biceps. Her stomach flooded with warmth. He looked incredible tonight.

He turned and caught her staring. A knowing smile tipped the corner of his lips. *Shoot. He caught me.* But she couldn't look away.

Blake launched his empty plastic punch glass into the trash can, his form reminiscent of glory days on the basketball court. Her pulse quickened as he made his way across the room. He stopped before her and offered his hand. "C'mon, dance with me."

Lauren took a long sip of her Diet Coke, then lowered the can back to the table. "This song's overplayed. Said so yourself. Besides, I think I strained my hamstring today."

He rolled his eyes. "Please. I watched you dancing earlier. There's nothing wrong with your hamstrings. Or any other part of you, for that matter."

Her cheeks flushed under his piercing gaze. She averted her eyes and reached for her Diet Coke again. He slid the can out of the way, his eyes never leaving hers.

"Are you done making excuses?" He grabbed her hand and tugged gently off the stool. Just one song. What could it hurt?

He nestled their hands next to his heart and drew her in close. She swallowed hard as she felt the warmth of his other hand pressed against the small of her back. Thank heavens for the music because suddenly she was at a loss for words. Shannon caught her eye over Blake's shoulder and winked, then disappeared as Jess whirled her away. Lauren tentatively followed Blake's lead, resisting the urge to rest her cheek against his chest.

"Relax." He guided them in a slow circle.

Relax. Right. She would concentrate on the music and ignore that chiseled jaw and perfect lips that beckoned to her. Warning bells rang in her head. *Don't kiss him.* That dimple was dangerous. She couldn't trust herself. One song and she'd find a reason to put some distance between the two of them. She had to.

Somehow the rest of her didn't get the memo. Her arm slipped around the familiar expanse of his muscular back and she floated around the dance floor. It was like they'd never been apart. His clean, woodsy cologne enveloped her. I could get used to this.

The logical part of her brain battled back with facts and details. *Portland. Think about Portland. You need a job, remember? Not to mention a new roommate. Besides, staying means telling the truth.* She winced. Twirling around the dance floor tonight, she'd forgotten, just for a few glorious minutes, what loomed between them.

The song ended much too quickly and Blake pulled back, a frown creasing his brow. "As much as I enjoy holding you in my arms, I think your brother needs you."

She stiffened. "Right now?"

"Seth is trying to get your attention."

Lacing his fingers through hers, he led her away from the dance floor, the sea of curious onlookers parting to let them through. Seth stood near the door with Molly, his bushy eyebrows knitted together. She shivered, despite the hot, stuffy air in the packed community center. Something was definitely wrong.

"Seth? What's going on?"

Seth licked his lips and dragged his gaze up to meet hers. "Y-y-you n-n-need to g-g-go home."

"Why?"

Seth held up his phone. Lauren leaned in close to read the text message on the screen from Mom.

We found something in the loft. If you see Lauren, please tell her to come home.

Her whole body began to tremble. Aunt Jane. *The ugly quilts.* She swayed, clamping her fingers around Blake's arm to keep upright.

"Whoa." He slipped his arm around her waist. "Everything okay?"

"Aunt Jane." Lauren managed to find her voice. "We argued today about my grandmother's care. I think she's determined to get the last word."

"Let me drive you home." Blake pulled his keys from his pocket.

"No." She shook her head. "I can't let you do that."

"I insist. Come on."

"W-w-want me to come, too?" Seth glanced at the screen one more time and then at her. Confusion and worry strained his features.

Lauren reached up and touched his cheek. "No. You and Molly stay here and have fun. Thank you for finding me." Her heart ached. What would he think of her when this was all said and done?

***

THE SILENCE IN the cab of Blake's truck was oppressive. Lauren watched him from the corner of her eye, his jaw set, his eyes locked on the road ahead. She longed to fill the space between them—observations about the weather, the latest Mariners game, or when Jess might propose to Shannon. Anything. Then she could pretend for three more minutes that this wasn't actually happening. Or should she warn him? *Hey, would now be a good time to mention*—she cringed, hating herself for manufacturing this downward spiral.

He dropped his hand from the steering wheel and she longed for him to reach for her one more time. Instead, he leaned over and cranked the stereo. Kenny Chesney's latest hit blasted from the speakers.

Blake slowed down and maneuvered the truck up the hill toward the Inn. *Stop! Turn around.* She wanted to scream.

There had to be a way to make this right. The fading sunlight cast long beams across the yard, bathing Aunt Jane's rented sedan in a rosy glow. Icy fingers of dread snaked up her spine. "I don't think I can do this," she whispered.

"Do what?"

"Go in there, now, with you."

Blake shifted the truck into park. "Now you're freaking me out. Let's see what's going on before we jump to any conclusions."

She clutched the door handle but couldn't move. Her heart pounded. Blake was already rounding the front of the truck. He opened her door and stepped aside. Sliding to the ground, her legs trembled again and Blake's steady hand cupped her elbow.

Her eyes found his and the tenderness lingering there forced her to look away. *How can I break your heart twice?*

"Come on. Let's hear what they have to say."

No. Every fiber in her being told her to turn and run but she forced her feet to follow Blake up the steps. He turned the knob and pushed the front door open.

Matt met them inside, his face ashen. He motioned them toward the living room. "We're in here."

Dad stood in front of the fireplace with his back to them, one hand propped on the mantle. He didn't turn around when they came in. Mom and Aunt Jane sat on opposite couches. The tension in the room was thick. A plastic bin full of quilts sat in the middle of the floor. *Did they know?* Lauren's stomach churned. "What's going on? Aunt Jane?"

"Hello." Jane stood and came toward them, her hand extended. "I'm Debbie's sister, Jane."

Blake tentatively shook her hand. "Blake Tully."

Jane's eyes widened and flickered to Lauren. "Yes, of course. It all makes sense. Then you'll want to see this." She went back to the couch and lifted the lid on a small white box.

"No," Lauren whispered. "What have you done?" She swallowed back the bile that rose in her throat. *This couldn't be happening.* Her vision began to telescope. Blake slipped his arm around her waist, pulling her against him, like a shelter from storm-tossed seas. She should be the one shielding him. His world was about to be shattered. Blake's eyes darted between her and Jane's hands.

"What's going on?" He dropped his hand from her waist and stepped closer.

"Debbie and I were sorting through our mother's things today." Jane presented the photograph to Blake. "Imagine our surprise when we found this." A picture of a swaddled baby with a knitted pink and blue hat filled Lauren's vision.

Lauren started to shake. "How can you do this?"

"Who is this, Lauren?" Blake stared down at the photograph, his fingers trembling. He dragged his gaze up to meet hers, his brow furrowed.

Lauren opened her mouth to answer, but the words wouldn't come. If only she could go back to that cold January day, when her decision altered the course of their lives. She would have done everything differently. Refused to sign. Picked up the phone. Told Blake the whole truth.

"Look. There's more." Jane grabbed another piece of paper. No, no, no.

"Blake, your name's on this one." Jane dangled the paper. "Maybe you'd like to read it?"

Lauren's vision blurred and she sank to her knees. "Please. Wait." She whispered as he stacked the paper on top of the photograph. *I can explain.*

Really? The voice in her head taunted. *He'll never forgive you.*

"Lauren?" Mom's voice sounded far away, like she was at the end of a long tunnel. "Say something. Anything. Please."

Blake studied the paper for what seemed like an eternity. When he lifted his head, anger flashed in his eyes. Those amazing eyes which once regarded her with love and trust.

"What—" He dragged a hand through his hair. "How— where? My gosh, Lauren."

Tears streamed down her cheeks. "I'm sorry." She sobbed. Her carefully crafted explanations were nothing but empty words now.

Blake's mouth gaped open. Then he clamped it shut, his Adam's apple bobbing as he swallowed hard and examined the photograph and paper again.

"Congratulations," Jane said. "Looks like you're a daddy."

Mom moaned and buried her face in her hands. Matt slid his arm around her shoulders.

"That's enough, Jane." With a curse, Dad stormed across the room and placed his hand on her shoulder. "I think you've done enough damage for one night."

"Let me get this straight." Blake's voice was ragged. "Is this my son? Our son?"

Mom leaned forward while Matt buried his head in his hands. Lauren felt the weight of everyone else's expectant stares. She wiped her nose on the back of her hand and nodded. "Yes. The baby's mine. Ours."

Dad blew out a breath and rubbed a hand across his forehead. Mom's face went pasty white. Blake's hand fell to his side, still clutching the evidence of her terrible secret. He pressed his lips into a thin line, shaking his head in disbelief. "No."

"Well, isn't this delightful." Jane clapped her hands. "I would congratulate you, Debbie. But I'd be talking to the wrong sister, wouldn't I?"

Her heart leaped into her throat. Wait. She got to her feet and stepped tentatively toward Aunt Jane. "What did you just say?"

"Lauren, I don't think now's the time—" Dad said.

She raised her hand to stop him. "No, I want to hear that again."

"Nobody's told you?" Jane's eyes widened. "Well, this whole night is full of surprises."

Lauren shot a glance at Mom. She huddled against the arm of the couch. Her shoulders shook and tears streamed down her cheeks. "What's she talking about?"

"We wanted to tell you. Please believe me." Mom dabbed at her eyes with a tissue.

Jane snorted. "Please. You ran me out of town and kept Lauren for yourself."

Lauren gasped and clutched her chest. Matt stood up and moved toward Dad, as if he anticipated an argument.

"That is not true, Jane." Dad's face flushed red.

"Take it easy, Dad." Matt placed his hand on Dad's chest.

"Blake, I'm going to have to ask you to leave. Now."

"Dad, wait." Lauren pleaded.

Dad shook his head. "We're not doing this tonight." He motioned for Blake to follow him toward the door. "Let's go."

Blake cleared his throat, feet firmly planted on the hardwood. "Believe me, sir, I'd like nothing more than to run as far from here as possible."

Lauren winced. *That makes two of us.*

He walked toward her, tears brimming in his eyes. *Please don't hate me.* He stopped in front of her and she swallowed hard. Less than an hour ago, she was wrapped in his arms, floating around the dance floor. Funny how quickly it all unraveled. Her heart pounded. His eyes dropped to the photo and he swiped at a tear that slipped down his cheek. He held up the picture but she refused to look. Couldn't stand it. "There are so many things I want to say right now."

"I'm sorry." She choked back another sob. "You have to believe me."

"I need answers." He cast a quick glance over his shoulder. "But it sounds like I'm not the only one. You've got to sort this out with your family. So I ... I'm going to go." He reached for her hand and pressed the birth certificate and the photograph into her palm. She let them both slip through her fingers and flutter to the floor, her whole body trembling.

"He has your nose," Blake whispered, his voice breaking. It was like a dagger to her heart. Then he was gone.

Her head throbbed. She felt hollowed out. Gutted. Questions swirled through the soupy fog that was her brain. She pressed her fingers to her temples and tried to formulate a complete thought.

"Are you happy, now?" she whispered, voice quavering as she glared at Jane. "You've single-handedly destroyed my life in one fell swoop."

"Lauren—" Dad stepped between them.

Jane smirked. "Please. I did you a favor. It's exhausting living a lie, isn't it? Maybe you and Deb could commiserate on that."

She glanced at Mom, still huddled on the couch. *How can you just sit there and take this?*

Mom stood and drew her shoulders back, rising to her full height. "Get out." She spat at Jane, pointing toward the door.

"Gladly. But I'm not finished here. I told you I'm taking Mother back to San Diego and I meant it. I'll be at the Anchor Point Inn when you're ready to discuss the details of her move." Jane gathered her purse and marched toward the front door without a backward glance. The cloud of expensive perfume that hovered in her wake turned Lauren's stomach. Aunt Jane slammed the door behind her.

Matt came and stood beside Lauren, placing his hand on her arm. "Hey." He dipped his head, concerned eyes seeking hers. "We love you. No matter what."

But his words did nothing to assuage the gaping wound in her heart. "I have no right to demand the truth, given all I've concealed from you, but I need to know. What was she talking about?"

"Are you sure you want to do this tonight?" Matt asked.

A surge of anger coursed through her. "Why wait? It's not like I'll be getting any sleep."

"Why don't we sit down together," Mom said. "Mike, will you get the pictures?"

Dad nodded and went into the kitchen.

"Need anything? Water? Coffee?" Matt asked.

"Water, I guess. Thank you." Lauren squeezed his arm. He was being so thoughtful, giving up precious hours of sleep to support her. Whatever Mom and Dad shared with them would change things. She could sense it. Regret and confusion enveloped her, weighing her down as she settled on the couch across from Mom.

"I never imagined it would turn out like this." Mom pulled a crumpled tissue from her pocket and dabbed at the tears on her cheeks.

Dad came back before Lauren could answer, a manila envelope tucked inside Mom's well-loved copy of *The Joy of Cooking*. Matt trailed behind him, carrying four bottles of water.

Adrenaline tingled through her veins as Dad tugged the envelope free. The ink had faded, but she recognized Granny's handwriting scrawled across the front.

"Honey, this is not easy for any of us. But it's time you heard the truth. Let's start with the photographs."

Her heart lurched. Photographs?

Matt set the bottles of water on the coffee table and sank onto the couch beside her. Dad handed her the envelope, his eyes moist with tears.

She lifted the flap, her gut churning in a vortex of equal parts curiosity and apprehension. Slipping her hand inside, she pulled three photographs out of the envelope. Her breath caught in her throat. A teenage girl with a wild mass of curly red hair sat up in a bed, holding a tiny bundle of pink-faced baby in her arms. The girl's green eyes were bright and a wide smile spread across her delicate face. She wore a locket identical to Lauren's. "Mom?" she whispered.

"Yes. The baby in the pictures is you. The redheaded girl holding you is my sister, Mallory. She is your birth mother." Mom pressed her knuckles to her lips.

Lauren's vision blurred. She shook her head. How could this be? Matt slid his arms around her shoulders. "No. How? I don't understand." *My mother is dead?* Goose bumps pebbled her flesh.

Mom sighed. "I'm so sorry. We should've told you a long time ago."

Lauren studied the other two girls perched on either side of the bed, each with an arm slung around the girl's shoulders and a hand on the baby's blanket. The curly brown hair and almond shape of Mom's eyes were unmistakable. That had to be her to the left of the redhead. The girl on the right looked a lot like Aunt Jane with the exception of the long blond hair. "So you just kept these pictures shoved in your cookbook, thinking I'd never find out?"

"To be perfectly honest, it was easier this way. You were a tiny baby when Mallory died. Jane wanted to raise you as her own. But Pop refused to let her." A hint of a smile touched Mom's lips. "He loved you so. I remember you spent one night in the orphanage and Pop couldn't stand it. Went down there first thing in the morning and brought you right back here."

Lauren turned the photos over and studied the handwriting on the back, processing this news about Pop. Then she spread them on the table. Matt leaned in for a closer look. The second included Granny and Pop with the redhead still holding the baby. Pop was frowning. The third picture was just the baby, a tiny fist pressed to her cheek while she slept, swaddled in a striped blanket. It was all so familiar. Lauren trembled all over, her brain a fragmented slide show of images.

"We wanted to protect you, sweetheart." Dad's voice was gruff. He cleared his throat. "You were never an orphan. We loved you from the minute Pop brought you home."

Orphan. Hot tears spilled onto her cheeks. She stared at the photographs in front of her. *Where was my father in all of this? Is my son going to wonder the same thing one day?* Pain pierced her heart and she covered her mouth to stop the cry from escaping.

Mom stepped around the coffee table and squeezed onto the couch beside her. "Oh, honey. It's okay, just cry." She slipped her arm around Lauren's shoulders and pulled her in for an awkward hug. Lauren stiffened. Mom's sweater was soft against her cheek and smelled faintly of laundry soap.

"Wait." Lauren pulled away. "What about the microfiche? You took these from the library, didn't you?"

Mom shook her head. "I didn't take them. A dear friend brought that by. She was volunteering at the library, converting the old records to digital. When she came across this particular story, she thought I might want to hang on to it. Until the time was right. She was only trying to help."

Lauren swiped the back of her hand across her nose. That explained her wild goose chase at the library. But still no one had mentioned her father.

"We've come so close to telling you. I know that sounds ridiculous now, but it's true," Dad said.

"My father?" Lauren whispered. "Who is he?"

Mom exchanged glances with Dad. The uncertainty that passed between them was almost palpable. Then Mom reached for Lauren's hand and captured it between both of her own. "Remember the day you got here and Granny called you Mallory? We were upstairs and I told you Mallory and her boyfriend died in the same accident? Honey, that young man was your father."

Matt, silent until now, sucked in a breath. "Good grief," he whispered, his hand trembling as he rubbed his forehead.

"We're so sorry." Dad's voice broke. "Please know that we love you and raised you as our own."

So that was it? Both parents gone in an instant and more than two decades spent concealing a secret? Although she had no right to be angry, she was. Livid, in fact. Dark spots peppered her vision. Nausea swept over her and she jumped up from the couch, her feet tangling with Matt's. "I-I can't do this. I'm sorry. I can't even think … I need to go." She ran toward the stairs and climbed to the loft. Tears were flowing freely and she gasped for breath between sobs. The waning twilight cast shadows across the room and her eyes struggled to adjust. She stumbled toward the bed and fell across it. Kicking her shoes off, she burrowed under the quilt and cried until she had nothing left.

CHAPTER TWENTY SEVEN

Blake gripped the steering wheel with one hand, knuckled a tear from his cheek with the other, as his truck found its way down Hillside Drive. A son. The news pierced him to his very core. And to think she'd never even tried to tell him the truth. Granted, he hadn't been in any shape to parent a newborn, but still⌐—to have no input at all⌐—He smacked the wheel hard with his hand. She had no right to make this choice without him.

His mind replayed their stolen moments together, spring of her senior year. He'd come home from college for the long Easter weekend. They were miserable apart and eager for the semester to be over. Things went too far that night, as they are prone to do, when two teenagers are nestled in sleeping bags in the bed of a truck.

"Of course," he whispered, shaking his head in disbelief. This explained her abrupt decision to leave town less than two months later. No amount of pleading on his part could change her mind, either. He'd always imagined she'd come back when she found what she was looking for. Turns out she was running. And apparently never looked back.

Driving down Main Street, he slowed the truck at the entrance to Mack's Bar and Grill. Blake's pulse accelerated in anticipation of how the whiskey would feel sliding down his throat, quenching his thirst and dousing the grief that roared through his soul. Somewhere in the back of his mind, his conscience sounded a warning to keep moving. But he was past logical thought at this point. He nosed his truck into the last available spot, shoved the gear shift into park and climbed out. Slamming the door, he jammed the keys in his pocket and headed for the entrance, riding on a wave of equal parts anger and adrenaline.

Once inside, Blake pushed his way through the crowd, a haze of cigarette smoke wafting from the usual suspects parked at the bar. Claiming an empty stool at the end, he ignored the curious stares and waved down the bartender.

"Shot of Maker's mark," he mumbled, rage clouding his vision. This was the quickest way to dull the pain.

The bartender affectionately dubbed Lefty for the port-wine birthmark splayed across his left cheek, stood on the other side of the bar, polishing a shot glass with a white towel tucked in the waistband of his worn Levi's. Blake could feel Lefty's steely gaze boring into his skull. *Don't even try to talk me out of this.* He craved a drink with every fiber of his being.

"You sure about that, son?"

"I'm a big boy, Lefty."

"True." Lefty poured the amber liquid into a shot glass, concern etched in the deep crevasses that lived above his brow line. Rubbing his beefy hand over his bald head, he slid the glass aside and leaned his massive forearms on the bar. "Want to tell me what's on your mind?"

"Not really." He just wanted to forget. The picture, the look on Lauren's face, the shock. All of it. His stomach churned. *Why? How was she even capable of that kind of deception?*

"Generally speaking," Lefty traded the shot glass for a tumbler full of Coke, "I like to keep my customers happy."

Blake frowned at the drink in front of him. "That's not what I ordered."

"Well, it's what you're drinking. Your dad and I go way back. To Vietnam and beyond. He would tan my hide if you fell off the wagon on my watch."

"One drink. That's all I need, man. You've got no idea what I'm dealing with here."

"I probably don't. But whatever it is ain't worth flushing eight years of sobriety down the drain. You can sit here all night if you want. But it ain't worth it. You hear me, son?"

"I've held it together a long time, Lefty. Eight years is pretty good, don't you think? Shouldn't I get some kind of reward or something?" Blake hated the bitter edge that tainted his words. Even worse, he hated that he was trying to manipulate his father's closest friend. *You're pathetic.*

"I've heard it all before. There's no bargaining here." Lefty set the Coke in front of him again. "Stay as long as you like, but that's the only drink you'll be getting from me."

Blake hung his head and watched the bubbles collapsing against the glass. What a waste. He'd spent so many months—years, in fact—only half-living. Waiting for her to come home. But Lefty was right. She wasn't worth it. And he was done trying to pretend she was.

CHAPTER TWENTY EIGHT

Lauren awoke to sunlight streaming through the window. *Make it stop.* She buried her head under a pillow and tried to go back to sleep. Just for a minute, she floated in that blissful space of unawareness. Then the events of the previous day flashed through her mind, each one more painful than the last. It was like rubbing salt in an open wound. She groaned and pulled the pillow away, tossing it aside. Her phone chimed and she rolled to the side of the bed. Where did she leave it? Her bag sat on the floor, slumped against the nightstand. Maybe it was in there. She rummaged inside until her hand closed around it. She pulled the phone out and squinted at the screen. A text from Matt.

Are you ok?

She dropped the phone back in her bag. No. She wasn't okay. Not even close. Sitting up, she swung her legs over the side of the bed. Her head hurt but it was nothing compared to the ache in her chest. *Blake.* Kind, generous, selfless Blake. He'd been absolutely transparent yesterday and she'd crushed him with her deception.

Her mouth was dry and her stomach growled. A shower could wait. Coffee was a definite must. She grabbed a sweatshirt from the chair beside her bed and slipped it on over her rumpled T-shirt. Dragging her fingers through her tangled curls, she opened her door and went downstairs.

The house was eerily silent. She couldn't even remember if they'd had guests last night. Dishes were piled in the sink and remnants of breakfast stuck to the counter. She craned her neck to look out the window. Mom and Dad's cars sat empty out front. Where were they? It was almost noon. Only a swig of coffee remained in the bottom of the carafe. She dumped it out and fixed a fresh pot. She tapped her fingernails on the counter while the coffee brewed.

Mom and Dad. She shook her head. Last night was a disaster of epic proportions, worse than she ever imagined. Of all the possible scenarios she'd played out in her head, Aunt Jane and a box of quilts never entered the equation. Then again, she'd been so consumed with her own secret that the hard truth about her own identity was a complete shock. A fresh wave of hurt and confusion washed over her. How did they keep such a juicy secret in this tiny town? Her cheeks grew hot. Was she the last one to know? Granny. Did she remember her real father? There were so many questions that demanded answers.

Her running shoes beckoned from the doorway of the laundry room. Not now. There weren't enough miles of road in Alaska to outrun this heartache. She downed a few sips of coffee, eager to get to the hospital before her courage dissipated. She ran up to her room, grabbed her phone and her purse then dashed back down the stairs. Her stomach roiled in protest. Coffee didn't exactly count as a meal. But she couldn't stay in the house another second. Grabbing the van keys, she jogged toward the front door.

Mitchell was sprawled on the porch. He thumped his tail and followed her with his brown eyes as she gripped the porch railing. A light breeze rustled the branches of the trees and a shadow slid over the yard as the sun went behind a cloud. Although the view was the same, everything else had changed. She was alone. Deceived by the ones she trusted the most. She stepped over Mitchell and ran to the van.

A custodian was mopping the floor in the waiting room when Lauren passed through the hospital's double doors. The acrid smell of disinfectant filled the air and the only nurse behind the desk at the nurses' station let Lauren pass with a cursory wave. So distracted by the long list of questions running through her head, Lauren didn't see Shannon coming out of a patient's room until it was too late. They collided and Shannon squawked, the chart in her hands falling to the ground.

"I'm sorry." Lauren squatted to retrieve the chart.

As they stood up, both gripping the chart, Shannon's eyes roamed Lauren's face. "You look like death warmed over. What in the world is going on?"

Lauren cringed. "You wouldn't believe me if I told you."

"Try me. C'mon, your grandmother is still with the physical therapist. Let's sit down for a few minutes."

Stepping into the break room, Shannon grabbed two bottles of water from the fridge and motioned for Lauren to sit down at the round table in front of the vending machine.

"Here?" Lauren glanced around.

"Sorry. I'd take you out dancing but I'm on for another hour." Shannon winked and twisted the top off of her bottle. "It looked like you and Blake were having a good time. Where did you go?"

Lauren gnawed on her lower lip. How did she even begin? "It's not what you think. Our evening didn't end on a happy note."

"You certainly don't look like the same Lauren Carter I saw last night. What's up?"

Lauren's hands fluttered to her throat, reaching for the locket and any measure of comfort it might bring. She took a deep breath and in a matter of minutes, told Shannon everything. Both the secrets the Carter family had spent years concealing and the truth about why she'd run off to Portland.

When Lauren was finished, Shannon pulled a tissue from the pocket of her scrubs and dabbed at the moisture on her cheeks.

"Wow," she whispered, twisting the tissue between her fingers. "I don't even know what to say."

"Please don't hate me."

Shannon knitted her brows together. "Hate you? How could I?"

"Isn't this the kind of thing you tell your best friend?"

Shannon reached across the table and squeezed Lauren's hand. "As your grandmother often says, most folks do the best they can. I'm sure you did what you thought was best for everybody at the time."

Lauren released a slow breath and looked out the window. "I don't know, Shan. I'm not sure Blake will ever forgive me."

"Have you asked him?"

Lauren dipped her chin, peeling the label off the full water bottle. "I'm sure he wants nothing to do with me now."

"I wouldn't be so sure. Blake's always been fiercely loyal. Why don't you go talk to him? What have you got to lose?"

That was the problem. It was already lost.

CHAPTER TWENTY NINE

W hen she finished talking to Shannon, Lauren fully intended to visit with Granny. But her therapy left her exhausted and Shannon urged her to come back later. Lauren couldn't decide if Granny truly needed a nap or Shannon wanted her to go and talk to Blake.

She left the hospital and sat in the van, the keys in the ignition, her head propped on the steering wheel. What next? Thank goodness she had that interview in Portland. At least she could go back, maybe find a smaller apartment and try to put the pieces of her life back together.

You're not finished here.

The voice whispered from somewhere deep within.

That's ridiculous. Last night had proven quite the opposite. Weary and confused, Lauren eventually lifted her head, started the engine and drove out of the parking lot.

Although she planned on going home, at the last second she turned the van in the opposite direction and drove down to the waterfront. Staring out at the deep green waters of the cove on a beautiful summer day always soothed her. Even as a young girl, when she was disappointed or angry or frustrated, she would ride her bike down to the harbor and sit for hours. There was a vacant parking spot next to her favorite bench so she pulled in and turned off the engine.

Climbing out of the van, she couldn't resist a glance across the street at Blake's shop. Her breath caught when she recognized his truck parked out front. Maybe she should go over, take him some coffee and tell him the whole story. *Forget it. He doesn't want to talk to you.* She turned her back on the shop and sank down on the bench with a heavy sigh. What a nightmare.

"Lauren? Lauren Carter? Is that you?" A very pregnant woman waddled toward her, the light breeze tousling her adorable blond pixie haircut.

"Christi?" Jason Cavanaugh's wife stopped in front of the bench, chest heaving with exertion. Lauren stood and gave her an awkward hug, trying to avoid the baby bump.

"I thought that was you. Jason told me you were back in town." Christi's eyes flitted toward Blake's shop and back to Lauren. "What are you doing down here?"

"Um, just needed a little fresh air. That's all. How about you?" Lauren studied her friend's curious expression. Does she know?

"Oh, I brought Jason some lunch. He's working on the boat today. Want to grab some coffee? I'm totally craving a latte."

Lauren hesitated. If she went into the Copper Kettle for coffee there was an excellent chance she'd run into Blake. On the other hand, they were bound to run into each other at some point.

"Okay." Lauren followed Christi across the street. "Congratulations, by the way. I had no idea you were expecting."

"Thanks. Two weeks to go. Although she seems pretty comfortable in there."

Lauren almost mentioned her own pregnancy going to forty-two weeks, but stopped herself before it was too late. No. Her stomach plummeted. She fumbled for a compliment about Christi's appearance instead.

Megan eyed them from her post behind the espresso machine as they entered the coffee shop. "Can I help you?"

Lauren rattled off her order and tried to ignore Megan's subsequent eye roll.

Christi giggled. "Just a decaf vanilla latte for me. Thanks, Megan."

While they waited, Christi brought Lauren up to date on the last nine years of her life. Lauren dodged almost all personal questions by circling back to the baby. Christi was more than happy to oblige, spilling all the details about their plans for the baby's room and their short list of potential names.

Megan looked up from her cell phone and cleared her throat. "Could you take my brother his coffee?"

Lauren swiveled toward the young girl. "I'm sorry. What?"

"Blake. He wants coffee. I'm not supposed to leave the shop. Can you take it to him?"

Lauren swallowed hard and glanced at Christi. Maybe she could deliver it. But if Lauren refused, that left her wide open to questions.

Christi smiled. "Go ahead. I've got a doctor's appointment, anyway."

Dang it. She nodded slowly, unable to speak.

"Good to see you." Christi patted her arm. "Maybe we can get together with Shannon and have lunch sometime."

"Sure, I'd like that." Lauren pasted on a smile. *Not that you'll still be speaking to me.* She knew her secrets were safe with Shannon, but scandalous news like this would spread like wildfire. Jane would make sure of that. It was only a matter of time.

"Here. Thanks." Megan slid the coffee into a cardboard sleeve and passed it to Lauren.

Heart pounding, Lauren grabbed the coffee and slipped out the door. Every step toward the shop next door felt like her shoes were filled with concrete. It was just coffee. They didn't actually have to talk to each other. She could hand it to him and leave.

The bell on the door jingled as she stepped in. Blake stood behind the counter, eyes on his computer and the phone pinned between his shoulder and his ear. His eyes met hers and he clenched his jaw. She took another sip of her own coffee and pretended she belonged there.

"Let me call you back, okay? Thanks." Blake hung up and stared at her. His piercing gaze cut straight to her heart. Dark circles ringed his eyes and a day's worth of stubble clung to his angular jaw.

Say something. She lifted the coffee cup. "Megan sent this over."

"Thanks."

The silence unnerved her. It was a long walk to the counter but she made it. Sliding the cup toward him, she wracked her brain for something to say. He pressed his lips into a thin line and looked down at the counter.

"Busy today?" She cringed at her lame attempt at small talk.

"Don't." His head shot up and anger flashed in his eyes.

"What?"

"Don't pretend like everything's okay."

"I'm not pretending. I brought—" Her knees quaked and her cheeks burned. *This was a mistake.*

"How could you?" His voice broke and he dropped his chin to his chest, hands braced against the counter.

She stumbled back. "Blake, please. Let me explain."

He snorted and shook his head in disgust. "You gave away my child, Lauren. *My son.* Yes, please. Explain it to me."

His words knifed at her heart, severing any hope that he might forgive her. Not that she deserved it. She pressed her palm to her lips to stifle a sob. Turning away, she hurried toward the door, tears blurring her vision. *That's right. Run. Just like you always do.* She should've never come here. What a fool she was for thinking he would listen to her.

CHAPTER THIRTY

B lake watched Lauren run out of the shop, hair streaming behind her as she jogged toward the minivan.

Go after her.

No. Don't even think about it.

She had him in pieces. All over again. One minute he longed to pull her close and mourn together for the child they'd created but released to someone else. The next, he wanted to grab her and ask a million questions. Did she hold him when he was born? What did he smell like? Was she alone when she delivered or was the rich doctor already in the picture? Most of all—and this is the one that nearly killed him—could his son ever find him?

Blake's knees grew weak and he sank into the chair in front of the computer. The thought of his own flesh and blood out there in the world, without him, was almost more than he could bear. Rubbing a hand across his scruffy chin, he tapped the computer to wake it from its hibernation and glanced over the reservations for the day. They were slammed. A party of fifteen had booked a white water rafting trip for the afternoon. That meant all hands on deck, so to speak. There wasn't time to wallow. Somehow he had to put on his game face and get the job done.

The front door opened again and Jeremy came in, his face ashen. "Hey."

Blake swallowed hard and managed a wave. "Hey."

Crossing the shop, Jeremy came around the counter and stopped in front of Blake. "A fist bump hardly seems appropriate in this situation, but I wanted to tell you that Mom shared, uh, what happened." He cleared his throat. "I'm sorry, man."

Blake held out his fist anyway. Jeremy bumped it, a half-smile tipping up one side of his mouth. "Thanks. I'm sorry, too."

Jeremy hoisted himself up on the counter. "I heard you stopped by Mack's last night. Why didn't you call me?"

"What were you going to do? Talk me out of taking a drink? Don't worry. Lefty pretty much had that covered." Even if Lefty hadn't refused to serve him, probably half the bar would've run him out of there. One of the perks of living in a small town. Laughter escaped his lips.

Jeremy's brows knitted together. "What's so funny?"

"Nothing funny about it. Ironic, really. Nobody in that bar was going to let a drop of whiskey touch my lips. But my girlfriend managed to leave town pregnant, gave our baby up for adoption, and no one said a word?"

Jeremy winced. "I don't think you're supposed to say 'gave up.'" He quoted the air for extra emphasis.

"Oh, excuse me if I'm not quite up on the current lingo." He picked his rafting helmet up off the desk and chucked it across the room. It crashed into the wall and landed upside down, spinning like a top. "Whose side are you on, anyway?"

Jeremy held up both hands. "Take it easy, man. This is new turf for all of us. I'm just trying to help. Saying 'gave up' just sounds so ... cruel. Like you didn't want him. I doubt that's the case."

He winced. Even though he gave his younger brother a hard time for his free-spirited ways, Jeremy's words were spot on. He drew in a ragged breath, puffed his cheeks and blew the air out slowly. "I just wish I'd known. You know? Maybe things would've been different."

After Lefty talked some sense into him last night, Blake left the bar and drove straight to his parents' house. Then he crawled into his old bed and sobbed until he had nothing left. His mom came home from her night shift at the hospital and woke him up for breakfast.

He'd shared the big news while she fixed her signature scrambled eggs, bacon, and coffee. Emphasis on the coffee. Blake didn't have the heart to turn down a meal when he knew she'd worked all night, but he could barely choke down more than a few bites. While he moved his food around on his plate, those were the words she'd repeated over and over. If only we'd known.

"Do you think Dad knows anything yet?" Blake leaned forward, elbows on his knees.

"I don't know. Dad's working almost around the clock on the new bridge project. I think he probably left before Mom got home."

"I've got to find a way to tell him myself." Blake glanced at his watch. He could drive by the construction site on his way out to the river, but that wasn't exactly the time or the place to break that kind of news to Dad.

"Well, judging by the looks of the kitchen, Mom's got a lot on her mind. That place was absolutely spotless when I stopped by."

Blake couldn't help but smile. Mom always cleaned like a woman possessed when she was upset. Needless to say, she didn't handle the baby bombshell well at all. In fact, Lauren better hope they didn't cross paths anytime soon. Mom was devastated. Their families were such fixtures in each other's lives for so long. This kind of betrayal was difficult to absorb. For everybody.

"Come on. Ride with me. We've got a big afternoon ahead and they're calling for a storm tonight." Blake grabbed his keys and followed Jeremy out of the shop, locking the door behind him. He'd have to catch up with Dad some other time, not to mention sharing the news with Megan. His chest tightened. *Here, baby sister, this is what you don't do.* Maybe he'd grab some steaks when they came off the river, fix a nice quiet dinner and spend some time with his family. Lord knows, he needed them now.

***

"M-M-MOM MADE C-C-COOKIES. Would you l-l-like some?" Seth held out a chocolate chip cookie on a napkin.

Lauren sat in an Adirondack chair at the edge of the yard, knees tucked up under her chin. She'd been there all afternoon, a one-woman pity party. Her mouth was dry, throat raw. Leave me alone. Mom and Dad—if she could even call them that— had been walking on eggshells since the recent revelation that they weren't actually her parents.

She wiped her nose on her sleeve. "No, thanks. You can have it, Seth."

"C-c-can't. Hot d-d-date. Might r-r-ruin my ap-p-puh-tite."

Lauren glanced up at Seth. He'd shaved his beard and his freshly-washed curls glistened in the late afternoon sunlight. His khaki pants were ironed and he wore a new denim shirt, tucked in and everything. She thought she detected the slightest hint of cologne. Her mouth dropped open. "Who are you and what have you done with the real Seth Carter?"

"Funny. I c-c-can clean up when I w-w-want to."

"Who's the lucky girl?"

A faint blush colored his cheeks. "Molly."

"Good for you, Seth. She was always such a sweet girl."

"Still is."

Lauren smiled. "You have fun tonight."

"Thanks. M-m-mom says d-d-don't stay out here all n-n-night. M-m-mosquitoes. And a s-s-s-storm's comin'."

Lauren nodded. "Thanks. I know."

Seth set the cookie and the napkin on the arm of her chair, patted her shoulder and walked away.

Lauren sighed and tipped her head back against the top of the chair. Mom was right. She couldn't stay in this chair much longer. The mosquitoes would eat her alive. She popped the cookie in her mouth, grabbed the napkin and headed for the house.

Guests were arriving as she got to the front door, an adorable older couple from Maine. While Mom helped them figure out how to get back to town for dinner, Lauren stowed their luggage in their room. When she came back into the kitchen, Dad was sitting at the table, his radio and a cup of coffee in front of him. He motioned for her to join him.

Swallowing hard, she perched on the edge of the chair across from him. "Hi, Dad."

"Hi, sweetheart. How are you?"

"I've been better." She smoothed the napkin out on the table and avoided his gaze.

"I'm sure you have. Look at me."

Lauren dragged her eyes up to meet his.

"Your mother and I, we are so sorry we never told you the truth."

"I know."

The front door closed and Mom came into the kitchen a minute later, sliding into the chair beside Dad. His radio crackled as another trooper called into the dispatcher. He turned down the volume.

"And the news about … your baby—" He bit his lip and looked away. Mom rested her head on his shoulder.

Lauren's chest tightened and she felt another wave of tears cresting behind her weary eyes.

Dad cleared his throat. "What I'm trying to say is that we love you. We've always loved you and nothing will ever change that."

Lauren nodded, swiping at the lone tear that trickled down her cheek. "I know."

"Sweetheart, talk to us. We know you must have so much on your mind. This isn't a burden you need to carry alone anymore," Mom said.

"That's the thing. I've lived like this for so long, I don't know how not to. And I tried to talk to Blake this morning and he pretty much wants nothing to do with me. Everything is such a mess."

"We're all going to have to dig deep on this one, sweetheart. This is a lot for us to handle all at once," Mom said.

"You think?" Irritation laced her voice. Mom flinched. Lauren instantly regretted her sarcasm. "I'm sorry. I should—"

"You don't have to apologize. Your world's been turned upside down. We get that," Dad said.

"And I get that you're probably wondering what in the world I was thinking. The orphan girl gives away your grandson. Doesn't seem right, does it?" *Take it easy.* But the anger and hurt bubbled up within and she couldn't tamp it down.

"We didn't—" Mom's face flushed.

"I couldn't stand the thought of disappointing you," she whispered, folding the napkin in half, then in fourths. "I was so ridiculously self-absorbed and the social worker said all the right things. A plan, the gift of a loving family, blah, blah, blah." But she'd given little thought to the emptiness she'd carry with her once her baby—Blake's baby—belonged to someone else.

Sirens wailed in the distance and Dad reached for the volume on his radio. He twisted the knob and a woman's voice came through the speaker. "Unit three, what's your ETA?"

"This is Unit three, en route to Crooked Creek put-in. ETA … about four minutes."

The hair on the back of Lauren's neck stood on end. She glanced at Dad. "Crooked Creek? Isn't that where Blake and Jeremy launch their trips?"

He silenced her with a sober glance, leaning closer to the radio.

"Unit three, I'm dispatching the swift water rescue team now. Reports of at least one victim trapped downstream."

"Copy that."

Lauren's blood ran cold. Swift water rescue. What if it's Blake? "Dad, we have to go."

A muscle in Dad's jaw tightened. "Sweetie, it could be anybody out there. Kids messing around, a fisherman who waded out too far … there's no way to know who's involved."

She jumped up, her chair clattering to the floor. The storm had moved in and raindrops pelted the kitchen windows. Low lying fog swirled through the trees, obstructing her view of the water. "Who would be out in this?"

"I don't think the storm was supposed to roll in this quickly," Mom said. "If you think you're headed out, let me fix you some coffee."

"I'm a trooper, Deb, not an EMT. The last thing they need is a bunch of gawkers, interfering with their rescue."

Lauren turned back toward the table, rubbing her arms vigorously to ward off the ominous feeling that seeped to her core. "I'm worried it's Blake. And Jeremy. Can't we just go see?"

Before Dad could respond, a male voice came through the radio again. "Dispatch, this is unit three. Confirming six victims in the water, four alert and responding to bystanders. Two adult male victims downstream, possible head trauma. Can I get an ETA on swift water rescue team?"

"Head trauma?" She gripped the rail on the back of the closest chair, her chest tightening. "Dad, please. If you won't go to the creek can we at least go to the hospital?"

CHAPTER THIRTY ONE

D ad drove into the hospital parking lot as the ambulance whipped into the circular drive in front of the emergency room doors. Lauren trembled. *Please. No.* Bile rose in her throat. Grabbing her purse, she was out of the car before Dad could turn off the ignition. A passel of nurses and doctors swarmed the ambulance. They snapped on latex gloves and barked orders as the back doors were opened. The white coats and scrubs blocked her view. She turned toward the main entrance of the hospital, determined to find out who was on that stretcher.

The automatic doors whooshed open and she stepped inside. She brushed a stubborn curl out of her eyes and looked around. A man snoozed in one of the orange vinyl chairs in the corner, unfazed by the chaos outside. Even the nurses' station was abandoned. An icy chill tingled down her spine. Without waiting for Dad, she headed for Granny's room. Maybe she'd find someone—anyone—who knew what was going on.

She stopped in the doorway, praying Shannon would be at Granny's side. But Granny was asleep in her bed, mouth hanging open. A magazine had slipped to the floor and she leaned over to pick it up.

"InStyle? You always were the fashionable one." Lauren flipped through the first few pages. Granny stirred but didn't open her eyes. She sighed and closed the magazine, sliding it back on the table next to the bed. *Oh, Granny. If only you were awake, I'd ask you to pray.* One tiny snippet of scripture popped in her head, long-dormant from her days in the high school youth group. *Pray without ceasing.* Although her prayers had probably seemed more like wish lists, she'd submitted her urgent requests to the Lord on the short ride to the hospital. If anything happened to Blake at this point, she'd never forgive herself.

Commotion in the hallway interrupted her thoughts. She heard footsteps running and Shannon's frantic voice. "I'll check in here, sometimes she visits Mrs. Watson." Shannon burst into the room and stopped short when her eyes met Lauren's.

"Shannon?" The color drained from her friend's face. "Are you okay?"

"Oh, Lauren." Shannon pressed her fingers to her cheeks.

Lauren's stomach clenched. This can't be happening. "It's him, isn't it?"

Shannon lowered her hands, eyes wide with fear. "I really need to find Sandy."

"If you're looking for Sandy then it has to be Blake. Tell me. Please." Her voice was one she didn't recognize as her own.

Shannon swallowed hard and grabbed her hand. It was warm against Lauren's clammy skin. "Dang it. This is a total HIPA violation but I can't not tell you. Blake is in serious trouble. He was in the water a long time, Lo. His body temperature is dangerously low, they're trying to rule out a spine injury. A near-drowning has tons of risks, I don't even—"

"Wait. Did you say drowning?"

Tears filled Shannon's eyes. "He was thrown from the raft, without a helmet, so they think he hit his head. Jeremy never lost consciousness but he's a wreck and doesn't really know what happened."

Lauren dropped her chin to her chest. Tears slid down her cheeks. What if Blake didn't make it? Her heart ached as though it might split in two. If only she had told him the truth from the beginning. He had begged her to stay but she was too stubborn to listen. Just had to run off to Oregon and handle everything herself. *And look where it got you?* She watched Granny still sleeping, oblivious to the drama swirling around her. *What now, Granny?*

She lifted her head and squeezed Shannon's hand. "Is there any way I could see him? Just for a minute?"

Shannon hesitated. She gnawed on her lower lip and then nodded. "Come with me. I'll see what I can do."

Lauren blew Granny a kiss and followed Shannon out of the room. She battled back a wave of nausea. What if it was already too late? *Hold on, Blake. I'm coming.*

***

"What do you think you're doing?"

Lauren nearly jumped out of her skin. She turned slowly and stared up into the piercing blue eyes of Ben Tully. He folded his arms across his chest, sweat ringing the armpits of his gray T-shirt. Grease stained the legs of his faded jeans and a frown dragged the edges of his mustache down. Shannon had deserted her in the hallway, just steps from Blake's hospital room, in an effort to find a way to sneak Lauren in.

"I just—I heard the call on my Dad's radio. I was hoping it wasn't Blake." She gulped back a sob.

Mr. Tully's countenance crumpled. He swiped at his eyes with his beefy fingers and nodded. "Me too, kiddo, me too."

"It's bad, isn't it?"

He cleared his throat. "His mom is in there now. I came straight from work. I'm waiting on her for an update."

Lauren's heart plummeted. If Mrs. Tully knew about the baby, and surely Blake had told her by now, she wouldn't let her anywhere near her son.

Shannon came out of Blake's room, her face ashen. She pasted on a thin smile but Lauren could see the despair in her eyes. She stopped and slipped her arm around Lauren's shoulders. "Hi, Mr. Tully."

"Shannon. How is he?"

Shannon's eyes darted between Lauren and Mr. Tully. "He's on a ventilator. Dr. Wheeler's on the phone with a swift water rescue trauma specialist in Anchorage right now. They're talking about inducing a coma."

Mr. Tully began to pace the hallway, rubbing his temples and murmuring through tears. It was more than Lauren could stand to watch. She grabbed Shannon's elbow and tugged her in the opposite direction. "A coma?" she hissed. "Are you serious?"

Shannon hesitated. "He's tolerating the ventilator but we're not sure one hundred percent oxygen is enough after what he's been through. I guess studies have shown controlled cooling through a comatose state helps the brain and the body recover." She bit her lip. "That's all I can tell you. I've said too much already."

"Ben?" They turned as Mrs. Tully came out of Blake's room. Her face was streaked with tears and Mr. Tully pushed past the girls to scoop his wife into his arms, her blond ponytail bobbing as her body shook. Lauren and Shannon turned away as Mrs. Tully's cries echoed in the hallway.

"This is awful. I shouldn't be here." Lauren turned to go. She felt empty inside. She had given up her right to be part of the Tully family a long time ago.

"Wait."

Lauren froze.

Mrs. Tully stepped toward her, dabbing at her red-rimmed eyes with a tissue. "Regardless of what's happened between you and Blake … recently, I know you want to see him. I think everyone deserves closure. I couldn't live with myself if I deprived you of that."

Her words were like a sucker punch. *Closure?*

"He's on shaky ground right now, Lauren. But he is stable and Dr. Wheeler said he could tolerate a visitor or two for a few minutes."

The lump in her throat kept her from speaking. She dared to look Mrs. Tully in the eye. *Please, please.*

"Five minutes. That's it."

Lauren steepled her fingers and pressed them to her lips. "Thank you."

Shannon squeezed her arm. "Come on, I'll take you in."

Lauren followed her to the door of Blake's room, trembling all over. Her mouth was dry and her chest tightened. She gripped the door frame and whispered a prayer for strength. All her hours of rotations in the hospital and working for Dr. Putnam hadn't prepared her for this. She drew a deep breath and stepped inside.

Her eyes traveled to the bed, absorbing each detail. He was lying on his back, with a gauze bandage wrapped around his forehead. Blood had soaked through the gauze, leaving a bright red stain near his temple. Gnarly purple bruises marred the skin around his eyes. The cervical collar that stabilized his neck made Lauren choke back a sob.

"D-does he have a spine injury?"

Shannon's brow furrowed while she studied the monitors that beeped a steady rhythm. "We're still uncertain about his right leg. He wasn't conscious long enough for them to test all of the extremities. They left the collar on for now, probably in case they need to transport him."

"Where?"

The paramedics had cut open his clothes and the remaining fragments of his white T-shirt crisscrossed his exposed chest like an angry gash. Lauren smoothed the bed sheet across his torso, tucking it between his arm and his body. The haunting push and pull of the ventilator unnerved her. The ghastly tube taped to his mouth sent an ominous shiver down her spine. Handsome, confident, selfless Blake … tethered to life by a complex series of tubes and machines. *How can this be*?

"The trauma specialist will decide if he needs to be flown to Anchorage. But let's not worry about that now." Shannon rolled a stool up beside the bed and patted it with her hand. "Come close so he can hear you."

Lauren sat down and reached for Blake's hand. His fingers were warm but unresponsive to her touch. She wrapped her fingers around his and squeezed. "Hey," she whispered. "It's me." She glanced at Shannon who nodded and offered an encouraging smile.

"You've had a lot of excitement this week." She smoothed the sheet again, tucking it tighter under his side. "I'm sorry I contributed to that."

This was excruciating. "Your mom says I only have a few minutes. There's some things I want you to know about our son, just in case I don't get another chance to tell you." Her voice broke, and she looked away, right at Shannon, whose eyes shimmered with tears.

Lauren dragged the back of her hand across her nose and sniffed. "He's eight now. You probably figured that out already. He lives on a farm in Milton-Freewater, Oregon. That's eastern Oregon, by the way. I haven't visited him but his parents write this great blog and they post awesome pictures. I'll show it to you when you—when you wake up."

One of the monitors behind her started to beep more frequently and she shot a glance at Shannon. "Keep going," she whispered, watching the monitor over Lauren's shoulder.

"I'm sorry I never told you about him. I regret that so much. I know you'd be a great dad." She watched his chest rise and fall as the ventilator pushed air in and out of his lungs. "I was scared and I thought I could handle it by myself. I hope you can forgive me."

"Lauren, look." Shannon pointed toward the monitor, her eyes bright.

She twisted on the stool to look at the numbers but none of it made sense anymore. She shook her head. "What? I don't get it."

"I think he hears you. As soon as you started talking, his heart rate picked up a little. Say something else."

That's crazy. If he could hear her, why didn't he open his eyes? She swallowed hard and squeezed Blake's hand. "His name is Shaun. The boy. Our son. His parents seem really cool. I wish—" she was babbling now. Her cheeks grew hot.

She stared at the monitor. Shannon was right. As long as she was talking, his heart rate picked up a few beats per minute.

"Mrs. T, you won't believe this," Shannon said as the door opened and Blake's parents came and stood behind Lauren. "When Lauren talks, Blake's heart rate increases. Show them. Say something else."

Lauren hesitated. She hadn't expected an audience.

"We're all pulling for you, Blake. Jeremy and Megan aren't here yet but I know they'll come as soon as they can. I heard Coach is finally announcing his retirement this week. Wouldn't you love to coach basketball this winter?" The monitor increased its beeping significantly.

Mrs. Tully moved closer and studied the numbers on the screen. Lauren noted his heart rate was increasing while his oxygen saturation looked questionable. She turned to mention it to Shannon, whose face was already clouded with concern.

"Shan—" Lauren pointed, her own heart rate increasing as a wave of uncertainty washed over her. The monitors standing guard around Blake changed from a steady beep to an ominous screech. Shannon's expression grew stern and she locked eyes with Mrs. Tully.

"Out. Now." Shannon pointed to the door. "I mean it, Sandy. Go."

Lauren cried out as someone grasped her shoulders and pulled her off of the stool. "What's happening?"

Mr. Tully had one arm around her and the other around his wife. She watched in horror as Mrs. Tully pressed her fist to her mouth and clutched her husband's shirt as he forced her out of the room. "No." she whimpered, her eyes wide in disbelief. He grunted as she clawed wildly at his arms. "Let me go, Ben. They're losing him!"

Lauren's knees buckled and spots of color flashed in her peripheral vision. Was it hot in here? Heart hammering in her chest, she reached for Mr. Tully's arm. *Help me.* Crumpling to the floor, she noticed that the linoleum felt so cool against her cheek before everything went black.

CHAPTER THIRTY TWO

I'm thirsty. She was absolutely parched but she couldn't find her water bottle. Her head ached and somebody was messing with her hand. Stop. She tried to swat them away but they just kept grabbing her wrist.

"I think she's coming around." A man's voice pierced her thoughts.

This bed is hard. She shifted to her side but her shoulder protested. And the light was shining right in her eyes. She grunted. Turn that thing off.

"Pupils equal and reactive to light," the voice said again. *What is he talking about?* It sounded similar to something Dr. Putnam had taught her. Pearls? Pearly? She couldn't remember. It was for assessing concussions. Wait. Concussions. *Blake.*

She opened her eyes and tried to put up a hand to shield them from the bright fluorescent light shining down on her. She turned her head slowly and found her face was just inches away from someone's knees and a white lab coat. Her eyes traveled up to find a man leaning over, staring at her.

"Ms. Carter? I'm Dr. Adams. How are you feeling?" He asked as he slipped a penlight back into his pocket.

"I'm thirsty," she whispered.

"We'll get you something to drink in a minute. How's your head?"

She thought for a second. "It hurts."

"You took a little spill, but I think you'll be fine. Can you try and sit up?"

She glanced around and realized she was lying on the floor in the hallway of the hospital. "What happened?"

"I wasn't with you but it sounds like you passed out. When was the last time you had something to eat or drink?"

She shrugged. "Yesterday, maybe. I don't really know."

He glanced at his watch. "It's just after five now. I'd like to get an IV going and keep you for observation, just to make sure everything is okay."

Observation? She tried to see past him to Blake's room. Didn't he know there were much bigger issues to deal with right now?

"Do you know what's going on with that guy in there?" She pointed in the general direction of Blake's room.

"Don't you worry. He's in good hands. Can you sit up?" Dr. Adams slipped a hand behind her shoulder and prodded her into a sitting position. Her vision swam and she felt nauseous as he propped her up against the wall. "There you go. How's that?"

She grimaced. "Not too good."

"Let's sit here for just a minute and then we'll move you to a chair." He touched his fingers to her wrist and checked his watch again.

"Do you think we could speed this up? I really need to get back in that room." She looked around for the Tully's or Shannon, anybody that could give her an update. The hallway was deserted except for her and the good doctor.

He smiled and patted her arm. "They're a little busy in there right now. Let's focus on getting you back on your feet."

A nurse she didn't recognize rolled a wheelchair down the hall and stopped next to her. "What's that for?"

"You," Dr. Adams said.

"I don't need—"

"There she is. Oh, Lauren, thank God." Lauren saw Mom coming from the corner of her eye. Mom stopped and knelt down beside her, pressing her hand to Lauren's forehead. Her eyes were filled with worry. "Is she going to be all right, Dr. Adams?"

Dr. Adams nodded. "I think so. She passed out, probably a combination of shock and dehydration. I want to keep her for observation but she's a little resistant."

Lauren's eyes flickered to his. "I'm not resistant. I'm just worried about Blake."

The creases in Mom's forehead deepened. "I heard there was a terrible accident. What's the latest?"

Dr. Adams ignored the question and rattled off instructions to the nurse. "Let's get Ms. Carter into a room and check her vitals, please." He offered her a hand and pulled her to her feet. She stood slowly, her legs trembling. After a few tentative steps she sank down into the wheelchair. She kept her eyes glued to the door of Blake's room until the nurse wheeled her around and she couldn't see anymore. This was ridiculous.

They rolled into the first available room and Mom sat down in a chair next to the window. While the nurse pulled the silver stand closer and attached the blood pressure cuff to her arm, Lauren stared at the clock on the wall and analyzed Blake's condition. Was it hypothermia? Could he survive an airlift at this point? Would they even be able to land the helicopter in this weather? Her stomach churned. If she didn't hear something, anything, she was going to go out of her mind.

"Have you seen Sandy or Ben?" Mom asked.

"We were all in Blake's room together and then he started crashing and they chased us out." She shivered. Mom's face went white and she gripped the armrests of the chair. Lauren glanced at the nurse. "Do you know anything about the guy down the hall? Blake Tully?"

"Open." The nurse ignored her question and held a thermometer in front of Lauren's mouth. She obeyed, hoping compliance might gain favor and more information.

Once she'd noted Lauren's blood pressure and pulse on a pad of paper, she removed the thermometer. "He's still hanging in there. But you didn't hear that from me. You understand? Stay here." She turned and left the room.

"I'm going to get you a bottle of water and see what I can find out," Mom said and slipped out behind the nurse.

Lauren counted squares on the ceiling tiles, flipped through an old Sports Illustrated magazine and watched the squirrels outside the window. After what seemed like an eternity, the door opened and Mrs. Tully appeared with Mom behind her.

Lauren's heart hammered as she studied their ashen expressions. Mrs. Tully's eyes were still red and puffy, her mascara smudged across her cheeks. Strands of hair had come loose from her ponytail, only adding to her disheveled appearance. "Hey, you gave us a little scare out there. How are you feeling?"

"I'll be fine." Lauren gave a dismissive wave. "How's Blake?"

Mrs. Tully leaned against the cabinet that housed the tiny stainless steel sink and crossed her arms. "Dr. Wheeler just came out to give us an update. Blake is stable but in critical condition. He did not go into cardiac arrest, as we originally thought. We're still talking about the coma. If he makes it through the night his chances of survival will be even better."

Lauren felt empty and numb. *If* he makes it through the night? "I don't understand. How can one bump on the head cause so much trouble?"

Mrs. Tully was silent for a minute, as though weighing the impact of her words. "Head trauma is pretty low on the list of priorities at this point. We're worried about complications of near-drowning. A small amount of aspirated fluid, in this case fresh water, can do a lot of damage. We're just taking it minute by minute." She stepped away from the counter, squared her shoulders and trained her eyes on Lauren. "I appreciate your concern. But for now I think it's best if only immediate family visits him."

Lauren's stomach coiled in a tighter knot. "I totally get where you're coming from, but don't—"

"This isn't up for discussion, Lauren. Ben and I have to do what's best for our son." Without another word, she turned and left the room.

Lauren could only stare after her, the painful reality sinking in. Of course they would shut her out. They obviously blamed her for that last scare. She could only imagine Ben and Sandra, huddled in the hallway outside their first-born's room, kicking themselves for ever letting her in Blake's room. *We just knew it would be too much for him, hearing the sound of her voice. Now look at him, barely hanging on ... never again. From now on, family only—*

Mom came and stood beside her, interrupting Lauren's painful reverie. The dark circles under her eyes had deepened to a deeper shade of violet, if that was even possible. Worry was etched in the lines between her brow. "He's a fighter, sweetheart. We're all praying he comes out of this."

Slipping her arms around Lauren's shoulders, Mom hugged her close. Lauren sat stiffly, resisting the embrace. But the hurt and sorrow were too much and she pressed her cheek against Mom's shoulder and let the tears fall once again.

"I'm so sorry. I know those probably sound like empty words but I'd give anything to make this all better for you." Mom pulled back, reaching for a tissue from the box beside the sink.

Lauren's chest heaved, fighting against the weight of the despair that nearly crushed her. The words did indeed sound empty. These last thirty-six hours confirmed what she'd always known. Every relationship that truly mattered in her life was based on a lie and try as she might, every single one eventually fell to pieces.

CHAPTER THIRTY THREE

L auren awoke as her bedroom filled with the first light of a new day. She rubbed her eyes and glanced at the alarm clock on her nightstand. The numbers glowed green against a black background: 4:30. Dr. Adams had released her from the hospital after dinner and Mom insisted she get some sleep. She vaguely remembered coming home and falling into bed, exhausted. A few solid hours of sleep helped her fatigue but did nothing for the ache in her heart. What if he didn't make it? *He has to. Please. Just one more chance.* With a heavy sigh, she climbed out of bed and trudged to the shower.

She twisted her hair into a bun on top of her head, turned the knobs until the water was as hot as she could stand it. Undressing, she stepped into the stream and washed quickly. The sooner she could get to the hospital, the sooner she could find out how Blake had fared overnight. Cutting off the water, she reached for her towel and dried off. The muffled tone of her phone ringing came from somewhere in the bedroom. A shot of adrenaline sent her scrambling from the bathroom. What if it was the hospital?

She traded her towel for her bath robe, shivering as she scooped her phone off the bed. Glancing at the screen, she saw Mrs. Putnam's name and smiled. Mrs. Putnam could use FaceTime? Who knew?

She swiped at the screen and waited until Mrs. Putnam's face popped up. "Mrs. Putnam? Is that you?"

"Hello, dear. Oh, my. Did I catch you at a bad time?" Mrs. Putnam smiled, patting her silver curls into place.

"No, I just finished a quick shower. How's Morocco?"

"Oh, it's lovely. Dwight and I have met so many interesting people and he's already done some surgeries. But I didn't call to talk about me. The Lord really prompted me to check in on you. How are things?"

Lauren bit the inside of her cheek. "So much has happened, I don't even know where to start. My family found out about the baby, Mrs. P."

Mrs. Putnam's eyes bulged. "Oh, my. How did that go?"

"They were shocked, of course. But it turns out they have a big secret of their own."

"How about that. What kind of a secret?"

"Long story short, it turns out my mom is actually my aunt."

She could see the surprise register on Mrs. Putnam's face. "Well, that's quite a revelation, isn't it? How are you feeling? Like a tremendous weight has been lifted from your shoulders?"

Lauren sank onto her bed. "No, not really. I feel worse."

Mrs. Putnam's brow creased with worry. "Why is that?"

"I told the baby's father, too. He had no idea. He's extremely angry. Then there was this terrible accident. He might not make it. If I—"

"Slow down, dear. One thing at a time. Who was in an accident?"

"Blake. The baby's father. He almost drowned. I'm waiting to hear an update this morning. The prognosis was not good."

Even from halfway around the world, Lauren could see Mrs. Putnam's troubled expression as she processed the news. "It's unfortunate that you're dealing with all of this at once. Not the best timing, is it?"

Lauren shook her head. "No. It's terrible. I'm supposed to go back to Portland tomorrow for an interview. But if I leave and Blake doesn't pull through, I don't know what I'll do."

"You must be overwhelmed, to say the least. I can tell how much you care for him." Mrs. Putnam tilted her head. "I guess I'm confused. If you're so concerned about Blake, why not stay?"

"Well, I feel like I should follow through on the interview. I can't live in Portland without a job. What if I'm evicted?" Lauren frowned. Those were valid reasons to go, right?

"I see you've given this some thought. But I'd like to offer a different perspective."

"Of course."

"When you get back to Portland and you have to deal with Holden and Monique on your own, yet you have these unresolved issues from home weighing on your mind … where are you going to run to next?"

Ouch. Lauren winced. "What are you trying to say?"

"You've lived a great deal of your adult life in a state of self-preservation, running from difficult situations. I don't think you should leave the people you care about the most right now."

"Wow, tell me you how really feel, Mrs. P."

Mrs. Putnam smiled gently. "Now is not the time for sugar coating. Wouldn't you agree?"

Lauren squirmed on the bed. "I don't know. I'm not sure I want to hear this right now."

"I'm on your side, remember?" Mrs. Putnam's eyes filled with warmth. "My prayer for you has always been that you will let go of the mistakes in your past and embrace all that God has in store for you."

"I'm trying. But as you pointed out, this is a lot for a girl to handle at once."

"Yes, it is. And you're free to make your own decisions. But God still reigns, even though you've tried your best to ignore Him and micromanage the details."

"You don't understand." Lauren stood up, clutching her robe closed with one hand and holding the phone in the other. "If God cares about me, why are my most important relationships always falling apart?"

"I think sometimes He saves us from ourselves and removes us from difficult circumstances. And sometimes He lets us run for a while, just to see how far we'll let our pride carry us."

Hot tears pricked her eyelids. "You think this is about pride?"

"I think it could be. But please don't lose hope. His grace is sufficient …"

Lauren shook her head as Mrs. Putnam recited another verse from memory. "This is so complicated, Mrs. P. If Blake doesn't—"

Mrs. Putnam held up her index finger and wagged it. "Now, what did I just say? Leave the micro-managing to Him. Blake will come around if that's what the Lord intends."

"I want to believe you. Really, I do. But I don't think I can stick around to see how this plays out."

"Then I'll keep praying that you'll let go of everything you're clinging to."

Fear ricocheted through her. *Let go? Of what?* She swallowed hard. "Thanks. I think."

"You're welcome, dear. Dwight and I are proud of you. I'll let you go now. I know this is a lot to think about. Keep me posted."

"I will. Good bye." Lauren disconnected the call and stared at her phone, Mrs. Putnam's advice still ringing in her ears. They'd never steered her wrong. From the minute she met them, she'd found solace from the messy, mixed up circumstances that composed her life. But things were different now. The truth was out. She needed to make a fresh start.

Putting her phone away, she pulled on a clean pair of jeans and layered one of Seth's Henley-style shirts over her T-shirt. After loosening her hair, she raked her fingers through her curls and stared at her reflection in the mirror. *This won't be easy. But you can do it.* Drawing a deep breath, she made her way downstairs.

Lights were on in the kitchen and she found her parents, Matt, and Seth huddled around the table, nursing their coffee cups. Her legs trembled, despite the pep talk she'd issued in the mirror a few moments ago.

"What are you all doing? It's way too early for a family meeting."

Seth stood and made his way toward her. "W-w-we are h-h-here for y-y-you," he stuttered, wrapping her in a gentle hug.

Tears welled behind her eyes again and she shut them tight. When Seth pulled back, he tugged on a lock of Lauren's hair and managed a sleepy smile. "D-d-don't care w-w-what they s-s-say ... you'll a-a-always be my s-s-sister."

It was all too much. A sob escaped and she pressed her knuckles to her lips. "I love you, Seth. You're the best."

"Hey," Matt protested, offering her a fresh cup of coffee. "What if I hug you like that and declare my undying affection?"

Laughter bubbled up after the tears and she couldn't resist wrinkling her nose at Matt as he slung his arm around her shoulders. "You're pretty incredible, too."

"Come sit down, sweetheart." Mom pointed to an empty seat next to hers. "I'll make breakfast in a bit."

Grabbing the half and half off the counter, Lauren sank into the chair and watched her brothers reclaim their seats.

Matt cleared his throat. "I stopped by to see Blake late last night. They wouldn't let me in. I even tried to play the pastor card, but no dice." His eyes flitted to Lauren's and then back to his coffee cup.

Lauren wrapped her hands around her coffee to ward off the chill. "He must not be doing well, then, if they won't even let you in."

"Sweetheart, we know you have a lot on your mind. Is there anything at all we can do to help you through this? It's all so surreal …"Mom trailed off.

"I do have some questions about my—adoption." Lauren glanced up from pouring half and half into her coffee. Seth and Matt sat frozen like statues, eyes glued to Mom and Dad.

Dad shifted in his seat at the head of the table. "Sure. Go ahead. You can ask us anything."

"Well, when I first got home, Mom described the couple that adopted Mallory's baby as people who couldn't have children. So—" She gestured toward her brothers. "How do you explain the arrival of these two?"

Mom and Dad exchanged a knowing glance. "Pop was adamant that Mallory's daughter remain with her family. Jane wanted to take you to California so badly but he just wouldn't hear of it. We hadn't gotten pregnant yet and so Pop just decided you would be ours."

"Within a month, we realized we were expecting Matthew," Dad said.

"And life was never quite the same after that," Matt chimed in.

"Isn't that the truth," Dad agreed.

Lauren shook her head. "I still can't believe nobody challenged you on that. I mean, there were reams of paperwork, a social worker, an entire agency worked to get Shaun's adoption processed—"

She bit her lip. That was the first time she'd casually mentioned her baby in front of her family. A moment of silent recognition passed between them, but this time she held her head high and smiled.

"I-i-i-is that his n-n-name? Sh-sh-shaun?" Seth met her gaze, his eyes wide with wonder.

"Yes. I'm very grateful that the nurses encouraged me to name him. The fact that his adoptive parents kept the name is a huge blessing."

"This whole situation just blows my mind." Matt shook his head. "How did you survive being pregnant and alone in a big city? Why didn't you call us? You have to know we would've helped you."

Lauren lifted her cup to her mouth, blowing on the hot coffee. Of course. Now the questions would begin. She took a sip, buying some time to formulate an answer. "Once I started running, I never quite knew how to stop. Like I said, the adoption was a process I could sort of detach from once Shaun was ... gone. It's the aftermath or I guess—the fallout—that I'm struggling with." *Fallout.* Blake's words to her in his truck on the way home from the airport flitted through her mind once again. He didn't know how right he'd been. She longed for an opportunity to tell him.

"Well, we're so glad the truth is out. And we hope it will set you free. You know you'll always have a home here." Mom slid her arm around Lauren's shoulders and pulled her close.

Lauren let the love of the only mother she'd ever known flow over her. When Mom pulled away, Lauren cleared her throat and looked around the table. "I still have that job interview in Portland on Friday. I—I'm leaving on the ferry tomorrow morning."

Mom gasped. "You're kidding."

"You j-j-just got h-h-here." The cloud of confusion that hovered in Seth's eyes dampened her enthusiasm. She held up her hand. "Wait. I didn't say it was forever. I want to follow through with the interview and I need to check up on my place. Life goes on, right?"

Dad dragged a hand over his haggard face, while Mom stared at her, crestfallen.

"Don't you think circumstances warrant you sticking around?" Matt's voice was strained, his eyes searching her face.

"They don't want me," Lauren whispered. "Mrs. Tully made that crystal clear."

"Why don't you let Blake decide that for himself when he wakes up?" Dad folded his arms across his chest.

Lauren dragged her finger around the rim of her coffee cup, her heart aching. "He was—is¬—very angry right now. The last thing he needs is me hanging around reminding him of all the ways I messed up his life."

"That's ridiculous." Mom got up and went to the counter, pulling the mixing bowl out of the cabinet. "You might be exactly what he needs."

"No." Lauren shook her head. "I need to go. At least for a little while. I can come back if I—if I need to."

"I'm sure we could find a job for you around here." Matt shot her a meaningful glance at his parents and then stood to re-fill his coffee cup.

"We were hoping you might consider taking care of Granny," Dad said. "She needs to be discharged from the hospital, but she can't stay here. There's a great new duplex available now. Will you at least consider it?"

"What about Aunt Jane? I thought she wanted to take care of Granny."

"That's not even an option." Mom cracked an egg on the edge of the bowl.

"Take it easy, Deb. We've been in touch with her ex-husband," Dad said. "He says Jane lives in a one bedroom studio now, above the boutique she still owns. According to him, there's no way she can move Granny to San Diego."

"I know it's all very sudden," Mom said. "But that's why we're asking you to stay."

Lauren hesitated, their resistance to her announcement testing the limits of her already frazzled nerves. "I'm sorry, I can't. Thank you for … asking. But I've made my decision. It's time to go."

She stood, pushed back her chair, and headed for the stairs before anyone launched another protest. The disappointment etched on their faces was more than she could stand. If this was what she needed to do, why did she feel like such a failure?

CHAPTER THIRTY FOUR

auren borrowed the van one last time and drove over to see Granny. The streets of town were deserted so early in the morning. She made it to the hospital in less than five minutes. The parking lot was more crowded than usual and her breath caught in her throat when she recognized Jeremy's truck. Of course he'd be here, standing watch for his brother. An image of Blake lying in the hospital bed, the monitors screeching in distress, flashed through her mind.

Please, Lord. Not for me but for his family. Please let him recover from this.

Snagging a handful of tissues from the box on the floor of the van, Lauren tucked them into her purse and slowly eased out of the driver's seat. A light rain was falling, so she broke into a jog and headed for the front door. Whether Granny recognized her or not, this would be her most difficult good bye.

The automatic doors whooshed open, signaling her arrival. She hesitated and glanced toward ICU. No. You can't. She drew a deep breath and headed for the nurses' station. Dr.

Adams stood behind the counter. He glanced up from the chart he was studying and smiled.

"Good morning. How are you feeling?" He tucked a pen back in the pocket of his white coat.

"Much better, thank you. It's amazing what a little sleep can do."

"Are you here for your grandmother or ..." He stopped short of mentioning another name, as if the whole hospital didn't already know who else she might be there to visit. She'd made quite a scene yesterday.

"Yes. I'm leaving tomorrow and I'd like to spend some time with her before I go."

"I see." His grey eyes clouded with concern. "I was under the impression—well, maybe I misunderstood— never mind. I've got to get back to my rounds. It was a pleasure meeting you, Ms. Carter. Safe travels." He waved and turned toward the ICU before she could ask any questions.

Lauren watched as he disappeared down the corridor and the heavy door slammed shut behind him. "What was that all about?"

The nurse seated behind the counter hung up the phone and glanced her way. "I'm sorry?"

Lauren pondered his cryptic comment. What impression was he referring to? An uneasiness crept in. "It's nothing. Thanks." She mumbled to the nurse and headed for Granny's room.

The smell of bacon and scrambled eggs wafted under her nose as she passed a food cart in the hallway, the loaded plastic cafeteria trays reminding her that she'd refused Mom's offer of breakfast. Food would have to wait.

She pushed open the door to Granny's room. "Good morning."

Much to her surprise, Granny was out of bed and sitting in a chair by the window, her Bible spread open on her lap. She wore a new magenta velour jogging suit, although the splint on her arm left one sleeve dangling, empty. Someone had already helped apply her makeup.

"Lauren." Granny splayed her hand and pressed it to her chest. "I was just praying for you and now you're here. What a blessing."

Lauren froze, unable to take another step. Goosebumps shot down both arms. Finally. Granny called her by name.

She crossed the room and leaned in to plant a gentle kiss on Granny's weathered cheek. Warm fingers grasped hers as she pulled back.

"Let me look at you, dear." Granny's eyes searched Lauren's face, her lips curving into a tender smile. "You resemble your mother more and more every day."

Lauren gasped and her fingers instinctively fluttered to the locket around her neck. "W-what did you say?"

"I see you're wearing her locket." Granny's gnarled index finger trembled as she reached up tentatively. "May I have a look inside? It's been years."

Lauren tucked her chin, heart pounding in her chest as she stared down at the heart shaped silver trinket nested between her finger and thumb. *Mother's locket?*

"You know about this?" she whispered, reaching back and loosening the clasp so Granny could hold the locket.

"Know about it?" Granny's painted-to-perfection eyebrows shot heavenward. "I gave it to her."

Lauren flinched. Why didn't anyone bother to mention this before?

She cupped the locket and chain in her hand and offered it to Granny.

"I'm afraid you'll have to open it, dear. This one armed bag of bones isn't good for much right now." She tipped her head toward her immobilized arm.

Her heart in her throat, Lauren used her fingernail to open the locket and placed it in Granny's outstretched hand.

Granny leaned toward the window, as if she needed the light to illuminate the faded photograph. "Hmm. This isn't the right picture."

Lauren's scalp prickled. She sank into the chair opposite Granny's. "It isn't?"

"No." Granny frowned. "This is you and me. Where's the one of your mother?"

"M-m-my mother?" Granny obviously wasn't as lucid as she thought.

"Yes. Mallory. This was her locket. She wore it constantly. It had a picture of the two of you in it. I bet you were only a day or two old."

Lauren bit the inside of her cheek, her heart about to split wide open.

Granny gazed out the window, as if she'd been transported back in time. "We found the locket laying on her dresser the day after the accident. Nobody could figure out why she took it off. It's almost like she knew—"

"Granny, you gave me that locket when I graduated from high school. I've never changed the picture."

Closing the locket and turning it over, Granny lovingly caressed the tiny letters and numbers. "Pop chose the verse but the engraver said it wouldn't fit. So they compromised. He wanted her to remember that God had a plan for her baby girl."

Granny passed the locket back to Lauren, her blue eyes shining with tears.

Fumbling for a tissue to staunch her own tears, Lauren accepted the locket with her free hand.

She had to ask. When would she get another opportunity?

"Granny, do you ... remember anything about my dad?"

Granny sat very still, her eyes closed. Lauren leaned forward, her pulse pounding in her ears. *Please. Remember something. Anything.*

"Kevin. His name was Kevin. He wore his hair long and shaggy, drove your grandfather nuts." She opened her eyes and a tiny smile crept across her features. "He was an adventurous boy, that one. But most of all''—Granny wrapped her hand around Lauren's and squeezed—"he loved you."

Lauren mopped her cheeks with a crumpled tissue, acutely aware of all she'd lost that one fateful night, yet humbled by her overwhelming love for the family that claimed her as their own.

"Knock, knock." Shannon came into the room and closed the door behind her. She pasted on a bright smile but Lauren saw the worry lingering just below the surface.

"Good morning." Lauren scooted out of the way so Shannon could speak to Granny.

"Hey, Lauren." She set her chart on the bed and leaned against the rail. "Mrs. Watson, I hear they're going to let you go home soon?"

Lauren stared in disbelief. Was this really the best time to tell Granny? With all of the details still undecided? She glanced at Granny, who appeared to be equally surprised.

"Is that right? News to me. Of course, nobody tells me anything these days." Granny frowned and flipped her Bible closed.

"Shannon, are you sure?"

Shannon reached for the chart and peeked inside. "Looks like the discharge papers just need Dr. Wheeler's signature. He's not here right now, with everything that's happened …" Her eyes darted to Lauren's and then quickly back to the chart. "I'd say she could be out of here as early as tomorrow."

Lauren swallowed hard and glanced at Granny. "Could we talk about this out in the hall?"

"Sure." Shannon patted Granny's arm. "We'll be right back."

"I'll be here." Granny gave a little wave of her fingers.

Lauren followed Shannon out into the hallway. Shannon leaned one shoulder against the wall, brows furrowed. "I take it this is a surprise?"

"Not to me, my parents told me. She is totally with it this morning, I didn't want to upset her, but the Inn isn't the best place for her to recover."

Shannon nibbled the nail on her pinky finger, a sure sign that she was holding out.

Lauren's gut twisted. "What are you not telling me, Shan?"

"I was told your family was counting on you taking care of her. I heard they rented one of those new places next to—"

"Oh, brother." Lauren tipped her head back against the wall and stared at the ceiling. "We just talked about this. I told them I'm leaving tomorrow."

Shannon sucked in a breath. "Leave? You can't go yet. Not while—"

Lauren held up her hand. "Don't say it. I'm not waiting for him to wake up. I can't."

"Can't or won't?"

"I'm not wanted here," she whispered. "He's better off without me."

Shannon pressed her lips into a thin line and shrugged her shoulders. "Go ahead, then. Run back to your big city life. We'll stay here and pick up the pieces, just like we always do."

Lauren pushed off the wall, stung by the accusation. "Wait a min—"

"Blake said you wouldn't stick around. Looks like he was right. Goodbye, Lauren."

Lauren watched her go, the pant legs of Shannon's scrubs swishing out a double-time farewell, as if parroting her last words. *Goodbye Lauren, Goodbye Lauren.* The echo remained in Lauren's head, long after Shannon retreated behind the double doors at the end of the hall.

Holding back tears, Lauren returned to Granny's room, dreading their last moments together. She was secretly relieved to find Granny with her eyes closed, a small smile on her lips. Lauren pressed a kiss to her fingertips and blew it in Granny's direction.

***

A FAMILY OF five from Michigan sat around the fire, their three young girls clamoring for the sticks Seth carved to roast their marshmallows. Someone—Lauren guessed it was Angela—had assembled a portable tray with all the necessary elements for building S'mores. Judging by the crumpled candy bar wrappers and the tell-tale smears on their cheeks, very little chocolate was making it into the graham crackers. But the girls were having a blast and that's what mattered. Matt and Angela's kids had joined in on the fun and the area around the fire pit was filled with laughter and conversation.

Lauren sat in an Adirondack chair, making a half-hearted attempt to enjoy her last night at the Inn, but the events of the previous days cloaked her in a sadness she just couldn't shake. Although it pained her to admit it, she was going to miss her family.

"Hey." Angela sat in the chair next to her, leg outstretched as she rocked Gavin's car seat with her toe to lull him back to sleep. "Are you okay?"

Lauren shrugged. "Having second thoughts, I guess."

"I'm sorry to hear you're taking off. You can always change your mind, you know. There's plenty of room for you at Granny's new place."

Lauren winced. "I—I can't, Ang. I'm sorry. I know someone needs to help her but I don't think I can stay here."

"But you aren't sure you should go, either."

She raised her eyes to meet Angela's and nodded. "Something like that."

"Could I tell you something?"

"I guess so." She tapped her fingernails on the arm rest and stared into the fire, mentally checking out of the conversation. She'd had enough intense discussions for one day.

"We don't get to talk very much, with the kids around and everything that's going on." Angela reached over and squeezed her arm. "But I wanted to tell you that we're proud of you. Honest."

Lauren placed her hand on top of Angela's. "Thank you. That means a lot."

"You made a very brave decision. I'm sure there's no one on this planet who loves that boy more than you."

Lauren puffed her cheeks and blew out a breath. There was one other person. But she'd deprived him of the chance to know and love his child. For that, she felt anything but brave.

CHAPTER THIRTY FIVE

Matt enveloped her in a warm hug. "I know it's been a tough week, but I'm glad you came to see us."

Lauren hugged him back, grateful for the embrace so he couldn't see her struggling to hold it together.

He pulled back and kissed her forehead. "Don't wait so long to come back, okay?"

"I won't." She bit her lip and scuffed the pavement with the toe of her running shoe.

"You sure you have everything?" He glanced at her luggage, tote bag and purse balanced precariously against the extended handle of each of her suitcases.

No! She screamed inwardly. *A huge piece of my heart still sits in that ICU.* She'd slept clutching her phone, praying someone, anyone, would call during the night and tell her that Blake had responded to the treatment. Nothing. Now the crew chief stood on the dock, loading the vehicles onto the ferry. The foot passengers would be next.

"I'll manage." She willed her lips to form a smile.

"I know you will. You always do."

"See ya, little brother."

Matt smiled but uncertainty still filled his eyes. "See ya, Lo-lo."

She grasped a handle with each hand and rolled her suitcases toward the end of the dock, her heart pounding in her chest. But she couldn't go without asking. She stopped and turned.

"Matt?" Her voice cracked.

"I'll let you know as soon as I hear something. Anything. Promise."

She nodded. "Thanks."

The trip down the gangway was the longest of her life. She paused halfway down to listen to the seagulls squawk from their perch on the dock pilings, filling her lungs with fresh air, savored the briny scent of saltwater one more time. *Home*. A hollow ache filled her chest. For all the energy she'd invested trying to escape it, Emerald Cove had left its imprint on her heart.

Once onboard, she wedged her bags between her legs and the railing on the aft deck and fumbled for her phone. There wasn't a cloud in the sky, which seemed wrong somehow, given her mood. Tapping her favorite camera app, she centered the snow-capped mountains on her screen and pressed the button to capture the image. There. A shot of her most favorite view to carry with her back to Portland.

The call came as the crewmember freed the spring line from the cleat on the dock. While the man on deck pulled the line in and twisted it into a neat coil, the engines hummed, vibrating the deck beneath her feet. Matt raced from the parking lot toward the boat. His white T-shirt billowed like a sail as he flapped both arms in the air and tried to hail the crew chief. Her phone continued to play the familiar melody of "Firework" but she stood, immobilized, as she read Matt's lips.

Stop.

In slow motion, she glanced down at the number on her screen. It was the hospital. Lauren swallowed back the panic rising in her throat. *This was it*. They were calling to tell her it was all over.

She answered the phone, every extremity quaking with fear.

"Tell me." There was no time for exchanging pleasantries.

"Lauren? Can you hear me?" Shannon said. "I have great news."

What? The faintest sliver of hope pierced the ominous fear that threatened to overwhelm her. She squeezed her eyes shut. "Is he ... did he—"

"He's awake. And he's asking for you."

CHAPTER THIRTY SIX

Lauren smiled into the phone. "I can't believe it. I don't even know what to say."

"Tell me you're headed this way, silly," Shannon said. "He keeps saying your name. Pretty persistent for a guy who's been comatose."

Lauren's heart soared. *He wants to see me.* But the distance between the ferry and the dock continued to grow and a surge of adrenaline set her in motion. Deserting her bags, she raced across the deck toward the crew chief.

"Can't you read the sign?" The crew chief barked above the engine noise, pointing at a placard prominently displayed nearby. "No cell phones back here."

"I gotta go, Shan. I'm on the ferry—I'll be there as soon as I can." She ended the call and gathered up her courage. "I— I've changed my mind. We need to go back."

"No can do, missy. The lines are off." He moved to step around her. Case closed.

"Please." She blocked his path and gripped the navy blue sleeve of his uniform. "I have to get off this boat."

"Captain can't exactly shift into reverse, you know." He frowned at her hand.

"My boyfriend just came out of a coma. He's awake and asking to see me. I'm begging you."

His face softened and he reached for the walkie-talkie clipped to his belt. "All right, all right. Who can resist a story like that?" He motioned for the wiry, gray-haired man on the dock to catch the lines while he spoke to the captain on the radio.

A minute later, he relayed the captain's response. "Looks like today's your lucky day. We're headed back."

"Oh, thank you!" She resisted the urge to hug him and flashed Matt a thumbs up instead.

Matt pumped his fist in the air then cupped his hands to his mouth. "I'll drive you over!" Tugging his keys from his pocket, he jogged back toward the parking lot.

The engines rumbled again and the ferry eased back toward the dock. The crew dropped the gangway and after tying off the line, the gray-haired man hustled over as she fumbled with her luggage.

"Here, let me." He grabbed both suitcases from her hands and hauled them onto the dock like they were Barbie-sized and filled with feathers. He lifted his hat and scratched his head as Lauren pulled a tissue from her purse and mopped the tears on her cheeks.

"Is this the rafter with the head injury we've been hearing so much about?"

Lauren nodded, smiling through her tears.

"Well, you tell him Lefty's got everybody down at Mack's pulling for him."

"I will. Thank you," she said as Matt pulled up next to her.

The butterflies cavorting in her stomach were almost more than she could stand. They rode in silence to the hospital, too stunned to even formulate words. She couldn't imagine what Blake would have to say. Did he even remember?

Matt drove up to the front door and she hopped out before he could even shift into park.

Shannon was waiting for her at the nurses' station, a huge grin stretched across her face.

"Here." She held up a Styrofoam cup with a lid and a straw. "I'm absolutely swamped this morning." She feigned exhaustion with a hand to the back of her forehead. "You'll just have to take this cup of ice to my patient. Think you can handle it?"

Lauren reached for the cup and felt her cheeks grow warm. Her heart thrummed in anticipation and she followed Shannon down the hall. "Doesn't his mom want to see him first?"

"She already did. She slept next to his bed last night. Once he woke up and she knew he was okay, she went home to tell Ben the good news." Shannon stopped outside Blake's door, her eyes wide. "Are you ready?"

Lauren's stomach did backflips and her knees trembled. She nodded.

"I'll leave you two alone." Shannon winked before disappearing around the corner.

Lauren tapped on the door lightly and pushed it open. Blake was lying in bed, looking out the window. But when she came into the room, he turned to look at her. The blue squares in his gown made his eyes seem even more intense. His lips curved into a gentle smile, sending her stomach into another series of flips and turns.

"Hey." His voice was gravelly. He stretched a hand toward her. "Come here."

She practically floated toward the bed and slipped her hand into his. He wrapped his fingers around hers and squeezed her hand.

She held the cup out to him. "I brought you a drink." She rattled it and the ice jiggled against the Styrofoam. "Well, ice chips, anyway."

He licked his lips. "Put it down. I just want to look at you."

Lord, have mercy. She smiled. "You do?"

"While I was sleeping, I kept hearing your voice. I was swimming through the murkiest water and my head, my chest … everything hurt so bad. I wanted the pain to stop, but I couldn't get away from it. But your voice. It saved me." He lifted her hand to his lips and kissed her palm. "Thank you."

Her pulse skyrocketed. "You're welcome."

"I know things probably didn't go so well the last time we talked." He winced and swallowed hard.

"Shhh." She offered him some ice chips. "Don't wear yourself out. You've been in a coma, for heaven's sake. We can talk later."

He shook his head. "No. We need to finish this."

She sank into the chair next to his bed, her blood running cold as she remembered his harsh words in the shop.

"Blake, I'm sorry. I'm sorry I didn't tell you about our baby. I don't expect you to forgive me. But please know that given the chance, I would do it all so differently."

He nested her hand against his chest, brow furrowed as his gaze roamed her face. "Why did you run?"

She brushed away a tear that leaked from the corner of her eye. "I thought if I told you, it would ruin all of your plans. You had that basketball scholarship and everyone was so proud of you. I couldn't stand to be the one that messed everything up."

"Seems to me there were two of us in the back of my truck that night. Don't you think I at least deserved to know you were pregnant?"

Lauren dropped her chin to her chest, thought again of all the times she'd reached for the phone that first year in Oregon and then changed her mind. "I'm sorry," she whispered again.

"Why didn't you keep him?"

"I wanted to. But I could barely support myself, much less a child." Her chin quivered. "I made an adoption plan, picked the family that I thought would raise him well. In the hospital, I had an opportunity to change my mind, but—"

Blake's eyes filled with tears. *Oh no.* She couldn't stand to see him cry.

"I would've done anything to help you. You know that, right? And I can hardly stand it that he's out there in the world. Without us." Blake swiped at a tear that oozed from the corner of his eye.

She gulped back a sob. "He has a great life. Much better than I could've given him on my own."

"I'm still in shock. I don't even know where to go from here." He was silent for a minute, his strong hands still holding hers. "But I'm proud of you for choosing to give him a better life. That was an incredibly selfless act."

Her legs trembled and she gripped the railing on his bed with her free hand. *Selfless?* She was anything but. He had it all wrong. She opened her mouth to protest but he pressed a finger to his lips. "I'm not done. Listen to me."

She steeled herself for whatever might come next. This was probably the part where he told her to get lost. That even though she'd admitted the truth, he couldn't get past that level of deception. *Let's get this over with.*

"I want you to know that I forgive you."

She blinked rapidly. *How could this be?*

Blake's thumb traced circles over her knuckle. "Did you hear me?"

She nodded slowly. "I don't know what to say."

His eyes traveled over her face. "Wait." He frowned. "There is one more thing I need."

Her heart stuttered. "Anything."

He slid his fingers up to her elbow and reeled her in until her face was just inches away from his. "This." He pressed his lips to hers, gently at first. When she responded, he deepened the kiss, sliding his hand into her hair and holding nothing back.

"Wow," she whispered, a shiver of desire shooting down her spine. "I think you should fall into the river more often."

"Stick around. There's more where that came from."

She planted a string of kisses along his jaw. "There's no place else I'd rather be."

EPILOGUE

S pecial delivery."

Lauren's heart stuttered at the sound of his voice. She opened her eyes as Blake ducked under the beach umbrella, two lidded coffee cups in hand. Breathing in the aroma of her new favorite Kona blend, she welcomed the cup Blake offered her. "Thank you."

"That's going to cost you." He sank into the chair next to hers, those incredible blue eyes staring at her lips.

She leaned in, her skin tingling as he tilted her chin with one finger and brushed his lips across hers.

He pulled back, a smile playing at the corner of his lips. "One more."

Warmth flooded through her as she kissed him tenderly. "I can't believe this day is finally here." She touched her forehead to his. "I love you so much."

"I love you, too. Keep kissing me like that and I'll bring you drinks all day."

She giggled. "But then we'd be late for our own wedding."

"Call me crazy, but I think they'll wait for us. I know the pastor pretty well."

Lauren took a long sip of her coffee, keeping her eyes locked on his. Their families were all about a destination wedding. Matt had counseled them through some pretty intense sessions. But the past was behind them. Time for a new beginning.

Blake wrapped a tendril of her hair around his finger. "It's been a whirlwind, these last eighteen months. I wouldn't trade a minute of it. But I can't wait to just be, you know? To savor these first few days of being husband and wife. To love you the way you deserve to be loved."

Her eyes welled up. "Blake Tully, that's quite possibly the most romantic thing you've ever said."

He pressed her fingers to his lips and kissed each tip, one by one. "Well, selfishly, I thought if we weren't spending all of our time sightseeing we'd channel our energy into … more meaningful activities." He wiggled his eyebrows.

She felt her cheeks warm under his mischievous gaze. "Now the truth comes out."

"Don't get me wrong. A guy can't really complain about winning state and getting married all in the same week. But I'm looking forward to a relaxing honeymoon."

"I'm proud of you, juggling it all so well."

"Thank you. I couldn't have done it without you by my side. I'm so glad you made it back for the championship game."

Lauren cringed. "That was close, wasn't it?"

She'd spent the first week of March in Portland, testifying in court. Apparently Holden sold narcotics to an undercover officer on more than one occasion. She shivered. It was unnerving to sit on the witness stand and provide evidence against her former fiancé. But she took comfort in knowing that if Holden was out of the picture, maybe Monique and other victims could finally get the help they needed to conquer their addictions.

Blake's first season coaching basketball was a struggle. The critics were harsh, blaming his losing record on everything from his former addiction to his near-drowning. Lauren knew their doubts were unfounded and Blake's determination paid off. In only his second season as head coach, he led the Emerald Cove Huskies basketball team to the state tournament. Funny thing, they just kept winning. Thankfully, Lauren had caught the last flight from Portland to Anchorage, just in time to see Blake's team win with a last-second shot at the buzzer, earning the much coveted title of Alaska state champions.

"I saw your Granny sitting in the lobby of the hotel. How do you think she's doing?"

Lauren smiled. Granny looked radiant at breakfast, charming the waiter and cracking jokes. "Believe it or not, I think this trip is exactly what she needs. She's a little out of sorts, but I know Shannon will look out for her today."

Jess and Shannon would stand beside them tonight, as best man and matron of honor, still newlyweds themselves. Megan, Angela, Jeremy and Seth would round out the bridal party, with Lauren's nieces and nephews serving as ring bearers.

Her brow furrowed as she thought about the one who would not be present when she and Blake exchanged vows on the beach at sunset.

"Hey." He tipped her chin and searched her face. "No frowns for the bride-to-be. What's wrong?"

"I just can't help thinking about Shaun today, that's all."

"I've been thinking about him, too." Blake tucked a lock of hair behind her ear. "We've come full circle, it seems like he should be with us."

"I told his parents we were getting married but she never answered my email."

Blake winced. "His parents. That sounds so ... weird."

She leaned her head against his shoulder and stared out at the waves breaking on the sand. "I will always love him. But I know they have given him what we couldn't. And that's what I cling to when I'm feeling sad."

"See? You thought your whole world had unraveled. And now look at you. God weaved something beautiful out of a tangled mess."

"Yes. Yes he did." She reached for Granny's locket and smiled at the man she loved more and more with each passing day. "God has big plans for us."

Blake leaned in and sealed her declaration with a kiss.

THE END

A sneak peek at *Love Flies In: An Emerald Cove Novella* coming Summer 2015

The envelope slid from the pocket of her fleece vest, refusing to be ignored. Tisha McDowell shoved it back in. *No way.* She reached for another smooth, flat stone from the dozen she'd lined up at her feet on the dock and chucked it out over the lake. Instead of skipping five times across the placid blue water—her personal best— it sank to the depths. Tisha growled and tossed the rest into the lake, each one landing with a single, disappointing *ploop*. She heaved a sigh and flopped into the white rocker, pulling her bare legs up under her chin. Good grief. *I haven't even read it yet and I'm already wrecked.* The anticipation of her mother's words scrawled in perfect cursive on monogrammed stationery weighed heavy, dragging Tisha's emotions into a tangled knot. If this latest installment mimicked its predecessors, Tisha would need days to recover. Between the bits of gossip Mama shared about who'd proposed to whom or which of her childhood friends was ripe with child, lurked thinly-veiled barbs and potshots about Tisha's own failures. While the premium card stock carried a trace of Mama's signature scent, it also dripped with contempt.

On the other side of the lake, a nail gun fired off steady rounds, piercing the solitude. So much for a relaxing day off. If she'd known the construction crews worked almost around the clock building Emerald Cove's new resort, she might not have agreed to house-sit for Jess and his wife, Shannon. But the view of the lush green mountains, their snow-capped peaks kissing a clear blue sky, coupled with the cozy, lakeside cabin trumped the extra noise. This marked her third summer working in Alaska as a sea kayaking guide. The stunning, raw beauty of her surroundings still took her breath away, especially on afternoons like this—warm enough for shorts and her lightest layer of fleece, yet a hint of a breeze to keep the mosquitoes at bay. Perfect.

Tisha turned her face heavenward, Pastor Matt's words from this morning's sermon percolating in her mind. *I'm kinda new at this prayer stuff, God, but Matt said we're supposed to bring it all to you. Here's the thing. We've been over this a few times. I can't read this letter. I'm through letting her—*

The tell-tale lump wedged in her throat. Again. No matter how many times she prayed, she always came full circle. Right back here. She could stick with her latest coping mechanism, which involved getting the essential updates from her little sister, Cami, and leaving her own envelope unopened. Mama always sent them both letters and this time was no exception. Tisha had picked up the mail from their rented post office box after church and sorted Cami's into a pile, depositing it on the counter in the tiny apartment they shared in town. Funny how Cami always breezed through her letter from Mama with a smile on her face, while Tisha buried hers in her underwear drawer. But this time, buoyed by courage or blinded by stupidity—she wasn't sure which— she'd grabbed her own stack of mail and brought it with her out to the cabin. Of course things were different for Cami. Her poor choices hadn't walked the family right up to the door of financial ruin. Mama apparently didn't feel the need to point out Cami's shortcomings on a semi-regular basis. Good thing Cami had agreed to spend the summer here, otherwise it would be hard to not resent her baby sister. Sooner or later, Tisha would have to tell Cami about her plan to buy Jess and Shannon's cabin. Once that news reached home, she could only imagine how Mama would respond.

While birds chirped in the trees surrounding the lake, a familiar hum filled the air. She studied the sky. A small plane circled above, the drone of its single engine growing louder as it descended. She stilled the rocker and scooted forward, the plane close enough she could see the red stripe running the length of its yellow fuselage, as well as the black numbers painted near the tail. Shannon and Jess hadn't mentioned anyone making arrangements to land at the cabin. Not that they owned the whole lake or anything. But surely they would include that with their detailed list of instructions. *'Help yourself to the drinks in the fridge, don't forget to water the plants, our Realtor's name is Lisa, and by the way ... a float plane will land on the lake Sunday afternoon.'*

It didn't seem to make much difference now. The plane was equipped with floats for landing gear and the pilot obviously intended to use them. Tisha gripped the arms of the rocker and tried to get a good look at the pilot, her pulse accelerating. She hadn't feared for her safety staying here alone. But this was one of the few times she wished Shannon and Jess had a dog. Maybe she could borrow a large breed with an intimidating bark for the remainder of her stay.

Water sprayed from beneath the plane's silver pontoons, kicking up tandem streams that glistened in the sunlight. Shielding her hand from the reflection off the windshield, she dipped her head for a better view. No co-pilot or passengers. The propeller began to slow, the engine noise decreasing as he taxied up to the dock. With a friendly smile, he offered a casual wave from behind the controls. Recognition pinged her chest. His eyes obscured by his aviators, she still couldn't place him, but he seemed familiar. A friend of her bosses, the Tully brothers? Maybe.

The door opened and the pilot eased onto one pontoon, then leaped over the gap, her perch rocking side to side as his boots hit the dock.

"Hi, there." He removed his sunglasses and anchored them to his T-shirt collar. When his hazel eyes collided with Tisha's, the warm smile from moments before evaporated.

Her mouth went dry. *Oh my word.* "Chase Binford?"

A Note from the Author

Thank you for taking the time to read Unraveled. I hope you enjoyed your visit to Emerald Cove, Alaska. In addition to the novella, Love Flies In, a full-length novel featuring Jeremy Tully as the hero is in the works and slated for a late 2015 release.

Speaking of upcoming releases, would you like to receive exclusive content and periodic updates regarding my future publications? Newsletter subscribers are the first to see my next book cover and read the opening chapters once your subscription is confirmed. Sign up for my newsletter via the sidebar on my website:

http://HeidiMcCahan.com

I love connecting with my readers via social media. You can find me here:

www.Facebook.com/HeidiMcCahan

Twitter: @HeidiMcCahan

Goodreads:

https://www.goodreads.com/author/show/8123834.Heidi _McCahan

One last shameless plug for authors everywhere: the best way you can help an author is to tell your friends about books you enjoy. If you have a few minutes, I'd appreciate it if you'd leave an honest review at Amazon and Goodreads. It would mean so much.

Happy reading, friends!

Heidi

ABOUT THE AUTHOR

HEIDI MCCAHAN is a Pacific Northwest girl at heart. She spent her formative years in Alaska, where her unique upbringing fueled her active imagination and loosely inspired her debut novel, Unraveled. Heidi graduated with a Bachelor's degree in Sports Medicine from Whitworth University and a Master's Degree in Athletic Training from the University of Tennessee at Chattanooga. After a brief career as a Certified Athletic Trainer, she married her husband, Steve. They currently live in North Carolina with their three boys. Heidi is a member of the American Christian Fiction Writers Association and a huge fan of coffee, dark chocolate and happily ever after.

Made in the USA
Monee, IL
08 September 2019